Love and the Divorce Lawyer

by

Barbara Newhart

Cover Art by *Tina Lynn Stout*

The Wild Rose Press, Inc.
PO Box 708
Adams Basin, NY 14410-0708
Visit us at www.thewildrosepress.com

Publishing History
First Edition, 2024
Trade Paperback ISBN 978-1-5092-5925-0
Digital ISBN 978-1-5092-5926-7

Published in the United States of America

Dedication

To my mother, who often said, "Change is the only thing in life we can count on." You are so right, Mom.

Acknowledgements

So many people are involved in creating a novel, and I thank you all. I also wish to draw special attention to my editor, Kaycee John, and the entire Wild Rose Press team for bringing Love & the Divorce Lawyer, A Mystery, to fruition. I feel so privileged to be one of your authors.

Next, my husband, Scott, and our family, have exhibited infinite encouragement and patience throughout this process, even when I'd proclaim, over and over again, "I just need five more minutes," or "It's almost finished," or "Just one more read through." Hugs and much love to all of you.

Paralegals, Darryl Swain Haberern and Joanne Ganger, worked with me when I practiced law, and now again, these two ladies graciously read my various drafts and provide their valuable input. I look forward to us working on many more stories together.

And finally, I wish to thank each of my readers for investing your time to join Josephina and Richard as they navigate this unpredictable minefield we call life. I hope they entertain you and brighten your day.

Chapter One

Anne Compton, Almost Four Years Ago

Anne placed the empty gun carefully on the table, then folded her hands next to it. Moments earlier, to prevent the judge from granting their divorce, she fired it at her husband. She and Peter had shared such wonderful dreams of their lives together. But that was a long time ago—before he broke their vows. For that, there could be no forgiveness. And yet, he escaped his sentence.

All because of her interfering lawyer.

Anne peered down at the floor at Attorney Josephina Jensen, the woman she hired to prevent the divorce, and who had failed her. To add to her treachery, Jensen stepped in front of the bullets meant for Peter. Now, the divorce would go forward, thrusting Anne with him into eternal damnation for his sins.

In the hallway outside, footsteps pounded the marble floors. The courtroom's double doors burst open, shattering glass and splitting wood.

Anne met the panicked eyes of her former fiancé, followed by the first responders. She smiled as a single tear dropped to her cheek.

Chapter Two

Present Day, Josie Jensen, Thursday Afternoon

"Face it, Josephina Jensen. You're a divorce lawyer."

"No, brother dear," the almost forty-one-year-old corrected as she twirled the stem of her wine glass on the bar. "I have a shattered pelvis and an assortment of scars from a couple bullet wounds to prove I *was* a divorce lawyer." She held her cane up in the air. "I am now a law school professor."

Reaching for his beer mug, Dan Jensen flashed his perfect bachelor-of-the-year grin. "I've got a great case for you. The divorce part is over. Judge Myers awarded the wife six million, plus a few million more in assets that are all in the husband's name."

"Let me guess," Josie interrupted, concentrating on opening the package of oyster crackers that arrived with her fish chowder. "The husband refuses to authorize the transfers."

"Correct. All you have to do is help the wife, now the ex-wife, collect."

Out of patience, Josie yanked the cellophane hard, spewing the contents in all directions. "Oh, good grief."

Dan swallowed a forkful of baked scrod and rice pilaf as she retrieved the crackers. "The couple has a chain of high-end grocery stores. They made a ton of money over the years. Plus, the stores are still operating."

When Josie didn't respond, he stilled her hand with his and gave it a squeeze. "You got this. You're a bloodhound when it comes to cases like this. It's easy money for you."

She glowered at him over her gold-rimmed glasses. "I remember you flying around the house in superhero costumes." She removed her hand. "Those gorgeous eyes and that infamous charm get you nowhere with me."

Deadpan serious now, Dan leaned in close, speaking fast. "The wife is Amy Castle. She's a cousin on my mom's side. Two years ago, I referred her to Barry Woodward because you were still recovering from your injuries. Barry did a fantastic job on the divorce. Sadly, he also put the moves on Amy, and they had an affair." Dan shook his head. "Really poor form. She learned over the weekend that he was married, and she fired him. So, would you please help her?"

Josie sat back and tackled one piece of information at a time. First, their family tree. She and Dan shared the same father but had different mothers. Yes, that could result in unknown cousins. Next, she considered the aforementioned lawyer. "Isn't Barry on his third wife?"

Dan resumed eating. "The fourth. She knows about the affair too. It's a disaster."

Josie balanced a piece of salmon on her soup spoon. "So, I'd really be doing this for you, right? To help ease your guilt over referring a family member to a brilliant, sex-addicted lawyer with commitment issues?"

He tilted his head. "Well, yes. And for Amy, an innocent victim of love, taken advantage of by her now ex-husband and deceived by her lover." When Josie didn't respond, he added, "She'll pay you a hundred thousand dollars, upfront, and you can bill her a c-note an hour. There's plenty more after that if you need it."

As if on automatic pilot, Josie's mind started listing each step of the process needed to hang the ex-husband. Then the sane, less greedy side of her brain kicked in.

Stop. You don't do that kind of work anymore.

Dan squeezed her hand again. "Please?"

Her resolve wavered. This not-so-humble, lawyer-of-the-year-type guy who just offered her a case other lawyers would beg for, was her life-long best friend and confidant. He also rarely said please. Twice. She pushed aside the chowder and swiveled in the bar stool to face him. "I hate you."

His broad smile beamed. "You love me." He picked up his cell. "Can I call her? She's waiting in the parking lot to meet with you."

Josie grabbed his hand. "I'm making no promises."

"Agreed. Just speak with her."

She scratched the scar on her chest. "Who's representing the ex-husband?"

Dan's cheeks and neck blotched red. "Oh yeah. About that." He rose and tossed a bunch of bills on the bar.

Warning bells erupted in Josie's brain. She grabbed the hem of his designer suit jacket. "Daniel Gabriel Jensen. Who is it?"

"Um, do you remember Richard Diamond?"

Chapter Three

Richard Diamond, Thursday Afternoon

"Mr. Castle is holding on line two."

"Thank you, Dana." Attorney Richard Diamond ended the intercom connection and drained a bottle of water.

Divorce caused even the most reasonable people to act unreasonably. And yet, Richard suspected his client, Malcolm Castle, displayed his "unique" form of unreasonableness long before his divorce commenced. To date, he held the record for the longest divorce case in the county, and the pandemic had nothing to do with the delay.

Richard didn't need to review Castle's file to recall the judge's final decision when he granted the divorce. With millions of dollars up for grabs, Mr. Castle was ordered to transfer six of them in investments, plus a beach cottage, a boat, and a car, to his former wife within thirty days. And here they were, a hundred days or so later, and no transfers. Richard wondered if his client intended to break the record for this post judgment phase of the divorce as well.

Was Richard ruffled? Not at all. Malcolm already paid him close to two million in legal fees for the divorce. And he said he would commit to spending another two million for Richard to run circles around his ex-wife and her lawyer in order to hold on to his fortune until the last possible moment. And then, only then, would he direct Richard to make a deal. He was not going to pay anything close to six million and it was up to Richard to make sure of it.

Richard inhaled a deep breath and held it for five seconds. Then he released a slow exhale. It had been a long day, and it was about to get longer. After another second, he pushed the phone's button for line two. "This is Attorney Diamond. How may I help you?"

"Hey there, Dickie Baby. It's me, Mal. I hear Amy's getting a new lawyer. A broad this time. She must have figured out, with some help, that this last one, who she was screwing, Wood something or other, was married. She gave him the boot Tuesday night."

Richard never asked why or how his client always had up-to-date details about his ex-wife's life. He didn't want to know. Malcolm Castle may be slick, but more important, his skewed beliefs about how the world should operate, including his marriage and his divorce, created the type of no-holds-barred challenge that Richard relished.

And Malcolm, along with Richard's other character-flawed clients, often expressed many prejudices, but they were not stupid. They ignored Richard's dark skin because of the favorable results he produced. As for being Jewish, the topic never came up. Black Jews were not common in this country. Black Jewish lawyers of Ethiopian descent were even less common.

Richard gave his well-appointed office an appreciative glance. Mal wouldn't pay his ex-wife, but he always paid his legal bills without question or delay. And the instant he didn't, Richard would fire him.

"What's the lawyer's name?" he asked, disappointed that Barry Woodward couldn't keep his pants zipped, or at least avoid getting caught.

There were few other lawyers left in the state who could handle a case of this magnitude. Like him, they treated the law as a game. The goal was to define the rules in each case, then be the best at figuring out how to enforce them or bend them. Which strategy depended on whose side you were on and how much money your client was willing to pay you.

"Some fat bimbo named Josephina Jensen," Castle answered. "I already checked her out. She teaches at the damned law school. She quit going to court a couple years ago after her wacko client, the wife, mind you, got a gun into the courthouse. Jensen tried to stop her from shooting it off and she got hit pretty bad. If she represents Amy, it will be her first time back in court, in the same building. With all that emotional garbage and you in my corner, I doubt she'll last a week. What do you think?"

Castle kept talking as Richard's memory replayed the nightmarish scenes that came to be known as the Compton Catastrophe around Hartford's Hall of Justice. He'd been down the hall when he heard the shots.

"Hey, Dickie, answer my question," Castle demanded, drawing Richard back to the present.

Richard typed Jensen's name into the attorney directory located on the state's judicial website, confirming what he already suspected. "You've got nothing to worry about, Malcolm." He noted the calendar hanging on the wall and changed topics. "Are you all set for next Thursday?"

"You mean when I become unavailable?"

Richard cleared his throat. "Court starts at ten. It is

my obligation to tell you to be there and on time."

"Consider me told. Just be sure to cover my ass at all costs."

"Consider your ass covered, Malcolm." Richard hung up and jotted down the time spent during the call and its content. Next, he returned his attention to Josephina Jensen.

Holding his chin between his forefinger and thumb, he leaned back in his chair and closed his eyes. He recalled her body, wrapped in a white sheet and packed onto a gurney with an oxygen mask covering her nose and mouth. Two silent paramedics, ignoring the media's flashing cameras and shouted questions, wheeled the stretcher out of the courthouse and down the ramp near the steps. They lifted her into the waiting ambulance and raced off, lights and sirens blaring at full blast.

The image, along with one other, never left Richard's mind. Over time, they had faded, but now they reemerged fresh as the day they happened.

Could Castle be right? Was she back?

Chapter Four

Josie

"Sit back down," Josie insisted, tugging at Dan's jacket.

The waiter returned just as her brother reclaimed his bar stool, interrupting the rant Josie was about to launch. "Shall I wrap your meal, madam?"

She looked at her barely eaten chowder and sandwich. "Do you want it?" she asked Dan.

He crinkled his nose. "After you played with it for the past half hour? No thanks."

When the waiter left, Josie reduced her voice to a near-threatening level. "Richard Diamond is a monster, Daniel. Thirteen years ago, he roasted us alive in that Masterson case. Do you remember what happened when the judge read his decision, after that awful eight-day trial? Our client burst out of the courtroom and howled through the halls like a mama orangutang searching for her missing babies. And what did Diamond do? He stood there in his thousand-dollar suit, preening like a peacock, his feathers spread in full bloom."

Straight faced, Dan pretended to study the dessert menu. "It's not that we lost. The judge just didn't give our client everything she wanted, the way she wanted it. Over time, the parents settled down and worked things out. And keep in mind, the playing field between you and

Diamond is even now. You can take him. In fact, consider it your opportunity for payback."

"We lost, Daniel," Josie spat back. "And I don't want payback. I haven't handled a divorce case or any case for almost four years, and I don't want to, ever again." She hated that her voice started to crack mid-sentence.

Dan clutched her forearm and sought her tear-filled eyes. "Stop letting Anne Compton ruin your life. You're an amazing lawyer and Amy needs you."

Josie darted her attention to the nautical paraphernalia covering the bar's walls. Even if he was right, she didn't want to do it. "I doubt very much Richard Diamond has mellowed over the years. He's like a clump of Roquefort cheese, its blue and green moldy disgustingness growing more and more pungent over time."

Dan laughed. "That just makes it more challenging."

Picturing Diamond in his element, Josie curled her upper lip. "He only represents wealthy, evil, greedy husbands and vengeful, spoiled, gold-digging wives. Their divorce proceedings last for years and always end with a trial. And for the rare times he loses, he files an appeal. There's no end."

"I agree." He hugged her. "That's why Amy's divorce took so long."

"And you want me to join that circus?"

He showed her his calendar on his phone. "Did I mention the contempt hearing against the ex-husband is scheduled for next Thursday?"

Josie straightened. "Are you listening to me at all? You act like we're discussing a sale on one of your fancy suits." She tapped her watch. "Luke and I are leaving for the Bahamas at eleven-fifty tonight. It's his birthday present to me. We won't be back until late Monday night."

Dan's grin and his eyes widened. "Then you'd better get started."

Before she could stop him, he sent a text.

"I'm not doing it, Dan. I'm not stepping one foot into any courtroom with that fiend."

Ignoring her, he stood and drained his beer mug. "You're gonna love Amy."

"I'm only agreeing to talk with her, Daniel."

He waved. "There she is."

Josie followed his gaze to the bar's entrance.

A pretty, well-endowed and well-dressed older brunette stood in the doorway. With a worried smile, she waved back.

Perfect. Just perfect.

Chapter Five

Richard

Richard pushed aside thoughts of the courthouse shooting and perused Josephina Jensen's list of clients on the case look up section of the judicial website. He recognized a small number of names from elite social circles and the media, though of course, not as affluent as his list. Otherwise, they would have ended up on opposite sides of more than that one case they'd had together several years earlier. She'd been younger then, and very green. And yet, before her ultimate defeat, she'd managed to impress him with a few curve balls she'd throw in his direction.

He changed screens to view the case details. There he could determine which ones Jensen settled and how many times she went to trial. In his opinion, a lawyer who settled everything was a weenie.

A half hour later, Richard aimed a dart at the bull's eye hanging on the wall several feet across from his desk. Watching it hit its target, he contemplated the information he learned about Jensen and blended it with Malcolm Castle's premonition. *Why would she choose the Castle case to make a comeback? And how did Amy Castle find her?*

Considering these questions, he left the room and pulled a bottle of water from the office fridge. After a long swig, he returned to his desk and accessed the Castle file on the same website. Thus far, Jensen had not filed her appearance form with the court, identifying herself as Ms. Castle's new lawyer. The hearing was a week away. If she was joining the case, he would expect her to contact him to request a postponement. And he would be most gracious in consenting to her request. He already knew it would take at least six weeks for another court date. His client would be very pleased.

Richard dialed his assistant.

"Yes?" Dana answered.

"Please let William know I want to see him at six-thirty tomorrow morning in my office. It's about the Castle matter."

"I will."

"Thanks. And have a nice evening."

"You too, Attorney Diamond."

Ending the call, Richard got to his feet and stretched. He could have emailed or called his associate's cell phone himself, but he detested both modes of communication. They left too much of a discoverable trail if they fell into the wrong hands. In fact, he blocked all Internet access in the building, except for legal research and the judicial website.

Sure, his two associates and six staff members grumbled. Richard did not care. It was his law firm and his livelihood on the line. His numerous high-profile clients counted on him to protect the confidential financial information they provided, along with their deepest and darkest secrets. As far as Richard knew, no one had figured out how to hack into the contents of a yellow legal pad or a client's paper file. And covering all bases, he'd installed a state-of-the-art security system and a fireproof vault to protect the files.

That being said, like Castle, Richard had many resources at his disposal. Presuming Josephina Jensen intended to re-enter his world, he decided to put them to use. And perhaps find a way to dissuade her from that decision.

He picked up the land line and dialed his investigator.

"Hello, Ed. Are you available to discuss an expedited situation? Excellent. I'll meet you in a half hour at the usual place."

Chapter Six

Josie

Josie took the exit leading to Interstate 91 and switched on her Jimmy Buffett playlist. She had just enough time for some last-minute shopping before heading home to finish packing for the trip. She also needed to decompress. The meeting with Amy Castle lasted over an hour. During that time, the distraught woman described, in a high nasal pitch, the legal and emotional horrors of her never-ending divorce.

Josie didn't doubt Amy's description. And she sympathized with the woman. Folks who hired Richard Diamond got what they paid for, to everyone else's detriment.

That's why Josie couldn't represent Amy. She'd been out of the game for too long.

A call interrupted her singing along about cheeseburgers in paradise. The caller ID told her it was Dan. After introducing Amy to her, he left them to handle some type of real estate crisis back at his office. "Crisis, my ass," she'd murmured, watching him hurry out of the restaurant.

Coward!

Using the hands-free function on the car's system, she answered the call. "Yes?"

"What did you think?"

Josie stopped at a light. "I think there's way too much traffic for a Thursday afternoon. And boy do I have a headache. Amy Castle seems like a down to earth, nice person, but does she ever shut up?"

"No. But she's a fabulous chef, a smart businesswoman, and like you said, a nice person."

Switching lanes, Josie spotted the department store up ahead on the right.

"Hello?" Dan asked. "What else?"

"Oops. Sorry. I think I just cut somebody off." She waved an apology in the rearview mirror.

"Josie!"

"Fine." She moved into the right lane. "I think she's got a long road ahead, but she'll get there."

"And you're going to help her, right?"

She huffed. "How many languages recognize the word, no, as a negative connotation?"

Dan just laughed.

"I suggested she call Everett Kramer. He's someone I'd consider hiring if I needed to and he's been around long enough to go toe to toe with Diamond."

"And if he's not available?"

Josie's phone beeped. "Our father's on the other line. I'll call you back." She pressed the green button and waited at another traffic light. "How are you, Dad?"

"Well, hello there, Josephina," Gabriel Jensen bellowed. "I'm just fine."

She smiled, picturing him shouting, "Yabba Dabba Doo!" He stood six foot nine inches tall, and owned three auto service stations in central New Jersey, and showed no signs of slowing down.

"I'm calling to wish my only daughter an early happy birthday. I can't believe you'll be fifty. How's it feel?"

"Fifty?" Josie balked, knowing he was kidding. "If I'm fifty, you're doing pretty good for eighty-two, Daddy-O."

"Touché, kiddo. What are you up to for your birthday?"

Another call beeped in as she filled him in on her weekend plans. "It's Dan again." She hit the ignore button.

"Oh yeah? How is my eldest son? He didn't call me back this morning."

Josie pulled into a parking space near the entrance to the store. "He's been busy torturing me about taking a divorce case."

"Why's that torture?"

She rolled her eyes. "Because, Dad, I love teaching. I love the schedule, the pension plan, and the medical benefits. And guess what? No guns allowed."

"But what about the dull, sameness of it all?"

"What about it? My ivory tower keeps me away from all the endless turmoil, just the way I like it. Why is that so hard for the two of you to understand?"

Josie switched off the engine but decided to finish the call before entering the store.

"Maybe you're right," Gabe teased. "You are getting older. You need your rest."

"You should know, considering your child bride." Her father had married his third wife, Roxanne, seven years after Josie's mom died.

"Thank God for those little blue pills."

"Yuck. Enough. That's way too much information."

Gabe roared his trademark deep laugh. "How about I come up there next Saturday and take you and Luke out to dinner for your birthday?"

"Luke will be away at a conference," she told him. "That's why we're going away now. But I'll be available. We can go into Boston. See a hockey game or something."

"Sounds good. Get the tickets and I'll pay you back. Got to go. Someone just crashed into the air meter. Love you."

Ending the call, Josie pictured him running over to the crash site, waving his arms while making some wisecrack that questioned the origin of the customer's driver's license.

Her cell rang again as she opened the car door. It was Luke, her husband.

"Count down, eight hours and a bunch of minutes till we reach warm sand, turquoise water, and tropical drinks."

"I know. I can't wait," Josie replied. "I'm just stopping at the store. Do you need anything?"

"Just you, darling. Naked."

"I'll be there."

"See you soon."

Giddy as a lovesick teenager, Josie entered the store, determined to find a few sexy additions to her wardrobe. Not that Luke needed any inducement. She aimed for the lingerie department, recalling how she met her husband of less than three years. He was one of the paramedics who saved her life after the courthouse shooting. His confident, soothing voice assured her over and over again that everything would be fine. Then she passed out. The doctors kept her in a drug induced coma for almost a week. The hospital staff told her he stopped by every day. When she woke, he continued to visit. One thing led to another, and they started dating. A year later, they eloped to Las Vegas.

As a divorce lawyer, Josie felt skeptical at first about starting a relationship with Luke. The older woman, younger man, victim/rescuer thing didn't interest her. But he was more than persuasive. And to his credit, they had a lot of fun together. As individuals, they each maintained busy lives, but they played hard together. This trip was an example.

Back to shopping. Josie spotted a slinky red ensemble that covered all her bad areas. Thrilled, she made the purchase and raced home. There, she grabbed the mail and sorted through it in the kitchen. A thick pink envelope fell out of an advertisement flyer. It was addressed to her.

Another birthday card, she presumed, opening it. The front displayed a caricature of an ugly, wrinkled, white-haired woman dressed in black, leaning on a cane. *Give him up, Baby* stood out at the top in large red, block letters.

"This is weird," she muttered. Warning signals flashed as she bent to retrieve four photos that had fallen out and onto the floor. Her naked husband, performing sexual gymnastics with a naked, skinny, big boobed, woman, stared up at her. A mass of blonde hair covered her face, but Luke's good looks came through loud and clear.

That son of a bitch.

Chapter Seven

Josie

Josie dashed upstairs to the master bedroom as fast as her bad leg and cane allowed. With shaking hands, she stripped off her suit and fumbled in the closet for something to wear. At the same time, her thoughts screamed. *Did Luke know she would get the photos today? Was all of this planned? Was the trip just a sick joke? Maybe he wasn't coming home at all.*

Dressed now in jeans and a blue button-down shirt, Josie carried the envelope and its contents downstairs to the kitchen and placed them on the counter. She doubled back to their family calendar. It hung on the wall near the brand-new, top of the line refrigerator. Always the lawyer, her inner voice wondered who would get to keep it.

"I will," she snapped back aloud, trying to figure out when Luke would have had time for an affair. Not that it would change anything, but she needed something to think about, anything to keep her from ranting and raving throughout their newly decorated home.

A few months ago, Luke started teaching a CPR course at the community college. It took up two nights a week. *Did he meet the woman there? Does he see her then? Where? How many times? Enough!*

Josie opened the card again. The author sure was

prolific. They'd typed on the entire inside and continued on the back about how much Luke loved this woman and Josie needed to stop being so vindictive and agree to divorce him. It ended with, *Sincerely, L & B,* typed at the bottom.

The electric garage door sounded. Josie stood still in the kitchen, listening to Luke park his truck in its usual spot. The engine clicked off. In her mind, she could see him climb out, shut the door, then walk around it, inspecting for any new scratches. Next, he'd dash up the three steps leading to the kitchen door. She heard him whistle one of his sixties rock band tunes as the doorknob twisted open. "Hey, babe, are you ready to go?"

She grabbed a frying pan from the dish rack. "I sure am, honey."

****

Luke greeted Josie with his usual cheery grin, then his eyes dropped to her hands. One held the photographs. The other held the frying pan, poised like a tennis racket, ready to strike.

She watched his brown brows draw together. His mouth formed a straight line.

Unable to speak, she held up one of the more graphic images.

As if sucker punched, his face bright red, he took a step toward her. "Josie…"

She backed away. "Don't move."

He stopped. "Can we sit down and talk about this?"

She recognized that same soothing tone from the courthouse fiasco. "Just breathe," he'd said. "Everything will be fine."

Right. Except this time everything would not be fine.

She kept her voice almost just as steady as his. "What if I don't want to sit down? What if I don't want to talk to you?" Meanwhile, fresh tears tumbled down her cheeks. She would have slapped them away, but her hands were full.

"I understand why you're upset. Just tell me what you want me to do."

"I want you to shut up."

"Can I sit down?"

She narrowed her eyes.

He pulled out a chair and sat facing her. "I'll take that as a yes."

Josie almost laughed. Luke had years of experience handling domestic violence situations. For him, this was just like an average day on the job. She eyed their carving knife set, sitting on the counter, within her easy reach. *Maybe I should make a move toward it. Just to give him a scare. No, he might use it as an excuse to call the police.*

They stayed like that for what felt like forever, just staring at each other. During that time, Josie's mind filled with questions and accusations, but she dismissed each one. What was the point? What could he say that would make this any better? Something like, "Oh, I didn't want to do it?"

Or, "I was thinking of you the whole time."

Or, "I didn't mean it. It just happened."

Or worse. "I'm leaving you. I'm in love with someone else."

Breaking their trance, Josie replaced the frying pan in the dish rack, then shoved the card and photographs into her purse which she'd left on the counter. She considered leaving them with him, but she knew she still loved this jerk. When she started to weaken, she would need them to remind her what he did. She reached for her keys.

"I'm sorry."

Hearing Luke's hoarse whisper, part of her wanted to take that frying pan to his head and smash his brain cells, presuming he had any, to smithereens. Another part wanted to feel his arms wrapped around her, smell the aftershave she'd bought him, and hear him tell her this was all just a nightmare. "Everything's fine. Let's go to the Bahamas and have fun."

But the first scenario would cause more complications and the second obscured reality.

Luke opened his mouth, starting to speak. She held up her hand to interrupt him. "Don't."

He stopped.

Josie wondered how soon after she was gone, he would grab the cell phone and tell "B" their plan worked. He would get his divorce.

She cleared her throat. "Forget about the trip. I already canceled it." She hadn't, but she would when she got out of there. "Please have the decency to move out. Take your clothes and whatever else you want. Then leave your keys on the kitchen table and go. Tonight."

Luke didn't try to stop her from leaving, and that killed her all over again. She drove a few blocks to a gas station and parked. Her meeting with Amy Castle echoed in her mind, along with images of Richard Diamond prancing around the courtroom, distorting facts and wrecking people's lives. Dan's plea repeated itself: "Would you please help her?"

Josie considered the pros and cons, and the overall unfairness of Amy's situation, and hers. Tossing caution to the wind, she dug her phone out of her purse and composed a text.

    —Hi Amy. After thinking over our conversation today, I would be happy to represent you, if you believe we'll work well together. I'm available to meet you Saturday afternoon, after two o'clock. Please let me know if that works. Josephina Jensen—

Chapter Eight

Amy Castle, A Few Hours After Midnight, Saturday a.m.

Amy woke, startled by screeching tires somewhere outside her home. A series of thundering crashes followed. She grabbed the night vision goggles she kept in her nightstand and got out of bed. Squinting into the darkness through her bedroom window, she expected to see Malcolm running from the scene of some kind of vandalism he'd committed on her property. It wouldn't be the first time, or the tenth. But the commotion was coming from one of the neighbors' houses down the road.

A raging scream echoed in the night. Then more curses and screams.

A porch light switched on.

That's Laura Schofield's house.

Amy had met her for coffee earlier in the day. Laura hadn't mentioned any new marital issues. In fact, she and her husband, Trent, had planned to go out to dinner that night, then to a comedy club.

As Amy's vision adjusted to the darkness, she made out a shadow thrashing around on her neighbor's front lawn near the circular driveway. A few feet away, she saw the back end of a huge pick-up truck. Its front end had crashed into the side of the garage. And a utility pole bent toward the street, its lines hanging close to the ground.

That's Trent's truck.

Amy yanked a pair of pressed jeans off a hanger and pulled open her dresser drawers in search of a sweater. Thanks to her wonderful but fastidious housekeeper, there was just too much organization to be able to find anything.

"Ah ha!" Locating the sweater drawer, she selected the beige one on top.

Dressed now, she jammed her feet into a pair of sneakers and searched for her phone. *Got it.* Outside, she ran across the damp yard to Laura's house. As she got closer, she recognized Trent, lying on the ground, hollering. Laura, a slight brunette, stood sobbing on the front porch. One hand covered her mouth.

This is not good.

Amy pounded 911 into her cell. "Hello. Yes, I'm calling to report a…a car accident." As she spoke, Trent struggled to get onto his hands and knees.

"He's drunk," Laura cried out, seeing Amy. "He cleaned out our entire stock portfolio. We had over two million dollars in there. He said people were going to kill him if he didn't give them the money."

Trent roared something unintelligible and tried to stand but toppled onto his side. Laura stayed put on the porch.

"Let's get you inside," Amy urged. "Where are the kids?"

"At my mother's. He was supposed to be home by seven. I didn't hear from him until he showed up like this…" She let out another wail.

Amy led her to the couch.

"He said we have to go into hiding. Dangerous people are searching for him. He said they threatened to kill me and the kids." She pushed a long strand of hair away from her face. "I'm done with him, Amy."

Do you think?

Laura sniffled. "I guess I need a divorce lawyer. Do you have any suggestions?"

Josephina Jensen came to mind. Amy liked her. The lawyer listened and asked questions that told Amy she understood the situation, though she wasn't taking any new cases. Dan warned her about that. But a few hours later, Josie sent her a text saying she'd reconsidered. They made a plan to meet on Saturday, to prepare for Thursday's hearing.

Now, though still petrified of her ex-husband and his lawyer, Amy felt some relief. And Dan said he would deal with Barry Woodward, her former lawyer and cheating bastard.

A wave of sadness washed over her. She missed Barry. They'd had so much fun together, despite her looming divorce. He was the total opposite of Malcolm, and an excellent lawyer, even up against the big, bad Richard Diamond. And that had infuriated Malcolm to no end—which made it so very delicious.

She thought back over the past year. Had she fallen in love with Barry? No. But it was close enough to the next best thing, even with their fifteen-year age gap. Finding out he was married stung, in a numbing, disappointing, but life will go on sort of way. After all she'd been through with Malcolm, she'd run out of tears.

Standing tall, Amy pushed back her shoulders. *Advice to every woman getting a divorce: Do not get naked with your lawyer.*

To Laura she said, "I do know someone. I'll give you her number."

Chapter Nine

Josie, Saturday Morning

Torah study started at nine-thirty every Saturday morning at Josie's synagogue. She was a regular but had planned to miss this week because of the Bahamas trip. After waking up that morning, anxiety-ridden in the New Hampshire condo she owned with Dan, she changed her mind and headed back to Connecticut.

During the drive, she rewound the past several hours since she'd stormed out on Luke Thursday evening. How did she end up in New Hampshire? Simple. She didn't know where else to go. Before heading there, she accessed their joint bank accounts. Not surprising, Luke left seventy-one dollars and nine cents, out of close to seven thousand in the joint checking, and four hundred in their saving account where they usually kept ten thousand for emergencies. When she checked the transaction date—the day before she received the card—her heart sustained another blow.

Nice, Luke.

Working on auto pilot, she'd transferred funds she kept in a separate personal account which Luke knew about, to another account she doubted he was aware of. She also changed the passwords.

Her next memory involved waking up late Friday afternoon with a massive hangover. After downing four generic pain relievers, showering, and dressing, she'd headed to a popular Chinese restaurant and ordered take-out. She brought it back to the condo and left it uneaten on the kitchen counter. At six the next morning, she tossed it into the dumpster on her way out of the complex and aimed for the highway.

Now, at nine-eighteen, Josie drove into her usual parking spot on the side street behind the synagogue. Cutting the engine, she considered her decision to take Amy Castle's case.

What the heck, right? The money was good and what was the worst Richard Diamond could do? She'd already been shot, and now her husband's run off with a bimbo, leaving photographs as proof. And yet, she was still standing. Sure, with a cane, but still upright. Right? *Beware, Attorney Diamond. I am not in a good mood.*

Josie made it into the building and up two flights of stairs, to the meeting room. As usual, the *Oneg* table overflowed with goodies, but her queasy stomach prevented her from selecting anything. She spotted a vacant seat next to Lucile Miller, one of the synagogue's retired office secretaries, and slid into it.

Lucile knew everyone. And many of their triumphs and their disappointments. She offered a pleasant smile. "*Shabbat shalom*, Josephina. It's wonderful to see you."

Josie accepted her outstretched hand. "*Shabbat shalom* to you too, Lucile."

The woman peered into her eyes. "Change is the most consistent thing we can count on in this life, my dear. For good and for bad. Always remember that."

Josie nodded once, taking back her hand. *Was my misery that obvious? Did people already know Luke and I separated? Worse yet, did they know he'd been unfaithful?* She scanned the room. The forty or so participants were greeting each other and settling into their seats, just like every other Saturday morning. All except one.

She froze. *Why was Richard Diamond sitting across the room, engrossed in the prayer book and jotting down notes?*

Josie counted the years since their paths had crossed. She couldn't be sure, but the time benefited him in that tall, dark, and mysterious kind of way. His black waves, styled around his ears and just touching his collar, were now streaked with occasional strands of silver, matching his close-cropped beard. And she'd never seen him wear anything other than a suit. A very expensive suit, paired with a crisp shirt, a fancy tie, and a matching handkerchief peeking out of the breast pocket of his jacket. But today he wore a burgundy V-neck sweater that covered his muscular arms. Under the table, she spied pressed jeans and shiny black western boots.

Stop!

To divert her attention, Josie opened her own prayer book, called a *siddur*, to the morning's Torah portion, but it was useless. She kept stealing glimpses of him through her eyelashes as her thoughts screamed. *No way! He's not Jewish. Or maybe he is. The topic never came up. I'd always considered him evil incarnate. And there's no way he could know I'm representing Amy Castle, right? I haven't told anyone other than her. Not even Dan.*

Always punctual, Josie's other half-brother, the younger one, Rabbi Mark Jensen, entered the room. Tall and lean, dressed in a dark suit and white shirt, with a multi-colored tie and matching *kippah,* he sent the group a welcoming smile that reached his caramel-colored eyes. *"Shabbat shalom,* everyone. Thank you for being here this morning."

Mark made eye contact around the room, resting on Josie. She sent him a tiny wave, making a face that conveyed, "Yes, I'm here."

He gave her a slight nod and moved on. After a brief prayer, he said, "Let's start by welcoming our new members this morning."

Josie's eyes widened. *The new members? Is Richard Diamond one of them—from that tiny congregation in Litchfield County? Shouldn't I know this?* She thought back over the past few weeks. Sure, she'd been distracted, working on her latest family law textbook that was due soon. But how could she have missed Diamond's name on the new congregant list?

Without meaning to, she looked in his direction.
Oh no!

Diamond sent her an inquisitive smile. He followed it with a slow nod. Then re-directed his attention to Mark who was making the introductions.

Josie sat there, spellbound. Until she heard Mark say her name. "And my sister, Josephina Jensen, is our Shabbat Coordinator."

Rising, she welcomed the new congregants, skimming past Richard Diamond. But she couldn't ignore his ebony eyes, filled with mischief, shooting lasers at her.

"My office is next to Rabbi Jensen. Please feel free to stop by any time, or you can call or email me. We're thrilled you've joined us."

As she started to sit, Mark added, "And this coming Friday?"

"Oh yes," she replied, standing straight again. "We're having a light supper this Friday evening, after the Shabbat service. Please join us and meet the other members."

Back in her seat, Josie focused on her *siddur*. All other distractions needed to vanish.

"Today we will read the Torah portion, *Toldot*," Mark told the group. "It begins in chapter 25 of the book of *Genesis*. Here we learn about Rebekah and Isaac's challenges to have a child. And when Rebekah does conceive, she has twins. Who can tell me how that worked out?"

Josie spent the next hour reading and listening along, again amazed by the authors of the Bible. Even way back then, they recognized how complicated family relationships could be, and they recorded it.

The instant Mark ended the session, Josie bolted out the side door and locked herself in her office. First things first. She pulled up the current membership list on her desktop. One Diamond was listed, highlighted in red, under new congregants.

Kaleb R. Diamond. Could it be him?
****

Josie accessed the judicial website and searched Richard Diamond's name in the official attorney registry. There it was, *K. Richard Diamond*. Except she'd never noticed the *K* before.

She consulted the membership list again. Next to Diamond's name she saw a notation linking him to the Litchfield congregation. Propping her elbow on the table, she rested her chin in her hand. *Of all places, did he have to join here? There were three other Reform synagogues in Hartford County, all within a twenty-mile radius. And he chose this one?*

A sliver of guilt crept into her dismay. For whatever reason, Kaleb Richard Diamond was now a congregant, and she was the Shabbat coordinator. Part of that position included welcoming new members. And she'd avoided doing that this morning by hiding like a wimp in her office.

Searching the surveillance camera monitors, Josie counted several folks, some familiar, others not, either leaving the building or chatting outside the sanctuary's doors in the reception hall. Many were there to attend this week's Bar Mitzvah ceremony, which was included in the formal Saturday morning Shabbat service.

Josie usually attended the less formal Friday night service. Luke, who wasn't Jewish or religious in any way, often joined her when he wasn't working. A few months ago, he started taking weekend shifts to cover for an injured employee out on sick leave. Now she wondered if his absences were a clue, one she hadn't picked up on.

Exchanging one troubling thought for another, Josie checked the hallway and reception area again. Seeing no sign of Richard Diamond, she hurried into the sanctuary and took her usual seat by the door. Nora Cohen, the synagogue's music director, played the opening prayer on the piano as the Bar Mitzvah, Jeff Becker, joined Mark on the *bema* with his proud parents.

It warmed Josie's heart to see her baby brother leading the ceremony. Eleven and fatherless when Gabe, a widower, married the boy's mother, Mark had been quite a handful. Gabe took his role in stride, adopting the boy and introducing him to faith and the Golden Rule. Specifically, treat people the way you want to be treated.

The youngster gobbled it up and at fifteen years old, he announced he wanted to be a rabbi. No one was surprised. College and rabbinical school flew by, and over the years, he spent a lot of time in Israel, as well as remote parts of the world where Jews were a slim minority. Being half-Jamaican, he said he felt compelled to reach out to them and others who didn't quite match the stereotypical mold.

And up until a few weeks ago, he'd worked as a traveling rabbi, leading the Litchfield congregation and another one farther away in the Berkshires. Neither could afford a full-time rabbi or a physical synagogue. Therefore, they shared Mark. He'd meet with each group twice a month for services, in someone's home or a rented space, in addition to weddings and funerals as needed. To supplement his meager salary, Mark taught religion and philosophy courses at the two local colleges.

Then, about six months ago, the assistant rabbi at Josie's synagogue gave his notice after accepting a position to lead his own congregation in White Plains. Mark applied and got the job. He found a replacement rabbi for the Berkshire congregants and brought those from Litchfield along with him.

Every few minutes, Josie peeked around the large sanctuary. Some of the new faces in Torah Study were present for the service, but not Diamond's. Thank goodness. She needed more time to process this. *But where did he go?*

Chapter Ten

Richard, Saturday Morning

Richard sat in his car, parked across the street from the synagogue, watching the live streamed Shabbat service on his cell phone. Yes, he knew it was ridiculous. But he wanted to avoid Josephina Jensen.

The cantor finished the last line of the call to prayer.

"Amen," Richard repeated. He sipped the coffee he'd purchased from the convenience store down the street and contemplated the synagogue's massive building. Topped with a gold dome and banked with dozens of stairs, it was a far cry from meeting with a group of perhaps thirty at one of their homes up in the Litchfield hills where he spent most of his weekends. There, he could escape the high stakes pressures of his law practice. And it permitted him to stay anonymous. Many people in that area did not even know he was a lawyer.

Richard and his fellow congregants meant it when they congratulated Mark Jensen on his new position, but they also felt the loss. They had been meeting together twice a month for close to six years. Though young, Mark shared a wisdom that touched their hearts and instilled pride in their heritage, even if they weren't strict observers. And like Richard, Mark was Black, or at least part Black. And he'd traveled to Ethiopia and other parts of Africa. This permitted them to share some of their unique, life defining experiences.

With that in mind, Richard decided he could rearrange his usual weekend routine and proposed merging the congregations. And now, here they were.

As things went, Richard had a prior engagement the night before that prevented him from attending this week's Friday service, regardless of its location. Eager to test out his new spiritual home, he expected to stay for this morning's service after Torah study but seeing Josephina Jensen put the kibosh on that. He didn't even know she was Jewish.

And what on this earth is a Shabbat Coordinator? Sure, it is a holy time, but was this place so big that it needed one person specifically designated for Shabbat duty?

And she attended Torah study too?

And she and the rabbi are siblings? What was that story?

Richard was eager to study in a setting outside his usual group. He figured it would provide different perspectives on the same Torah passages they read year after year. And today's session exceeded that expectation. Except the female Jensen's presence kept distracting him. In another setting, and in another universe, Richard would have seized the opportunity to seek her out and exude his infamous charm, saying something like, "It is so wonderful to see you, Attorney Jensen. I know it has been a long while, but you are even more gorgeous now. How is teaching at the law school? I hope those soon-to-be lawyers are wowed by your brilliance."

But Richard had no desire to schmooze inside any

synagogue. His family members in Ethiopia were not permitted to worship openly in any capacity without the risk of imprisonment or even death. Knowing this, he had grown up here in the U.S., keeping Shabbat sacred. A time of peace. And a privilege.

And yet, on a more primitive level, Richard admitted Josephina sure looked good. Her shiny, brick red, wavy hair just reached her shoulders. She had pulled it away from her face, revealing high cheekbones and pretty, blue-green eyes that picked up the assorted blues in her sweater. During that single case they had against each other years ago, he watched those eyes flash freeze to ice, or melt into a calm lake, depending upon her mood.

Richard almost laughed. If she represented Amy Castle, he was sure to be on the receiving end of her irritation again. Soon.

Finishing his coffee, he decided to put this unexpected development into perspective. He was glad the woman recovered from her shooting injuries. The event never should have happened. But it did. And time does not operate in reverse. To her credit, she moved forward, here at the synagogue and teaching at the law school. And she had met with Amy Castle this past Thursday. He checked the judicial website that morning. Still, she had not entered the case. And yet, that deer in the headlights stare she sent him at Torah study suggested otherwise. And then she vanished right after the session ended.

Richard thought about the Castle case. If Jensen joined that arena, and if she was up to her game, he did not expect her to roll over. That meant all the ingenuity he employed to delay the inevitable would no longer work. Jensen would have the distinct advantage of court orders against his client, and her client had plenty of money to pay her to enforce them. Any lawyer would jump at the chance to represent her. Even him if he were not already on the other side.

Richard mulled over his client's options. And he wondered again if Jensen could be persuaded not to dabble in his pond.

Enough. For now, when the service ended, he would head to his home in the hills and spend the day chopping wood and contemplating this week's Torah portion. He smirked. Warring twin brothers and conspiracies to steal an inheritance. Nothing had changed after all these centuries.

And tonight, after the third star shined in the evening's sky, Richard would contact his investigator to learn what he'd dug up on Ms. Josephina Jensen.

Chapter Eleven

Josie, Saturday Afternoon

After almost an hour's drive down Route 9 South, then onto I-95, Josie took the third exit and spotted the car dealership Amy Castle mentioned in her directions to her beach cottage. Eleven miles later, Josie practically drove into Long Island Sound, separated only by a short, sandy beach. Taking a moment, she absorbed the peaceful scene, then backtracked and located the gravel road she was supposed to be on, bordered by tall, groomed hedges on both sides. Up ahead, an oversized dolphin-shaped mailbox stood next to a driveway entrance.

Turning onto the drive, Josie decided the description, beach cottage, was a vast understatement. Instead, she faced a gorgeous, modern-styled Cape Cod with blue weathered shingles. The front door was painted a bright turquoise, and the numerous windows were trimmed in white, accented with window boxes filled with bright red geraniums.

During their initial meeting, Amy told Josie she and Malcolm bought this property right around the time they opened their first store there in Madison. Another store, farther down the shoreline in Mystic, followed a year later. A third in nearby Westerly, Rhode Island, came next.

For the first few years, the Castles used the cottage during the summers and on holidays. Then, when their sons left for college, Amy moved in full time to keep a closer eye on their area businesses.

During the divorce, Malcolm fought hard to keep the property. But Amy fought harder. The judge, in his final orders, awarded it to her and Malcolm retained their main residence in Salisbury, some eighty miles away in the state's northwest corner. Amy was fine with that. The house was built to resemble a vast castle, to match their last name. Though prestigious, with movie stars as neighbors, it was too large and expensive for her to maintain on her own.

Josie idled the engine and called Amy who answered on the first ring.

"Pull into the third garage on the right. If you park in the driveway, Malcolm will have your tires slashed."

She winced as visions of imaginary bullets soared past her. This was exactly the type of situation she wanted to avoid. But it wasn't too late. She could put the car into reverse and drive away. And it was Shabbat. She shouldn't be working anyway.

The garage door closed behind her.

Now it was too late.

Leaving her car, Josie walked past a high-end silver SUV and a bright blue electric model sedan. Amy greeted her at the inside door. She'd tied her hair back into a high ponytail and wore a form fitting, leopard print blouse, black pants, and flats.

"Thank you so much for coming here," she said. "Please excuse the security concerns. Believe me, they're necessary."

Josie followed her through a wide hallway leading

into a huge, modern kitchen. White with accents of blue, yellow, purple, and green filled the bright room. Floor to ceiling windows displayed a huge patio outside, adjacent to an immaculate lawn, then a sandy beach with bluish water touching its shore.

Wow.

As she admired the view, Amy leaned toward her and whispered, "I need to ask you a favor. My neighbor is in the living room. She's got a horrible situation with her husband and needs some advice. Would you talk with her for a short while? I'll pay you for your time."

"Sure," Josie answered, changing mental channels. She recalled Dan saying something about Amy introducing her to other wealthy unhappy ladies who wanted a divorce. *But did he always have to be right?*

"Laura Schofield," Amy announced, having Josie go first into what looked like a living room. "This is Josie Jensen."

A woman, perhaps in her mid-thirties, with dark hair, pale skin, and sad, bloodshot eyes rose from the couch. She dabbed her eyes with a shredded tissue, then shoved it into the pocket of her cream-colored pants that hung loose on her small frame. Weight loss, Josie knew, was a common sign of a troubled marriage.

"Hi, Laura," she said, hoping to sound low key, yet encouraging.

The woman averted her eyes. "I don't want to waste your time. I'm just not ready to do this." She grabbed her purse and headed toward the front door. Opening it, she half-turned to Josie. "I know I'll need you at some point, but…"

Understanding, Josie nodded. "Amy has my number. Feel free to call any time."

Did I say that?

****

"I'm pretty sure she'll call you," Amy said, as they watched Laura sprint home. "Her husband is a gambler with a drinking problem. He owes some nasty people a lot of money." Leading Josie to another part of the house, she added, "My situation is bad, but not like that."

Josie understood. "I hope things work out for her."

"And when they don't, I'll make sure she calls you."

They exchanged sad, knowing smiles.

Then Josie stopped herself. *Wait! That's what I don't want!* Frustrated with herself for being such a marshmallow, and yet disheartened by the woman's obvious pain, she followed Amy into a large dining room. There, an enormous table, piled high with documents, awaited her. Banker's boxes filled with even more documents lined the length of the parquet floor.

"Would you like something to drink?" Amy asked. "I've got wine, beer, soda…"

"Any soda with caffeine would be great." She pulled back an apple green velvet-covered chair, with thin, pink pinstripes. Her own dining room came to mind. She and Luke just finished remodeling it, along with their kitchen. It cost more than they'd expected but they loved the results. And yet it didn't compare to Amy's exquisite taste.

A dismal feeling churned in her stomach. *Who would get to keep their house?*

Amy carried in the drinks, including a bottle of wine, jarring Josie back to her purpose for being in this gorgeous home by the sea. She removed a yellow legal pad and a pen from her purse as the woman settled across the table.

Time to begin.

"The other day when we met at the restaurant, you described your divorce. Today, I'm interested in details about you and Malcolm, and your marriage. The average person doesn't defy court orders. I need a picture of what I'm up against. Then we'll get into the actual finances."

Amy drained half the wine in her glass, then folded her manicured hands on the table. Meeting Josie's gaze straight on, she said, "Fire away."

That moment cemented Josie's decision to represent this woman who projected a certain fragile strength and grace under adversity. She'd been wronged and now the law was on her side. The Amys of this world were the reason why Josephina Jensen became a lawyer. No, a *divorce* lawyer.

"Tell me about how you and Malcolm met." She raised her hands at the beautiful, no doubt expensive, surroundings. "And how you built this massive fortune?"

Amy positioned herself in a way that said she had told this story many times before. "We met while working at a small grocery store near the center of town in Torrington. It was the only one within a forty-five-mile radius, before the larger chains expanded into that part of Connecticut.

"Malcolm started there when he was fourteen, bagging groceries for tips and taking care of the parking lot. By the time I was hired seven years later, he knew every aspect of the business. I was new to the area, having just graduated from high school in Maine. My elderly aunt lived in town and asked me to move in with her. I agreed and got a job in the store's bakery department. Malcolm asked me out during lunch on my third day."

Amy paused to drain her wine glass and refill it. "Even back then, Malcolm had one goal and that was to get rich. Filthy rich. We continued to date, and he proposed on my twenty-first birthday. He'd just been approved for a small business loan to buy out the store owner and my aunt had passed away a few months earlier. She left me her house, mortgage free, and about fifty thousand dollars between life insurance and some savings."

Josie held up her hand to interrupt. "What did you do with your inheritance?"

Amy sat up proud. "We lived in that house for almost twenty years. It was small and old, but it was in a great location, on a huge lot. It sold for four hundred thousand after a bidding war."

"Good for you. And the fifty thousand?"

"We put it toward the business."

Finishing a note, Josie said, "So you contributed to the finances, right from the beginning."

"Oh yeah," her tone resolute. She straightened a pile of documents in front of her. "And worked all the time, every day, nights, weekends, and holidays included." She paused, then added, "To be fair, Malcolm worked too. He loved it. I loved it too, for a while. But then I decided I wanted more."

She crossed her arms to her chest. "The first twenty years were good, but outrageous. Our sons, Scott and Jason, they're twins, started bagging groceries when they were eight years old." She fixed her eyes to the upper left, accessing her memories. "It wasn't terrible. I think we were in love, at least in the beginning, and we worked well together. I always thought we shared a common purpose in what we were doing."

Amy brushed a loose strand of hair from her face. "Thinking back, things began falling apart after the boys left for college." She shrugged and formed a sideways smile. "Even though, if you ask them, they claim it's always been bad. You know how kids can be." She scratched her nose. "And maybe they're right. Maybe I just didn't notice until it was just the two of us again." She took another drink, then continued.

"I handled all the baked goods, the prepared foods, and catering for all of the stores. Combined, they make up a third of the company and always produce high profits."

Josie continued taking notes. "And the judge clearly recognized your contributions when he awarded you control of those departments. I presume you now have your own corporation, in your own name?"

Amy sat back in her chair. "Yes, Barry, my lawyer…" She dropped her gaze to her hands. "Um, my other lawyer. He did that as soon as all the deadlines to appeal the judge's decision expired." Looking back to Josie, she added, "Thank goodness we already had a separate location, just for all the cooking and baking and packaging. The judge gave me that too." She grinned. "Malcolm was furious. He wanted the entire business, and to keep all the earnings. At least now I can go to work and not see his nasty face."

"I'm sure he kept Richard Diamond hopping."

Amy sent her an eyeroll. "He sure did, but I was able to prove I created all the recipes for every baked good and prepared meal we sold. I also trained the staff and spent every day cooking and baking. I still do."

"And so here you are."

"Yes." She rose to walk into the adjoining kitchen

and opened the fridge, then she closed it and said to Josie, "Thirty-five years and eleven stores in three states later, we accomplished his goal. Then, to celebrate our accomplishments, we ended up in divorce court where he told me, to my face, that my contributions were meaningless."

It was the same sad story Josie heard many times during her years in practice, and it fueled her determination to make sure justice was served.

After a short break, she stood and stretched. "Let's make sure we're on the same page." She took a step forward. "Is it okay if I pace? The cane can be distracting, but it helps me think."

"Pace away," Amy said, leading with her hand into the kitchen. "I'm listening."

"I believe your goal here is to get all of your money from Malcolm as soon as possible and in the most efficient way." She made it into the kitchen, then faced Amy.

"That's correct."

Heading back into the dining room, she continued. "Malcolm and his lawyer have the opposite goal. They want to continue dragging everything out as long as possible and drive up the legal fees as high as possible. Then, when you're exhausted and disgusted and close to broke, and Malcolm accepts the fact that there's no way out, he'll agree to pay you maybe a fraction of what you're entitled to, and make you feel grateful that he paid you anything."

Amy pursed her lips and nodded. "That's what Barry said too, but I just don't understand why Malcolm thinks he can do that. The judge made his decision. It's not like we're poverty stricken. The business makes a ton of money."

Wringing her hands, she drew her eyebrows together. "We've had four hearings scheduled since the divorce, all because he won't pay me. Three of them got postponed because either he or his lawyer or the judge wasn't available. He didn't even bother showing up for the fourth one, and the judge let him off the hook. He just rescheduled it to this Thursday."

She rested her elbows on the table and rubbed her temples. "Shouldn't Malcolm be punished for this? Can't the judge throw him in jail until he agrees to do what he's supposed to do? The case is over. It's time to move on."

Josie returned to her chair. "You're right, Amy. But to Malcolm, it won't be over until he says it's over." She reached across the table for her hand. Squeezing it, she winked. "So, let's convince him it's time."

Amy's sad eyes widened, then narrowed. "You have a plan?"

"I do." She'd been percolating an outside-the-box idea ever since she decided to represent Amy. It was risky—and sure to start fireworks—and it just might work. Everything depended on how Richard Diamond and his client played their cards.

"But first I need the final divorce judgment." She pointed to the piles and boxes. "It should be here somewhere."

Amy stood, eager to help. "What am I'm looking for?"

"It's the final court order that proves you're divorced and lists all of the judge's orders. Your copy should have a gold stamp on the first page along with the court clerk's certification."

Amy took the first pile and after a brief search, held out a packet. "You mean the judge's decision?"

Josie shook her head and pulled her laptop from her purse to locate the Castle case on the judicial website. "That's the judge's memorandum of decision for the trial. There, he detailed the events that occurred and explained what evidence he relied on in dissolving your marriage and making his financial orders. It needs to be redrafted into a specific format, then signed by him and the two lawyers, in order to close out this part of your case."

Studying the docket entries, she frowned. "That's so weird. It's not here. The judgment process is supposed to be completed within thirty days of the decision."

"Why is it important?"

The question turned Josie's frown upside down. The situation was too risky to disclose the details, so she said, "Let's just say that when we get the final judgment documents, if Malcolm and Diamond continue to refuse to cooperate, we can make some moves that could switch the playing field to your advantage." Then she added, "Even if it doesn't work, it will bring Malcolm's behavior to the forefront, and he'll be held accountable."

Amy tilted her head and locked her gaze on Josie, as if she walked on water. "Truly?"

"Truly."

****

It was almost eight o'clock when Josie returned with Amy to the garage. Considering her next moves, she said, "When I get back to my office, I'll contact a state marshal to serve Malcolm with a subpoena that orders him to appear in court on Thursday."

"I agree," Amy said, "But just know that none of the

marshals my other lawyers hired were able to serve him with anything. It's like he always knew they were coming."

Reaching the door, Josie leaned against the wall to maintain her balance as Amy continued.

"Even in the beginning when I tried to have him served with the divorce papers. Wanting to be decent, I made the mistake of asking the marshal to call him first, to arrange a meeting. But Malcolm had other ideas. He hung up on the marshal and had me served the next day. From that point on, he went around bragging how he divorced me."

Hoping to sound reassuring, Josie said, "I'll have Marshal Linda Reed contact you. She's the best around and you know Malcolm better than anyone. I'm sure the two of you can make it happen."

Now in her car, Josie tucked Amy's check into the zipper compartment of her wallet. Though she'd accepted it from Amy with a quiet thank you, she admitted now that this was a big deal. For so many reasons, aside from the money.

Josie drove out of Amy's neighborhood and reached Route 9's dark, narrow entrance. Meeting with her provided a helpful distraction. But now, betrayal and embarrassment about Luke loomed over her, like an impending tornado threatening to touch down on her head. She hadn't heard from him since leaving the house Thursday night.

Was that good? Or bad? She didn't know. Her intellectual side told her to start their divorce. *The marriage was over. Why wait?* But her emotional side confirmed the wounds were too fresh.

From out of nowhere, engines roared, knocking

those thoughts from her mind. A set of high beams in the rearview mirror raced toward her. They weren't slowing down.

What the heck?

Horns blared.

Driving off the road was her sole option. Her car jolted forward and rumbled as it veered downward into a ditch.

Did they just hit me?

Her car jolted and rumbled again as another vehicle sped past.

Josie followed the vehicles' rear lights as they crossed in and out of the oncoming lane until they faded from view. *Is one chasing the other? Thank goodness no one is coming from the other direction.*

Facing forward now, Josie's headlights shined into the very dark woods mere feet away. At least the lights stayed on. As did the engine. She switched the gear into reverse and gently pressed the gas pedal. The car moved a little, then stopped. She tried again, pressing harder this time. The engine revved and the tires spun, but the car rolled back into the original spot.

Josie looked out the windows on both sides. No headlights shined from either direction. In fact, she couldn't see anything, except pitch black darkness. *Where the heck was a bright moon when you needed one?*

She decided to get out and assess the situation, but it wasn't an easy feat. Her cane sank deep into the damp, uneven ground as she attempted to hoist herself upward. On the third try, she made it, catching herself before pitching forward. She shined her cell phone's flashlight on the car, finding the front half leaning downward into the ditch and its back end elevated off the road.

Hence the spinning wheels.

Not knowing what else to do, Josie permitted her potty mouth to pierce the dark silence. Back in the car, she locked the doors. Motor memory directed her finger to hover over Luke's assigned speed dial button on her cell phone. Would he come if she called him? Would his girlfriend let him?

She swallowed a rising wave of nausea.

Truth be told, she wanted to forget the whole infidelity thing. She wanted Luke to tell her it was all a mistake. A misunderstanding. They would push it out of their thoughts as if it never happened and pick up their happy life together again.

What happy life?

Tears rimmed her eyes. She sniffled and straightened in the seat. It was time to pull up her big-girl panties and face facts. No, that caused even more anxiety. She tried inhaling from her diaphragm, counting to ten. She made it to six but couldn't hold it and ended up exhaling all the air out in one big swoosh.

Well, that didn't help.

Too impatient to try again, she switched on the car's overhead light and pulled her auto club card out of her wallet. As she punched in the phone number, she muttered, "I've been a member for decades and never used the roadside service. They'd better hurry."

While on hold, Amy's warning about her ex-husband's destructive tendencies repeated in her head. *But there was no way Malcolm Castle could be responsible for this. Or Richard Diamond. Neither had any way of knowing I was meeting with Amy. It was just kids, fooling around. There's not a lot to do out here in the boonies on a Saturday night.*

"Excuse me, ma'am?" The dispatcher's voice over the phone interrupted her internal monologue.

"Oh, sorry. This is Josephina Jensen. My member number is…"

Josie finished the call and settled back to wait for the service truck. Then she heard the revving engines and blaring horns again. She double checked her doors. Yes, they were locked. She held her cell phone ready to dial 911 as the headlights drew closer. She watched through her passenger's side window as two vehicles, maybe they were the same ones, sped toward her. The first one made her car shake. The second trailed close behind. She saw a flash of something white fly out of the second vehicle. It landed on the road.

Didn't they see the posted signs about littering?

Eighteen minutes passed before Josie noticed blue and white lights in the darkness. A tow truck, with its own red and yellow lights appeared and lined up its back end to her car.

Josie heard the police radio as an officer approached. "I'm at the scene," he said, into his shoulder mic. He read off the license plate number, then described the car and the location and added, "Charlie's Auto Shop is here."

Josie lowered the window and handed the officer her license and registration. He was young and polite as she answered his questions.

"Two trucks ran me off the road. They popped up out of nowhere, like they were drag racing. I couldn't pull over fast enough."

"It happens," the officer assured her. "Do you know what kind of vehicles they were? Pick-ups or big

SUVs?"

Josie thought about it. "I don't. It all happened so fast and it's so dark out here." She answered a few more questions, including, "No, I have not had any alcohol this evening."

A heavily bearded tow truck guy, wearing a fluorescent green and orange vest, walked over to them. "Can you get out of the car, ma'am? I'm ready to pull her out."

"Sure." Reaching for her purse and cane, Josie said, "I think one or maybe both of them hit my car's back end."

"You got clipped, all right," the officer agreed, after helping her out of the car and shining his light on the area. "In two places."

He added it to his report as the tow truck guy handed her a clipboard.

"I need for you to sign that I was here."

"Sure."

Josie gave it back to him, with the ten-dollar bill she'd grabbed before leaving the car. As he thanked her for the tip, she noticed something out of place lying on the ground. Trash probably. Then she recalled something flying from the second truck as it rushed past her. She walked toward it, aiming her cell's flashlight. It was trash. An empty white box, the kind with the clear plastic window that lets you see the donuts or pastries inside.

Josie stepped closer, then stopped short, reading aloud the red words on the box. "Castle's Cakes?"

As comprehension seeped in, icy rain drops pelted her head.

Chapter Twelve

Late Saturday Evening

"I want details. You covered the license plates, right?"

"For sure."

"How far did you push her car off the road?"

"Far enough that a tow truck had to get her out of a ditch."

"Perfect. And you threw the box out the window afterward?"

"Sure did. On the second pass, just like you said."

"What'd she do?"

"We hung back, out of sight, using those night goggles you gave us. She picked it up."

"Then what?"

"She looked at it, then she stuffed it in her pocket."

"Good. She got the message. Maybe it will make her think about what she's getting herself into, but she can't prove nothing. Anybody could have thrown that box out the window. Everybody eats Castle's Cakes. There's even a Castle's store a few miles down the road. Shit, the world is full of litter bugs."

"For sure."

Chapter Thirteen

Josie, Early Sunday Morning

Josie didn't remember falling asleep, but she woke with a sudden start when her cellphone's ring pierced the air. Reaching for the incessant nuisance, she made out the time and the name on the caller ID.

"Daniel, it's not even seven o'clock yet."

"Why didn't you tell me Luke moved out?"

She sat straight up in bed. "How do you know?"

"Spill it."

"It's no big deal." She wasn't ready to rehash the details. "How did you find out?"

"Tell me what happened."

Hearing her brother's caring tone, she felt her nose drip.

"Do you want to meet me for breakfast someplace? Or I could come over."

"No, but you go first." Her voice cracked as she reached for a tissue. "Who told you?"

"Don't worry. It's not public knowledge."

Josie fell back onto a pillow. "Good."

"At least not to the English-speaking public."

She bounced up again. "What?"

To her continued horror, Dan laughed. "Relax. My Polish cleaning lady told me."

"Excuse me?"

"Yeah. My cleaning lady is your cleaning lady's mother. Remember?"

She scratched one of her scars. "No."

"She left me a voicemail saying your lady went to clean on Friday. She couldn't find Luke's hamper of dirty clothes and his closet and dresser drawers were empty. She wanted to know if she should charge you less because there was much less laundry than usual."

Josie shuddered. "Great. By now an entire contingency of Polish cleaning ladies and their families, stretching from Enfield down to Stamford and even over in Warsaw, know I've been dumped. Who am I going to get to clean my house now?"

She knew she sounded like a cuckoo, but it felt better to seethe on that problem.

Dan laughed, then turned serious. "We'll find you another cleaning person. Stop stalling."

Reluctant, Josie gave him the gritty details, staring up at her bedroom ceiling as she spoke. Silence followed the recitation.

After too many moments she implored, "Would you please say something?"

"I can't believe it. You two are always so…"

"Happy?"

"Yeah."

"I thought so too. But I was wrong." She frowned at the rain pelting the windows.

"What did you do after you confronted him?"

"I told him to move out and he did."

"And then you went to the Bahamas by yourself?"

"No." She sat on the edge of the bed. "I postponed the trip and got as far as our condo in New Hampshire. I came back yesterday and spent most of the day with Amy

Castle."

It took Dan less than half a second to catch her meaning. "You're representing Amy? That's fantastic! And what perfect timing. I know you're upset about Luke now, but pretty soon you're going to get fire-raging mad. And that can be a good thing because Amy's ex and his lawyer are legitimate targets to take it out on."

Josie wrinkled her nose. "That's ludicrous. And how true."

"Have you thought about what you're going to do with your house? If you're gonna keep it, let me know if you need to refinance to buy Luke out. I'll connect you with one of my bank clients and I'll handle your closing, at no cost, of course. And I've got a realtor in mind if you want to sell and buy something else."

Again, the house. The first marital asset divorce lawyers, real estate agents, and mortgage folks ask about. Everybody's got their hand out.

Josie sighed. "Thanks. We haven't gotten that far, but I'll let you know."

She wanted to shrivel up and hide under the covers. She loved this house. She bought it on her own a few years before marrying Luke but couldn't deny he'd helped with many of the updates and improvements. She could afford it on her own. But did she want to?

Filled with uncertainty, she took her cane and the phone with her downstairs to the kitchen.

"What about your prenup?" Dan asked.

Ah yes, she thought. The prenuptial agreement. That piece of paper you pay for, but pay no attention to, because you're so delusional over the idea of living happily ever. And when the marriage doesn't work out, you can't find the dang thing and you have no idea what it says. And most judges toss them out anyway.

Josie's eyes misted again. "What about it? I have to find it."

"Hey," Dan said. "Just know I'm around if you need me."

Wonderful. There went her leaky eyes and nose again. "Thanks. I appreciate it."

"Oh, I almost forgot."

She filled a glass with orange juice. "Yes, brother dear?"

"You may get a call from Debra Tate. I'm not sure when. It could be today, or several months from now, but when she calls, please talk to her. She's been unhappily married for about forty of her forty-some year marriage. She's a great lady and she deserves better. She's also my aunt on my stepfather's side. Her mother, who I call Grams, reached out to me yesterday, asking for the name of a good divorce lawyer. And, like a good brother, I told her about you."

Josie carried the glass to the kitchen table and sat down. "You've got to be kidding."

"I kid you not," he replied.

"I'll have a word with her, but first I have a question."

"Sure."

"How many more unhappy relatives do you have?"

Dan laughed, but Josie didn't join in. Hanging up, she reached for a pen and notepad. Time to plan her day.

By five after eight, she'd scrolled through the contacts on her phone and located the number for State Marshal Linda Reed. Unlike marshals in movies and on TV who chased bad guys and protected witnesses, Linda, along with eighty other men and women in the State of

Connecticut, was a state appointed process server. That meant she was authorized to serve court papers to people who were getting sued or who had some type of involvement in a court case. It was a business. All the marshals had their own offices and they made a ton of money. The good ones, like Linda, were invaluable to lawyers who spent most of their time litigating.

Josie dialed Linda's number. Yes, a few years had passed since they'd spoken, and yes, it was Sunday morning, but she had no doubt Linda had been up for hours, waking those cagy individuals who avoided her during the week.

"Josie Jensen?" Linda gasped, answering on the fourth ring.

"How are you?"

"I'm thrilled to hear from you. So, what's going on? I doubt a call at this hour on a Sunday is just to catch up."

"You're right," Josie replied, starting her laptop. "I need your services. I just hope you won't hate me when it's over."

"No way that could happen."

"I'm going to keep you to that. Are you ready?"

"Go for it."

Josie gave her a brief sketch about serving Malcolm Castle. "Tomorrow is the best day to get him. My client says he's a master at avoiding service. She knows his schedule and she's more than willing to help."

"This is going to be fun," Linda replied.

"Let's hope so. I'll have the documents ready in a few hours. Can I drop them in the big mailbox outside your office door?"

"Sure thing."

"Great. I'll include the client's number for you to

contact her."

"It's a plan. And welcome back."

Josie's gut lurched. "Oh no, no, no. This is just an isolated case." But as she said it, Dan's aunt Debra and Amy Castle's neighbor, Laura Schofield, squeezed their way into her consciousness.

Linda laughed. "I hope not."

Ending the call, a tiny part of Josie sort of hoped not too. Then she recalled being run off the road last night. *Was that an intentional message sent by Malcolm Castle, via his donut box?*

Or was it just a coincidence?

Chapter Fourteen

Amy Castle, Monday Afternoon

"I'm down the street from Malcolm's office now," Amy told State Marshal Linda Reed, on her cell phone. "Parked in the silver SUV."

At long last, she had an active role in her own case. Since the divorce started, she'd been forced to sit back and wait for everything and everyone else to do something. Wait for her lawyer to call her back, wait for Malcolm to pay the mortgage, or reinstate her car insurance, or provide the business records that the accountant needed to finish their taxes. And when he didn't, because that's just Malcolm, she was forced to wait for a court date. That took at least a month. Then they would waste thousands of dollars on lawyers for a judge to tell him to do it or threaten to throw him in jail. That cycle went on for more than four years and she was sick and tired of it!

Not that this should have been a surprise. Malcolm controlled every aspect of their marriage. What made their divorce any different?

"I see you," Linda replied. "I'm passing you now in a white, living room on wheels SUV."

Amy waved. *This was so exciting. Malcolm would never suspect her of being a marshal. He might even try to date her.*

"If you go right on that next street up ahead, you can see into the parking lot through the trees. There you'll find his red sports car parked close to the building, near the side door. I call it his flying saucer."

"You've got to be kidding."

Amy laughed, watching the marshal take the turn. "It's one of fifteen in existence. I know this because my former lawyer challenged him about buying a car worth over a million dollars during our divorce proceedings. In the meantime, he'd taken control of all our money and refused to pay our bills. Both houses went into foreclosure, the electric company and gas company turned off their services, and my fifteen-year-old station wagon conked out in the middle of the highway during rush hour."

"This is going to be fun," Linda quipped.

"I'm glad you think so." She glanced in the rear-view mirror for any unusual activity. "I want to thank you again for attempting this."

"My pleasure. Are you sure he's in the building?"

Amy checked the time. "I am. He would never allow anyone else to drive that car and he never strays far away from it."

"Good. Are we clear on the plan?"

"Yup." She put her car in drive. "I go to his office suite to get my monthly profit-sharing check, because he refuses to mail it or use direct deposit." She had to add that last part because it annoyed her to no end. "When I'm inside, I'll text you because he always leaves right afterward, using the stairwell exit to the same door, close to his car. You'll wait outside there, where he won't see you right away. When he appears and closes the door behind him, you'll serve him the papers."

"Let's do this," the marshal exclaimed.

Amy hit the phone's end button and relished a rush of excitement. Josie said that if Malcolm was served, but didn't show up at court on Thursday, she would ask the judge to order him to pay her attorney's fees for that day and to have him arrested.

He'll go wild.

She drove into the lot and parked. For decades, she had her own parking space near the entrance, with her name on a posted sign. The very same day Richard Diamond filed the divorce in court, Malcolm put a huge garbage dumpster in the space. Amy removed the sign, but he reposted it. They went back and forth for months. The dumpster remained there today, along with the beat-up sign, but she'd painted over her name.

Before climbing out, Amy conjured up her bitter ex-wife expression. Malcolm would suspect something if she wasn't her nasty yet pathetic and pleading self. Per usual, she made sure she looked great. Today she wore red leather pants and a butter yellow leather jacket over a low-cut black sweater, with red, pointed-toed, high heeled boots.

Let him drool.

Flinging back her curled locks, Amy sauntered across the lot and into the building toward Malcolm's office suite. His assistant left at three o'clock each afternoon. He insisted that Amy pick up her check on the last Monday of each month, between three-fifteen and four. He didn't want anyone around when she was there. And if she was late, he'd make her wait until the next month. That's because he knew it would take at least that long to get a court date, where her lawyer would ask the judge to hold him in contempt and for attorney's fees.

But Malcolm never let it get that far. Instead, he would have the payment delivered to Amy's house late the night before court. That way, if she still wanted a hearing, the judge would think she was acting petty, tattling that the payment was late. And either way, she'd still get stuck with a bill for the time her lawyer spent dealing with Richard Diamond, before and after she received the check.

Malcolm was just too good at being so bad.

Faking annoyance, Amy pretended to balk as she pushed the buzzer to his suite. Her watch showed three-twenty-five. The door unlatched and Amy entered. Exhaling, she plopped onto the brown leather couch and grabbed an outdated magazine to pass the time while she waited for His Highness to show up. Because he always made her wait.

As Amy flipped through the worn pages, she decided that after she got all her money, she would ask Josie to get a court order directing Malcolm to deposit the funds into her account each month. She should not be forced to deal with this continued nonsense. Then she thought about the marshal waiting outside. *Let him play his games. Today he was going to get served.*

When Amy's watch read three-thirty-two, she tried the office door that led to Malcolm's inner suite. As expected, it was locked. She sent him a text and banged on the door.

"You know I'm here, Malcolm. Get out here."

Then she heard a car door slam and an engine rev. She ran to the side window above the parking lot.

Why that little shithead! Sure enough, she watched his fancy car squeal out of the parking lot.

Where was that marshal?

Amy's chest tightened to such a point, she feared her heart and lungs were going to burst. She fumbled in her large purse for the folded-up paper bag she kept for this kind of emergency. Living with and divorcing Malcolm resulted in all sorts of psychological and physical medical conditions. She never left home unprepared.

As she breathed into the bag, her emotional stamina faded to a new low. Malcolm was going to get away with it again. She had so much hope when she hired Josie Jensen. And the marshal sounded so convincing. But now it was clear nothing was going to change.

Chapter Fifteen

Josie, Monday Afternoon

Josie's moment of reckoning stood before her in the form of a huge courthouse. Though she had a decent grasp of the Castle case, she needed to examine the court's physical file and the trial exhibits. That meant she needed to enter the courthouse, the place she'd vowed to avoid forever.

Earlier, deciding to dress for the occasion, she dug into the closet in her spare bedroom. Sure, she always dressed well to teach her classes, but in here she kept her special court outfits.

It took more than a moment to locate the deep purple pantsuit and teal silk blouse, buried in the back. Neither had been worn since the pandemic. Correction, since the shooting which took place a few weeks before the pandemic became official. Next, she selected a cane from her assortment. Who'd have guessed that the Internet, and now even some of the drug stores, offered so many decorative options? Like a fashion accessory. She hadn't bought them. No, Luke did. He started the collection when she graduated from using the walker. It became a thing. Every few months, he'd present her with another one, with a unique design or color he thought she'd like.

A wave of sadness knocked her off balance. She

leaned against the wall and closed her eyes. He'd always been so thoughtful toward her. Affectionate too. What happened?

Back to the present.

Josie chose to arrive at the courthouse at three o'clock that afternoon. Late enough for most hearings to be over and early enough for the staff to still be present and working.

She peeked at the ten steps leading to the two sets of doors, framed with brass, on the landing at the top. Why did she know how many steps there were? Because she used to count them as she ran up them, wearing four-inch heels. Single-minded and adrenaline-pumped back then, she was eager to take on her opponent.

Not anymore. Today, she wore black patent leather wedges with one-inch heels and moved to the left, toward the ramp that eventually reached the landing. Yup, this will be her route from now on.

How things change. In just an instant. Just like Lucile said last Saturday at Torah study.

Determined to ignore her nerves, Josie focused on the doors. The sun's late afternoon rays reflected off the shiny metal.

"Just get up there!" she scolded herself aloud.

Tentative, she placed her good foot on the ramp. Then the left.

No bullets so far.

For some odd reason, a childhood tune popped into her thoughts about putting one foot in front of the other. Obeying the lyrics, Josie continued the journey, recalling where most of the nooks and crannies were hidden in this majestic, square building. She pictured the high ceilings covered with magnificent murals. They contained historical scenes from Connecticut's rich past.

Ugh. How I missed this place.

Almost at the top, another memory surfaced. The one where she was wheeled out of those doors on a stretcher, down the ramp, and into a waiting ambulance.

It took two-plus years of multiple surgeries, along with endless physical therapy to learn how to walk again, and occupational therapy to figure out how to live with the resulting physical and emotional carnage. When she was able to work, there were no more fourteen to sixteen-hour days battling for her clients. Instead, she entered a law school classroom to teach others what she did best.

All because her former client, Anne Compton, managed to smuggle a weapon into the courthouse and then used it.

Josie felt the beginning signs of a panic attack. It started with a tightening in her throat and a heat flash burning the back of her neck.

It's just one case, and like Dan said, I'm just a well-paid debt collector. His aunt and Laura Schofield could find someone else to represent them.

With that in mind, Josie pushed back her shoulders and aimed for the shiny brass door handles. But when she made it to the landing, she couldn't get her arm to budge from her side.

Her cell phone rang. Unstuck and relieved for the interruption, she retrieved it from her purse and checked caller ID. "Dan?"

"Are you inside yet?" he asked. "The building closes in two hours."

"Thanks for the obvious."

"Do you need an escort? I'm down the street at the state capitol. Give me five minutes."

"No, but thank you."

"Where are you?"

"At the top of the stairs, leaning on one of the outside pillars."

A deep male voice, coming from nearby, laughed. Recognizing it, Josie froze. She checked with her peripheral vision. "Oh no."

"What?"

"Diamond and another guy are coming toward me."

Chapter Sixteen

Richard, Monday Afternoon

William Singer leaned toward his mentor and uncle by marriage, Richard Diamond, as they walked toward the courthouse. "Do you think she sees us?"

"I hope so," Richard answered, pulling up the collar of his dress coat. He watched the red-headed figure dressed in purple, using a cane to maneuver up the ramp to the building's entrance.

"When you asked me to join you for this pretrial, I had no idea we'd spot the infamous Josephina Jensen you mentioned last Friday morning."

"Yes, what a coincidence."

Singer stopped. "Do you really think she's gonna represent Amy Castle?"

Richard kept walking.

"Holy shit! You've got her under surveillance?"

"There is nothing holy about it." He watched the woman face the street below, holding what he suspected to be a cell phone in one hand.

"She's been out of commission for years now," William added. "Did they ever figure out how her client got the gun inside the courthouse?"

"No, I do not believe they did."

"Man, what a disaster. I know all the increased courthouse security can be aggravating, but that situation proved it was necessary."

"Yes, it did."

"Hey, if Jensen starts practicing again, do you think that experience will affect her edge? Years ago, I had a trial against her and she scared me so shitless, I settled the case halfway through, just to get away from her. I wonder if she's mellowed now."

"She scared you more than me?"

They laughed in unison.

As Richard hoped, Josie looked around. What he didn't expect was the electrical current jolting through him as their eyes met across the distance.

She must have felt it too because she bolted inside the building. The corners of his mouth tilted. Perhaps this was a foreshadowing of things to come.

"How long has Ed been watching her?" Singer asked.

"Who said he is?" Richard replied, increasing their pace.

He felt no need to corroborate or to lie. Just like there was no need to mention that the woman sped away from her house Thursday evening and ended up in New Hampshire. Or that her husband loaded his pick-up truck that same night and drove off. Or that on Saturday morning, she made it to Torah study at his new synagogue. Then she spent the remainder of the day at Amy Castle's place in Madison. As for being run off the road...

Singer blew out a whistle. "So, Castle's watching his ex-wife and we're watching her lawyer?"

"I did not say that."

"You didn't have to."

Richard ruminated on a conversation from earlier in

the day. A fella named Luke Penway called his office to seek representation for a divorce from his wife, Josephina Jensen. Would Richard consider meeting with him?

Some lawyers may have declined the call, remembering Jensen as a former colleague and a zealous opponent. Or they may recoil over the events of the shooting and feel sympathy for her. But to Richard, both were contrary to operating a thriving law practice.

Instead, he agreed to an hour-long consultation on Zoom, along with a five-hundred-dollar consultation fee paid up front.

During the meeting, Richard provided the ins and outs of the divorce process. More important, the unsuspecting husband provided a wealth of information about his soon-to-be ex-wife. It was well worth the deviation from his usual seven-hundred and fifty-dollar consultation fee. And it amused him that this man was willing to toss away his marriage for a young filly who reeked of trouble. The sex may be good now, but she would turn on him sooner or later. Those kinds of women always did.

Finding Jensen at the courthouse today, combined with the other information Richard possessed, increased his belief that her official involvement in Castle verses Castle, part two, was about to commence. Therefore, the new dilemma of the day boiled down to whether it was appropriate for him to represent the spouse of an adversary while they litigated one of the courthouse's most contentious cases. He told Penway he would get back to him.

Richard decided not to wait. He reduced his pace and called his office.

Chapter Seventeen

Josie

From her spot at the top of the courthouse steps, Josie whispered to Dan on her cell. "They're on the sidewalk near the bottom of the steps, huddling close like they're making fun of someone. Probably me."

"Maybe you should wait for them and say hello. This could be a good thing."

Josie stamped her good foot. "Are you out of your mind?"

"Think about it. It will give you an opportunity to introduce yourself and start discussing how to get Amy's money."

"Like hell it will." A burst of energy shot through her limbs, propelling her like a rocket through the double doors, to the metal detector. Calming her heart rate, she breezed through courthouse security and arrived in the vast rotunda-like main lobby.

So far, so good. A few people occupied the benches outside one of the four courtrooms on this floor, but she didn't recognize them. She rounded the corner to the clerk's office, cursing at her shoes and her cane, clicking in rhythm on the black and white marble floor. The sound echoed upward toward the domed ceiling several flights up.

Reaching her destination, Josie spied Valerie

Gordon, the deputy chief clerk of the family law division. Still sporting a blonde, pixie haircut and large framed glasses, Valerie stood behind a long counter, topped with a sheet of bulletproof glass that separated the staff from the general public.

The clerk recognized her, waving her over to the end of the counter. "Josie! It's wonderful to see you. How have you been?"

"Things are good," she replied, appreciating the welcome. "It's great to see you too." And she meant it. Valerie was one of those unflappable people, always pleasant and professional. She got things done, and at the same time, she maintained an even keel, regardless of the constant chaos swirling around, created by divorcing couples and their warring lawyers. Not to mention her large staff and the dozen judges she managed.

"So, what do you need from this office?" Valerie asked, her smile curious.

Josie checked left then right, and then behind her, making sure neither Diamond nor his cohort were in sight. Satisfied, she dug out the blue appearance form from her purse. "I need to see the Castle file."

Reading it, Valerie's eyes widened. "You're Ms. Castle's new lawyer?"

"Is it that bad?"

Now it was the clerk's turn to make sure they weren't being overheard. "Did you know she's hired and fired four others?"

"I understand." Even though she didn't know the number was that high. *Dan owes me big time for this one.* "What do I need to know?"

"It's not my place to comment."

"But general observations are permitted."

They both laughed.

"How about this," Josie offered. "If you had to pick a side to represent, which one would you want? Him or her?"

Valerie leaned toward her. "Let's just say they're both determined to have their way, Josie." She paused, tilting her head in thought. "But if I had to choose, I'd say her."

"Good. That's what I've also heard."

The clerk moved to her computer and typed. "Let me find all the boxes."

Josie suppressed a groan, recalling the bunch she'd plowed through at Amy's house. "Um, how many are there?"

"I think we're up to thirteen." She looked closer at the screen. "Yes. Thirteen."

"How litigious of them."

Valerie laughed and tapped more keys while Josie tried to maintain a blank expression.

"The computer says they're with Judge Myers." She lifted a phone receiver and pushed four digits. "Let me find his clerk." After a few seconds, Val said, "Hi, Tom. Amy Castle has new counsel. She needs to see the files. Are all the boxes still with you? Great. She's on her way."

Hanging up, Valerie told her, "He'll meet you in the conference room attached to Courtroom 509."

Josie felt herself lean against the counter. Almost four years ago, the shooting that changed her life forever took place across the hall, in Courtroom 510.

Chapter Eighteen

Amy Castle

Amy moped out of the Castle building, unable to stop her tears. Back in her car, she locked the doors and squeezed her eyes shut. *Malcolm won again. Malcolm always won.*

She had no idea how long she'd been there when she heard a loud tap on her window.

Startled, she opened her eyes to find an attractive blonde calling out her name. Perhaps in her forties, the woman wore cream slacks and a red blazer. She held up a gold badge to the window.

"Ms. Castle? I'm State Marshal Linda Reed."

"Oh." Amy started the engine and powered down the window, unable to hide her disappointment. "I know you tried."

The woman's blue eyes and smile widened at the same time. "We got him, Ms. Castle. Mission accomplished."

"What?" Sitting up straight, Amy hit the unlock button and motioned her toward the passenger seat.

Once inside, Linda announced, "I just served him, and boy is he furious." She tapped the small device on her shoulder. "And I recorded it all on my bodycam."

"How? I watched him drive away."

"He must have gone out another way because he

didn't come through the door as we'd planned. But I had my deputy waiting in his car, just in case he tried to take off. We were able to follow him. He was driving so fast down Cottage Road, a cop signaled him to pull him over right before he got to that busy intersection with a gas station and the fast-food place. He had no choice. It was either blow through the red light there and risk an accident or stop for the light."

Amy couldn't wait to hear more. "What did he do?"

"He stopped and we reached him as he was yelling at the cop. He must have suspected something because he took off as I got closer. He went through the light and continued toward the highway."

Amy's mouth dropped open. "You mean he drove away from the police?"

"Yes, ma'am, he did," Linda answered, her eyes aglow. "The officer chased him for over a mile, lights and sirens blaring. You should have seen the other cars on the road move out of the way. My deputy and I followed, not as fast of course, but we could see everything. The entrance ramp for the 291 East connector toward Boston was coming up. I thought he was going to jump on, but just in time, two cruisers came right at him from the other direction. He would have T-boned them if he didn't stop. The first cruiser pulled up alongside of him, boxing him in."

The marshal paused to catch her breath as Amy absorbed the information.

"The cops drew their guns and ordered him out of the car, but he refused. I watched him shake his head at them as he hollered into his cell phone. Then another cruiser arrived, and a big guy got out. Using his door as a shield, he aimed what looked like a rifle through the open window and yelled out through a loudspeaker, 'I'll get the tires.' "

Amy imagined every detail of the scene. "Oh no. They were going to shoot at his precious car?"

The marshal nodded. "That got him to open the door. The cops were so mad, they dragged him out and leaned him up against the car to handcuff him. There was lots of yelling. It was great."

"This is better than TV. Then what happened?"

"I walked right over to them, introduced myself, and held out the papers to him. He tried to run again but the cops held him. He screamed and tried to kick at them. Then the big one, holding the rifle, told me to put the documents between his cuffed hands and his back."

Amy couldn't believe it. "Did he try to wiggle away?"

Linda grinned. "You betcha, but the cops held him still and I shoved the papers right in there, announcing in front of everyone, 'You've been served.' When we left, he and the police were still there. I presume he's being arrested."

Amy's chest felt tight again, but this time with relief, not hyperventilation. She leaned against the headrest and closed her eyes. Opening them, she squeezed the woman's hand. "Thank you, Marshal Reed. You can't know how much I appreciate this."

"My pleasure." Linda opened the door. "I'll get my proof of service right over to your lawyer for court. Best of luck to you and be sure to let me know if you need anything else."

Beyond elated, Amy watched the marshal drive away. Then, unable to stop herself, she drove to the location Linda described. Sure enough, Malcolm was still there, sitting on the curb. His hands were cuffed behind him, and his shirt tail hung out over his chubby stomach, as he yelled at the tow truck driver who was maneuvering his car onto a flatbed.

Reducing her speed, Amy recorded the scene on her cell phone, then honked the horn. Malcolm's head snapped in her direction. She waved, sticking out her tongue at him as she passed by.

It felt better than good sex.

Gotcha, you huge turd!

Chapter Nineteen

Josie

"Get a grip!" Josie scolded herself. She knew when she took Amy Castle's case that she'd be returning to this floor of the courthouse. All family law cases were addressed on the fifth floor because it contained several conference rooms adjacent to the courtrooms, for mediations and to separate misbehaving spouses. Hoping she'd masked her panic, she thanked Valerie for her help.

The clerk nodded with a smile. "Welcome back."

Not for long.

Now inside the ancient, creaky, elevator, Josie hoped that the less-than-smooth ascent wasn't due to a fraying cable that would send her crashing down into the basement. When it did arrive at the fifth floor, it stopped with a thud.

She pushed the open button when the doors didn't part, then waited as they uttered their protest, whining and screeching the whole way. She poked her head out. The hall was empty. Straightening, she moved forward, keeping her view slightly to the left, to avoid the dreaded Courtroom 510 on the right.

A tall, lanky young man stood at the doorway leading to Judge Myers' courtroom. He wore the typical clerk's uniform of khakis, a navy jacket, a rumpled white shirt, and a neutral tie askew just below his Adam's apple. Gold-framed aviator glasses rested on his nose and dark hair curled at his collar. He sent her an awkward smile and wave.

It took a moment for Josie to place him. "You're Thomas Rivers, from my Monday and Wednesday night family law class." Then she added, "And last year's trial techniques seminar."

"And I'm Judge Myers' law clerk during the day," he confirmed, seeming pleased she'd recognized him. "Five other students work here too. Let me show you where the Castle boxes are."

Following the clerk through the courtroom and into the adjoining conference room, Josie hid her dismay. *There goes the sanctity of my law school position.*

Six students would see her duking it out and maybe getting her head handed to her on a rusty platter by Richard Diamond. Plus, they'd be privy to any gossip that might re-surface about the shooting.

That's just marvelous.

Compartmentalizing, Josie made a face at the row of boxes lined up on the long conference table and on the floor against the wall. "Have you been involved with the post judgment motions for contempt?" she asked the clerk. "Ms. Castle told me that every time a court date was scheduled, it was then postponed."

"Yes." Thomas removed an overstuffed folder from the box labeled 13 and flipped through its contents. He stopped at a stapled packet and showed it to Josie.

"This is the court's internal docket." He pointed to a list of dates. "You can see here, the judge hasn't been around a lot this term. He took a vacation after this trial ended, followed by a month-long trial in New Haven, to fill in for Judge Newberry who broke his hip. When he got back, the first scheduled date was postponed because Attorney Diamond was on vacation."

"Of course." Josie heard her own sarcasm.

Rivers didn't react. He flipped to the next page. "On the next court date, Attorney Diamond had an emergency in Stamford. On the one after that, Mr. Castle himself, had some kind of emergency." He paused, looking at Josie. "And he failed to show up for the fourth date. The judge granted Attorney Diamond's request for a postponement and now the case is on for this Thursday."

Rivers closed the folder. "In case you didn't know, Judge Myers is scheduled to start another big trial in New Haven in mid-December."

That gave Josie hardly three full weeks to either get Amy's money, or at least make a huge dent in the process. Otherwise, they'd be going to New Haven, or worse. They could be scheduled here in Hartford before a new judge. That meant she'd need to educate him or her about Richard Diamond's antics. That could take months. She suspected Diamond already knew this. In fact, he was probably counting on it.

Josie wondered if Marshal Reed had any luck serving Malcolm Castle.

"Is there anything I can help you find in the boxes?" Rivers asked. "I know this case inside and out." He rolled his eyes to the ceiling, then back to her. "The trial was wild."

"I have no doubt." Josie started to decline his offer but then a thought occurred to her. "Do you know what happened to the final divorce judgment? Perhaps the judge has it in his chambers?"

The clerk consulted the docket and the remainder of the folder. "I don't remember seeing it. I'll ask the judge.

I know he wasn't too happy when he received a copy of the motion for contempt. I doubt he'll be thrilled to hear that the judgment hasn't been finished. Let me check on it and get back to you."

"Thanks."

"Are you all set for now?"

"Yes," Josie replied, anxious to begin working. "You've been a great help."

He paused before leaving. "See you in class."

She smiled at him. "That's right."

Alone at last, Josie settled at the middle of the rectangle table facing the door and reached for the same bulging folder the clerk referenced. When finished, she kept going and tore through eight of the boxes. A whiff of fabulous cologne caused her to look up.

"Josephina Jensen?" Richard Diamond questioned, as if surprised. He took up the entire door frame and had to duck to enter the room. "I can't believe it. Two times in what, three days? How incredible."

That's one way to describe it.

His baritone voice filled the room as his eyes piqued with curiosity, first at her, then at the boxes. As he spoke, she appreciated his well-tailored medium-blue suit. It outlined his athletic physique and complemented his pale-pink shirt and periwinkle tie.

Always the peacock.

"Are those the Castle files?"

Before she could respond, his cell phone rang. He held up his forefinger to her.

"One moment." He pressed his phone to his ear and moved outside the room. "Richard Diamond here."

Josie used the opportunity to pack up and ease past him before he could finish the call. On her way out, she heard a loud nasty voice swearing through his phone. Her own vibrated in her purse. Once out of his sight, she read the text. It was from Amy Castle.

—*The marshal served Malcolm!!*—

Josie rubbed her forehead. *That must be him now, bawling out Diamond.*

Chapter Twenty

Richard

"I'm telling you, Dickie. That lady marshal and her goon almost got me killed. And now they got me arrested."

Richard maintained his appalled tone as Malcolm Castle ranted again about the claimed abuse he suffered earlier while being served a subpoena from Josie Jensen's state marshal. The first rant-filled call came during the first police stop. Richard had to cut it short because he was in the middle of a pretrial conference with the opposing counsel and the judge, but he directed William Singer to head over to the police station.

Knowing at the time that Jensen was in the courthouse somewhere, Richard set out to find her when his conference ended. And he did find her. But now he was forced to listen to his client's further tale of woe.

"The damn cops chased me down Cottage Road like I was a criminal, with that marshal witch behind them. It's just not right, Dickie. You gotta do something. I want you to make sure she gets her badge taken away."

Malcolm Castle wasn't Richard's first client to avoid being served court documents. These guys went to all lengths. And up until now, Castle had little trouble fending off the marshals. But odds being what they were, a canny marshal finally caught him.

Richard received a text from William as Castle continued to whine. The official charges against Castle ranged from threatening a police officer to reckless driving, reckless endangerment, and resisting arrest. No doubt they would make him stew awhile before releasing him from custody.

He wondered which state marshal Attorney Jensen hired.

He'd find out soon enough.

"You told me not to worry about Jensen," Castle roared. "But she signed the subpoena. I want her off my ass now!"

"Everything is under control, Malcolm."

"You say that, but how do we fix this? I ain't paying Amy one more dime until I'm ready, Dickie. And I ain't ready. In fact, I'm heading to my new place in Florida just as soon as I get out of this dump and I ain't coming back until next week. If then."

"Perhaps not," Richard replied. "You may not be able to leave the state while you are out on bail. I expect it will be a condition of your release."

"And you're just going to have to fix that too, Dickie. Right?"

Richard did not appreciate the snide tone. He'd played Malcolm's divorce better than an endless symphony conducted by one of the great masters. But now, the instruments showed wear and tear from overuse and repair, making restoration no longer feasible. The time had come to pack them away somewhere, just like this case.

"First things first," Richard replied, curtailing his annoyance. "Attorney Singer is working on getting you out of there. We can discuss your concerns after you are at home, not while you are sitting in a bugged police department detention room."

Castle grumbled. "I get your drift."

"Good."

The line disconnected.

Richard left the courthouse and walked the short block back to his office. He suspected Josephina Jensen was long gone.

In her shoes, he would have bolted too.

He retrieved his phone and pounded in a number.

"This is Attorney Tabor."

"Good evening, John. Rich Diamond here. I'm calling about that referral my office sent you earlier."

"Yes, Rich. Thank you again. That was very thoughtful of you to send Mr. Penway to me. I feel so honored. I…"

Richard cut him off. "When are you meeting with him?"

"Um, he'll be here at six. And he's agreed to pay the full amount of the retainer fee you suggested. I'll be sure to send you your one-third share when the funds clear."

"Much appreciated. Enjoy your evening."

Richard disconnected the call before Tabor could say more. A weasel is a weasel, but they can be useful on occasion.

That should slow Jensen down some.

Chapter Twenty-One

Josie

Huffing, and puffing, and limping, Josie reached her car and jumped inside, locking the doors at the same time. Her cell phone rang as she engaged the ignition. She ignored it. She needed to get out of the area quickly before Diamond left the courthouse and saw her.

After reaching Lincoln Street, she made a left. The highway entrance was one traffic light away and that led to the law school, two exits away. She followed a city bus across Capitol Avenue, then passed the legislative office buildings on her left and right.

There was something about being in a state capitol, where laws were made, upheld, and changed on a continual basis. The constant excitement electrified the air. Did she miss it? She didn't think she did. Until now.

Her cell rang again as she eased into a line of traffic. This time she answered. "Josie Jensen."

"It's me, Amy. Did you get my text? Malcolm was served! I can't believe it."

Josie heard relief, vindication, and a hint of deviousness in her client's voice. "I'm so glad."

And Josie did feel glad. And relieved, and terrified. That meant the games had begun. And it begged the all-important question. Would Diamond's reaction be proportional, such as having Amy subpoenaed to court too? It wasn't necessary. Nothing was going to keep her away. But it would paint the written record in a better light for Malcolm, for the casual reader who didn't know the parties.

Or would Diamond and his client toss out a live grenade?

Either scenario was possible.

"Your marshal is my hero," Amy continued. "She brought a deputy with her and they scared Malcolm so bad, he got pulled over for speeding. Then he drove off. The cops stopped him, and he got arrested."

"Excellent," Josie replied, but her thoughts screamed, *Arrested? Serves him right.* But it also worried her. *Was Castle that much of a loose cannon? He couldn't just take the marshal's papers without creating a scene?*

"So, what's next?" Amy asked.

Josie asked herself the same question. "We need to prepare you for court on Thursday. How about we talk on Wednesday morning? Nine o'clock?"

"That works," Amy answered. "I'll call you then."

Another call rang from Josie's phone as she exited off the highway.

"Hey, Dad."

"Daniel said you took that big case. Good for you for getting back into the game. And a hundred grand is pretty impressive."

Josie knew he'd think that. Her brother's adoration of money was hereditary. "It's just this one, Dad. As a favor to Dan."

"Yeah, but he said this could lead to other big ones."

"We'll see." It was easier than rehashing that same old discussion. "Are we still on for Saturday?"

"I should be there by noon."

"See you then. Love you, Dad."

"Love you too, kiddo."

The law school's exit was a half mile away. She activated her blinker as her thoughts returned to Amy and Malcolm Castle. She wondered when she would hear from Richard Diamond. And what he would say or do.

****

Back in her office at the law school, Josie had thirty-nine minutes to get some work done before her evening class started, and she needed every microsecond of it. And of course the phone on her desk rang and lit up. She recognized her young assistant's extension from the registrar's office on the first floor.

"Hi, Rivka. What's up?"

"State Marshal Reed is here. She says you're expecting her."

"Oh yes. I'll be down."

Josie started to hang up when Rivka asked, "Would you like me to bring her up? I have that form the dean asked you to approve. It's for the syllabus for the new class you're teaching next term."

After the stress of the day, she settled back down. "That would be great. Thanks."

Moments later, the two women arrived as Josie prepared a check for Linda's fee.

"That Malcolm Castle is one feisty little man," the marshal commented, holding out the proof of service documents to her. "Good luck in court."

Josie hadn't seen Linda since just prior to the shooting. Almost as tall as Josie, and not much older, the marshal wore a baby-blue suit and an ivory blouse. No one would guess her occupation. And that was the point.

"Amy told me the story. I wish I was there to see it happen."

"I'll email you the bodycam link."

As they spoke, Josie realized Rivka was waiting and made the introductions "State Marshal Reed, meet Rivka Abrams, my office assistant."

"Do you plan to be a lawyer too?" Linda asked.

The exact opposite in appearance, the petite, curly haired brunette, wore a long black skirt, black low-heeled boots, and a black turtleneck. She lifted her chin and blushed. "I do."

"Rest assured, you've got the best mentor by far."

Rivka agreed and placed the document Josie needed to sign on the desk. "Your class starts in a few minutes."

"And you're good for her," the marshal added, causing them all to laugh.

As the ladies left, Josie packed up for class and thought about what Linda said about Rivka. Over the past ten months, she'd come to rely on the young woman's efficiency and attention to detail. In addition to being a full-time undergrad, she worked part-time for the law school's registrar, making sure that Josie, along with her law school professor colleagues, addressed all the administrative parts of the job, outside of teaching, that they deplored.

When Rivka first started the job, she told Josie she was raised Orthodox, in a very conservative, traditional, Jewish neighborhood in Brooklyn. She was living here now with her aunt who was studying to be a nurse.

"Like all the girls in our congregation, my mom got married on her seventeenth birthday and had us four kids right after. Money was really tight after my dad died, so she decided to go to college and get a career to earn enough to support us. Now she works as a pharmacist in White Plains."

"That's huge," Josie marveled, then drew her brows together. "How did that go over with your community?"

Rivka's dark eyes glimmered with pride. "Oh, we had to move. You find out who your friends are when you start questioning the crowd. But Mom won't back down. She's determined that my three brothers and I have the skills to get good jobs, even if the boys decided to devote their lives to studying Torah. She tells them, 'God gave all of us a brain and twenty-four hours in a day. That's plenty of time to study and to earn a decent living.' "

Josie had listened to her story, fascinated that they shared the same religion, and yet they observed it in such different ways. She practiced Reform Judaism which, while also firmly based on Torah, focused on more of a contemporary world view, while blending in the past's sacred traditions and spiritualism.

Josie switched her attention to the documents Linda provided. Malcolm Castle had been served in-hand, meaning face to face, instead of the documents being left at his home. That type of service was permitted, but obviously not as good. Especially in contested cases like this one. She wondered again when she would hear from Diamond.

The scars on her thigh and chest started to itch and her bad leg throbbed.

Josie ignored the physical signs of anxiety. She locked her office door behind her and retrieved her vibrating phone from her purse. Luke's name glowed on the caller ID screen. This was the first time he'd tried to contact her. The itching and throbbing increased and her stomach threatened to upchuck its contents.

He knows my teaching schedule. Why is he calling now? Should I answer and be late for class?

No, Josie decided. He could wait. He'd already tossed her personal life upside down. She couldn't let him interfere with her job too.

Ignoring the hum, she entered the elevator and thought about her class. The students were smart and engaged. And no matter how many times she'd taught a specific course, each group brought with them a fresh perspective. More than half of their families were divorced. This gave them similar but also some unique perspectives, depending upon how the adults in their lives handled the situation. Josie believed it was crucial to share those experiences with the students who came from intact families. And vice versa.

Josie entered the lecture hall and found Thomas Rivers in his usual seat in the middle of the third row. He smiled a greeting. She shot one back and began the evening's lecture.

"Good evening, everyone. Tonight's topic is the financial affidavit."

"Is that what tells the lawyers how much money the clients have to pay for their divorces?" someone shouted from the back.

Many students laughed.

"That's not far off," Josie replied, connecting her laptop to the projector. "Its purpose is to create a financial snapshot of the couple's assets. Let's examine what's involved."

A half hour into the lecture, the side door opened. "Ms. Jensen?" An average sized woman with short dark hair motioned for her.

Josie presumed she was from the registrar's office downstairs. The final exam schedule still needed to be finalized. "One minute, class."

Even with her cane, Josie liked to walk up and down the length of the room when teaching. It kept both her and the students engaged.

Slower than she'd like, she made it to the door, still talking. The woman held it open, motioning for her to step into the hallway.

At that instant, Josie realized the woman was not from the registrar's office.

****

Josie's dreaded reality hit her full force. No longer could she avoid the inevitable, because it was happening, right then and there. Ready or not.

Luke had directed a state marshal to serve her divorce papers while she was teaching a class.

The woman, who resembled nothing like Linda Reed, held out a stapled set of documents. "I'm State Marshal Isabell Martini. Please take this, ma'am."

The sound of the woman's voice echoed in drowned out slow motion, like she was speaking underwater. Also in slow motion, Josie complied with her request.

"You've been served," the woman announced, and left down the hall.

Boy, that old saying sure was true. Josie really did want to clobber the messenger. Why couldn't the woman have served her at home? Or called ahead? Then she remembered Luke's call right before class started. The one she didn't answer.

Finding the door handle, she returned to the lecture hall and scanned her students.

Sure, the marshal wasn't carrying a big sign that

read, "Serving divorce papers to Professor Jensen." No one who observed the scene would know what just happened unless Josie flipped out and told them. The truth was, she almost wanted to.

Lawyers weren't usually present when their clients were being served. And now, after all these years, Josie knew how it felt. It sucked. She wished she'd served Luke first. But she couldn't fester now. She had a class to teach. Pasting on her most neutral expression, the one she perfected when learning the extent of the damage to her leg, she picked up the evening's lecture where she'd left off. And yet, as the hour ticked by, something kept pecking away at the edges of her thoughts. Something she just couldn't decipher.

At the break, a half dozen students met Josie at the lectern. Most times, she enjoyed this time. They'd fill her in on internship and job opportunities, and the latest school gossip. And there were always a few brown nosers and worry warts, asking for extra credit and trying to clarify her grading procedures. Just wait until they worked in the real world.

Tonight, Josie feigned listening, nodding where appropriate as she aimed for the exit. "I'll be right back," she promised. "There's something in my office I need to take care of."

Alone in the elevator, she scanned the cover sheet of the five-page divorce document. She already knew what the complaint said. More important, she wanted to know if Luke hired a lawyer.

Finding the section, Josie's eyes bugged out and her shoulders and jaw dropped. She re-read the name. *Jonathan Tabor? Luke hired Jonathan Tabor? He's the worst of the worst divorce lawyers in the entire state.*

Maybe the entire country.

Then Josie read the court location. Her hands shook the papers.

That asshole planned to file the divorce in Hartford? That was her courthouse. Heck, she almost died there. No way was she going to battle her personal life there. Richard Diamond may be a beast to deal with, but at least he was smart and had some class. Tabor was a different animal altogether. Unless he'd undergone a personality transplant during the past four years, he was a greedy, incompetent, and overpriced jerk who ripped off his unsuspecting clients. He made a circus out of even the most irrelevant points and annoyed everyone, including the judges.

Leaning against the back of the elevator, Josie poised herself for battle. *There's got to be something I can do to stop this.*

A possible solution came to mind halfway through the last hour of class. She just hoped she had enough time to pull it off.

****

By the time class ended, Josie had mentally plotted each step of her plan. She gathered her materials and headed toward the exit. "I can't stay," she told the students hoping to speak with her. "But feel free to email me with any questions about anything."

Back in her office, she locked the door behind her and grabbed a soda from the mini fridge. The divorce complaint beckoned to her from the center of her desk.

A tear fell from her eye and started its journey down her cheek. Brushing it away and sniffling, she settled in her chair and popped open the can. As the cold, fizzy caffeine traveled down her throat, she turned to the last page of the packet. There, the person bringing the divorce lists what they want the judge to order at the time the marriage is dissolved.

The first two requests were typical. A judgment of dissolution of the marriage and an equitable division of the marital assets. "Yes, but also the marital debts," Josie added aloud, recalling their last credit card bill.

Reading further, she squeezed the can in her grip.

"Alimony?" she questioned aloud. "Luke wants alimony? We've been married less than three years. Plus, our prenup rules out alimony to either party."

But the next section raised her pitch to a near shriek. "And he wants part of my lawsuit settlement from the shooting?"

The settlement was the result of claims she brought against Anne Compton for shooting her and the judicial department for its lax security that permitted the gun to get inside the courthouse. It covered all of her medical expenses and a large sum was placed in a trust that provided her with an annual income and funds to pay her future medical bills. She felt pretty confident no court would award Luke any of that, but how dare he ask?

Josie drained the half-crushed can and dialed her brother. Waiting for him to answer, she pushed the cell's speaker button and accessed the judicial website on her personal laptop.

"What's up?"

"Luke had me served during my class tonight. And get this? He's seeking alimony and part of my settlement trust."

"He's such a loser."

Josie rubbed her nose. "And that's not all. He hired Jonathan Tabor, who just happens to be the worst divorce lawyer known to the profession."

Hearing Dan's chuckle intensified her fury. "I'm glad you find this amusing. Do you want to know what else?"

"There's more?"

"Of course, why should that be all?"

His chuckle morphed into a full-blown belly laugh. "Tell me."

Biting back a harsh retort, she said, "The divorce complaint and summons direct the case to be filed in Harford. Can you believe it? That's my courthouse, Daniel. I spilled my blood there. And listen to this."

"I'm all ears."

She turned back to the first page of the packet. "The address Tabor lists for Luke is an apartment in Colchester. I looked it up online. I suspect it's his girlfriend's place."

"This is excellent," Dan assured her. "Divorces involving Colchester residents go to the New London judicial circuit. Since Tabor listed that address, he made Luke a Colchester resident. File a motion to transfer the divorce to New London. And I think there's even a court rule that addresses your situation. Just a sec. I'll try to find it."

Josie knew what he meant. "I've got it right here. Section 9-41 provides that any personal lawsuit, such as a divorce or other civil matter, filed against a lawyer where they predominately practice, shall be transferred to another court, unless the parties agree otherwise."

"See? Things happen for a reason. You were meant to help Amy. With her active case in Hartford, and the Colchester residence, you can throw a double whammy at Tabor. And just for fun, include copies of the photos of Luke and his girlfriend when you send him his copy of the motion to transfer. That should take things down a few notches."

Typing now, she said, "I'm going to do something better."

"Care to share?"

****

Josie's laptop clock showed nine-twelve. She dialed Linda Reed.

"Can I presume another adventure is in the works?" the marshal asked, laughter filling her voice.

"So sorry to call at this hour, but I need your help again." She continued to type as she spoke.

"I'm listening."

"I'm getting divorced. My husband needs to be served tonight." She spoke the words fast, to prevent her voice from cracking.

After a pause, the marshal said, "I'm so sorry, Josie".

"Thanks. Me too. Anyway, time is of the essence." She hit the print button.

"No worries. I'm still out serving. How can I help?"

Josie checked the time again. "Can I meet you somewhere with the divorce documents in about an hour? And I know this is imposing further, but after he's served, can you get me back your proof of service as soon as possible so I can file everything at the New London courthouse first thing tomorrow morning?"

"Sure. Do you know where he'll be tonight?"

"I do. He's working at an ambulance company in Hartford, next to the hospital. He'll be there, in between calls, until midnight. Otherwise, he listed a home address in Colchester."

"Which is in New London County, out of my jurisdiction. I get it. That's why this needs to be done before he leaves work tonight."

Josie let out a deep breath she didn't realize she'd been holding. It was so nice to work with people who didn't require you to spell out every detail of a situation.

"Correct."

"Then here's the plan," the marshal replied, energy filling each syllable. "If I can't get him, I'll have a New London marshal lined up to serve him at home and get the docs right back to you. No worries, legal beagle. We've got all bases covered."

"Thank you."

At ten-twenty, Josie met Linda at a late-night diner. Soon after, she reached her street, anxious to crawl into her bed and end this very long day.

She squinted through the glare caused by the street's lights hitting her windshield. Something wasn't quite right.

Why is my house so dark?

Chapter Twenty-Two

Josie, Tuesday Morning

At six minutes after nine, Tuesday morning, Josie stood in line at the clerk's office in the New London judicial circuit courthouse. As planned, Marshal Reed served the divorce documents to Luke last night in his employer's parking lot and got the affidavit of service back to Josie two hours ago. Now it was a race to the courthouse. So far, Tabor hadn't filed his documents in Hartford, but could he be standing in line there now, just as she was here? And did he tell Luke to cancel the electricity at their house?

As Josie had no answers, it was first things first. She needed to get the divorce filed now. Then she would deal with the power company. Oh, and she needed the locks at home changed, *again*, because Luke changed them. She figured that out when she tried to get inside the house last night. With the electricity out, the electric garage door opener didn't work. She tried to use her key to get into the house through the front door, and as she was fighting with the lock, she received Luke's text.

—Don't lock me out again. Your new key is under the mat on the deck.—

Screw him, Josie thought for the millionth time as she moved up in line and returned her thoughts to last night.

Due to heavy rains causing recent power outages, she and Luke kept a small generator in the back yard. After connecting it to an electric heater, the refrigerator, and a lamp, she settled on the living room couch. That was when she realized the brand new, big screen television was missing, along with the new leather recliner they'd purchased last month.

Ugh.

She'd either been selectively burgled, or Luke took another swipe through the house. She decided to go with the latter. Armed with an extra flashlight and blankets, she watched reruns of her favorite TV shows on her cell phone until she passed out.

Up at the crack of dawn, Josie skipped a cold shower, grabbed coffee on the road, met up with Marshal Reed, and waited in the courthouse parking lot until it opened for business. Now she felt exhausted and crabby. And she had to teach a class in two hours.

When it was her turn in line, Josie moved to the clerk's window and presented the necessary documents, along with the filing fee. Without warning, her knees started to buckle. Holding on to the counter, she opened her mouth to talk with the woman behind the plexiglass, but at first no words came out.

At that moment, Josie knew she couldn't do this divorce on her own. Though she'd listed Dan as her attorney on the paperwork, that was just temporary, to prevent Jonathan Tabor from contacting her directly. She'd put off the question of which lawyer to hire because she was hoping maybe she and Luke could handle the process themselves. It wasn't complicated—when the people involved used common sense. But with Tabor on scene, as well as last night's antics, she suspected the common-sense option was no longer available.

"Here you are." The sympathetic clerk handed Josie the receipt for the fee and a stamped copy to prove the date and time the paperwork had been filed. If Tabor challenged it, they could compare the times of the filings. He'll be pissed if she beat him to it. Luke too, she supposed, but it served them right. If they wanted a circus, they were going to get it.

In New London. She hoped.

The entire filing process took less than five minutes. It felt like an eternity.

Eyes downcast, Josie mumbled a thank you and turned to get the heck out of there.

"Oops! Excuse me," a surprised voice boomed.

Josie had collided into someone, a sturdy, male someone, toppling them both. The man placed his strong arm around her waist, attempting to draw them upright, but their combined weight threatened to tip them over.

"Richard?" she exclaimed, horrified.

He crinkled his forehead. "Josephina? Are you hurt?"

"No, I'm fine." Meanwhile, her bad leg screamed its objections. "Are you okay? I'm so sorry."

He raised an inquisitive brow. "What a pleasant surprise. This makes it three times we've run into each other in the past four days. This time, literally. Do you have a case here?"

Josie's throat closed up. She managed a tight-lipped smile and a short nod as they disengaged and she limped toward the exit, cane in hand. There was no way she wanted him to know about her divorce.

"See you Thursday," he called out.

"See you Thursday," she squeaked back, as he made his way to clerk's counter.

Watching him, Josie couldn't help but wonder. *This was just another coincidence, right?*

As if in response, she recalled her mother saying, "There are no coincidences in life, Josephina. Always remember that."

****

At school, and on time, Josie began her lecture on what she called Strategies in Family Law. With three classes left in the term, this was when she strived to put all of the semester's information into perspective.

She raised her chin toward a young man in the first row. "Tell me, Mr. Hastings. What does the term, strategy, mean to you?"

"As a lawyer, or just in general?"

"There is no more, just in general," a woman to Josie's left called out.

Another man added, "No kidding. Two years of law school took care of that. We're all warped now."

Josie agreed. "Fine. Let's pretend, for now, just in general. What does strategy mean?"

"A plan to outmaneuver someone. Like in war or playing paintball."

"Or chess," someone called out from the back. "It's a plan to win."

"Excellent," Josie responded. "Now, should that behavior, or concept, be permitted in the practice of family law? Think about it. We are officers of the court, first and foremost. Right? We're obligated to perform within ethical guidelines while dealing with people's lives at their lowest, and their children's lives. How can we do that, and also win for our clients?"

She pointed to a blonde woman midway up. "Ms. Keller?"

"Not everyone agrees with what ethical means. That's why people end up in court and ask a judge to decide."

Josie nodded. "Correct. That's how law is made."

"But people interpret it differently," a young man from the middle interjected.

"So, they hire us," a woman to her left added. "To figure out ways to make the law fit what they want."

"Are all strategies permissible, as long as they're considered legal?" Josie asked. "Raise your hand if you say yes."

Several hands shot into the air.

"I disagree," A young woman in the front piped up. "In most family law cases, two people who used to be in love and committed to forever, are now ending their relationship and all the hopes and dreams that went along with it. The stakes are high and much more emotional than a typical car accident with minimal injuries. Especially if they have children."

"And expensive," Josie added. "The more a couple argues, the more the lawyers get paid. Which means the less money a family has for things like food, shelter, clothes, vacations, even college. And split that number in half, to support two households. So, let me ask you this. What does it mean to win in family court?"

A student in the back who rarely participated declared, "Whoever gets to keep the most money wins."

Several students chuckled.

"Or whoever gets to keep the kids wins."

"Or both."

"No one wins," the same woman from the front

corrected. "It's more about survival. Cutting the ties, picking up the pieces, moving on, and starting all over again."

Josie passed out two versions of the same assignment, one for each side of the room. "Break into small groups and discuss how you would advise a new client about dividing their assets and debts and determining child custody and a parenting plan. Include what you know about alimony and child support. And estimate how long you believe the case will take and how much it will cost by the time the divorce is granted. Be sure to take into account what the client wants, and what their spouse wants. You have twenty minutes. Then we'll discuss your ideas."

Her phone lit up as she returned to the lectern. Luke's name appeared at the top of the text. She hadn't responded to him about the lock change, and she'd wondered how long it would take him to react to being served last night. By now he should also know she filed the divorce in New London and yet his lawyer had still not filed in Hartford.

Here was her answer. But did she want to know?

She checked the class, confirming her students were occupied with the assignment. She pushed the button to read the text, then winced.

—You just made it worse for yourself.—

Her cheeks burned. She re-read the words, wondering what they could mean. The worst for her was opening that card and seeing those photos of Luke with that other woman.

Another text followed.

—And thanks for taking that big Castle case in Hartford. My lawyer says half the money you get belongs

to me. And have fun doing it while he keeps you tied up in court on your own divorce.—

After the shock of the veiled threat lessened, all sorts of questions swirled in Josie's thoughts. The loudest asked, *How do Luke and Tabor know I'm representing Amy Castle?*

Chapter Twenty-Three

Josie, Wednesday Afternoon

Josie spent an hour that morning on the phone with Amy Castle, preparing for Thursday's hearing. Then she taught two classes. Dan called just as she reached her office. "Did you see my text about my Aunt Debra?"

"Not yet," Josie answered, hobbling to her desk. "Is this the woman you told me about on Sunday?"

"Right. She turned sixty-five on Monday and her mom died in her sleep early yesterday morning. She left a decent-sized trust, making Debra the sole beneficiary during her lifetime. It includes a house, cash, and investments."

"Very nice," Josie commented.

"It sure is, except Debra got a call from a real estate agent later in the day. That jerk of a husband is already trying to sell the house out from under her. She wants to hire you to stop him and start the divorce."

"He sounds like a delight already."

"She has money to pay you and it gets even better."

Josie sat down and started up her laptop. "Tell me. I can't stand the anticipation."

"Debra lives in Suffield. That means another Hartford judicial circuit case to support your change of venue argument for your divorce."

You mean if I agree to represent her? She opted for,

"I guess that's something."

"You'll like her. She said she figures she has at least another twenty years left in this life and she wants to make them the best she can."

"She sounds like a gutsy lady."

"Yet very genteel, unless she gets her dander up like it is now."

"I'll keep that in mind." Josie pulled up the judicial website again to see if Tabor filed his documents yet.

Still no.

"Call her now if you can," Dan suggested, in his very pleasant, yet very nagging way.

"I will," she promised, jotting down the contact information he provided.

****

Later that afternoon, Josie drove down a pleasant, tree-lined street filled with historic houses bordering the town green. Arriving at Debra Tate's address, she thought again about the past few days. So much had changed so fast.

A tall, attractive older woman, dressed in a blue pants suit and mid-heeled matching pumps, waited outside of a Victorian-style yellow house, with white trim and a red door. She greeted Josie with a warm smile, exuding a rare tranquility, though her hands trembled slightly, clasped at her waist.

"It might feel like your entire world is spinning upside down right now," Josie told her. "Just remember that things will work out. You'll be okay."

The woman's blue eyes shined. "Thank you for saying that."

Eager, but with grace, she led Josie through a bright, pretty kitchen. Though somewhat dated in style and appliances, it felt cheery and opened into a dining room with a large bay window. A vase of pink and yellow roses, with babies' breath and ferns, sat in the middle of a cherry table. It was set for two, with crystal glasses and a gold-rimmed dish pattern Josie recalled from one of her mother's collections. The colors of the chairs and placemats matched the flowers.

Admiring the scene, Josie felt a warm welcome wash over her. And a reminder of how much she missed her mother…

"I made tea," Debra announced, as they entered the tastefully furnished living room decorated in shades of blue and yellow.

Josie was about to decline, but she spotted a tea set in another vintage pattern she recognized. It sat alongside a bowl of luscious strawberries on the table in front of a blue velvet loveseat.

"I'll get the fresh whipped cream," Debra said, heading back toward the kitchen.

Daniel! It must be him. There was no other way for this woman to know I loved strawberries.

The woman returned, sending Josie an eager smile, and set another bowl on the table. "I'm so thankful you were able to meet with me here."

Because I don't have an office, except at school.

Debra poured the tea and moved the creamer and sugar bowl closer to Josie. "Please help yourself to the strawberries."

"My mouth is watering, but only if you'll join me."

Pleased, Debra filled a plate, then settled on the rocking chair across from her. Josie followed suit and started the divorce conversation. The woman chimed in soon after and it didn't take long for Josie to hear herself agreeing to represent her.

So, what was one more client?

She thought of Amy Castle, and then Laura Schofield, who may not be far behind. These women were embarking on a well-deserved adventure, determined to improve their lives. That took courage, extreme courage. And they trusted her to help guide them.

As Debra handed her a check for the retainer fee, Josie asked, "When would you like your husband to be served?"

"Sunday," Debra answered without hesitation. "Philip is leaving Thursday morning on a fishing trip. He'll be home late Sunday. I'm using the time to move in here. This is my mother's home. She died last week and left it to me in a trust."

Dan had filled me in, but gee, he wasn't kidding when he said she was ready to act now.

"Does Philip know your plans?"

Debra shook her head and clasped her hands in her lap. "No, and he's going to be furious. I don't want to be cruel, but knowing him as I do, I don't think I have a choice."

She raised her eyes to the ceiling, then back to Josie. "You see, for the past several years, I've told him I wanted a divorce. And each time I backed down. I even left for a short time."

"So now he doesn't believe you're serious."

She nodded. "It's become a joke to him."

Josie gave her a reassuring smile. "Then let's begin. First things first. Divorce is all about money. Your homework is to create a list of all of your marital assets. For example, real estate, pensions, investments, etc."

Debra frowned. "I just have a small pension. Everything else is in Philip's name. He's always reminding me that it all belongs to him, alone."

Josie smirked. "A lot of men, the ones who tend to be a bit controlling, think that. But guess what?"

Debra leaned forward, curiosity filling her blue eyes. "What?"

"They're wrong," Josie replied, grinning and winking.

"They are?"

"I promise." She fished her phone out of her purse and hit Dan's speed dial number. "So, let's call the other Attorney Jensen and see if he can work his real estate magic by having an appraiser come to your house while Philip is away. That way, you won't need his cooperation later."

Debra's eyes shined. "Oh, I'd like that."

Chapter Twenty-Four

Josie, Thursday Morning

For Josie, the dark hours leading to daybreak on Thursday dragged by. Filled with nervous energy, she hobbled back and forth through her kitchen, dining and living areas, working and reworking her strategy for dealing with Richard Diamond in court that morning.

At worst, she reasoned, Amy would leave the courthouse today empty handed. The judge would order a new hearing date, and they would try again at that time. Except Amy was paying her a lot of money to get results and quick. And Malcolm Castle was paying his lawyer even more, to prevent those results.

Exasperated, Josie stopped pacing and collapsed into a kitchen chair. "Let's face facts," she said aloud. "I'm scared."

She was scared of reliving the scene when her client pulled out that gun, and the shock of those bullets ripping into her. And she was scared that the awful experience she'd had with Diamond years ago, when he'd beat her in court, would repeat itself. Even worse, she worried she was missing something in Amy's case, like she did in that one, and he would humiliate her all over again.

Digesting that reality, she saw the divorce complaint from Luke's lawyer. It sat on top of a pile of other papers on the table, including their prenuptial agreement.

"And I'm humiliated about my personal life." That last sentence came out in a whisper.

She recalled the photos of her husband and that bimbo, and getting served at school, and getting locked out of her house, and having no electricity.

On her feet now, refusing to psych herself out, Josie selected a song on her phone's play list. The intro beat of *Rocky III's The Eye of the Tiger* filled the room. This, and the other *Rocky* songs were her go-tos during those endless months of surgeries and rehab following the shooting.

As the song built momentum, so did Josie. She tore the divorce complaint into four quarters and dropped them into a ceramic bowl. Then she set them ablaze with the lighter she used to light the Shabbat candles each Friday evening.

Watching the flames burn, she whispered, "To hell with you, Luke. And to you, Richard Diamond, and to you, Malcolm Castle." After a moment, she added, "And to you too, Anne Compton."

The alarm on Josie's phone rang as the last flame fizzled into black ash. She checked the time. Six o'clock on the dot. Time to get ready for court. Heading upstairs to change, she decided to wear her cream suit with a green silk blouse.

Green. The color of money. The goal of the day.

Along with ducking any flying bullets, real or imagined.

****

The time on the car's console glowed eight-twenty-two. Amy Castle sat beside Josie in the passenger seat. They were two short blocks from the courthouse and stuck in traffic.

"Thank you for letting me drive in with you," Amy said, inspecting her make-up in the visor's mirror.

In general, Josie didn't drive clients to court, but Amy was special. And courthouse parking could be a nightmare. She needed to make sure they both arrived on time and in one piece.

"You know, none of my professors ever mentioned the perils of finding a parking space within a mile of a busy courthouse," Josie remarked, envying Richard Diamond for being savvy enough to have his office within walking distance. "Who knew being a lawyer meant spending an hour or more in a panic, circling nearby streets in bumper-to-bumper traffic, dodging other would-be anxious parkers, all seeking an available spot. Even an illegal space was acceptable, as long as you got into the building on time."

Amy laughed. "I bet they never discussed the weather in law school either."

At that, they scowled at the sleet, mixed with dime-sized hail, pounding the windshield and splattering in all directions.

"At least we have a secret weapon." Josie pointed to her handicapped parking pass on the dashboard.

Amy's face clouded. "I'm so sorry for what happened to you."

Josie knew she was referring to the shooting. "I don't like how I got this parking perk," she replied. "But it sure comes in handy."

"It must have been awful."

Josie concentrated on the line of cars ahead. "It was."

The traffic light switched from red to green. Horns sounded from all directions as she inched forward.

"I know you didn't want to handle court cases anymore, but thank you for agreeing to help me."

Josie drove into a designated spot in the small lot adjacent to the courthouse. Parking, she noticed Amy's clenched fists at her sides, and her eyes squeezed shut. Her bottom lip quivered.

Switching off the ignition, she pushed aside her jumbled feelings and let out an audible sigh. "What Malcolm is doing is wrong. He knows it and his lawyer knows it. In fact, his lawyer knows it so well, he's been doing his darndest to keep Malcolm away from the judge."

Amy checked her make up in the visor's mirror again. "So today, we want to make sure the judge knows Malcolm isn't following his orders?"

"That's one goal. And I'd like you to get all your money today, but as I told you before, Malcolm isn't going to roll over without a fight. I predict we'll be here a few more times before this matter is straightened out."

"I understand," she said, clasping her hands in her lap.

Josie's gaze returned to the console. Eight-forty-one. She noted Amy's red nose and the tears swelling in her heavily mascaraed eyes. She hoped it was waterproof. And she felt the same emotions, but this woman was relying on her not to show it. "Just try to remember that the bad part is over. You're divorced and you have court orders."

Amy stared at the courthouse's foundation through the windshield. "I know. It's just that…"

Okay, it's time for some encouragement.

Josie retrieved her cell phone. "Before we go, I want to play this song that I think fits today. Are you game?"

Amy shrugged. "Sure?"

Josie hit the programmed button on her phone.

As the music started, she handed Amy the lyrics. "You might remember this."

She laughed. "*The Eye of the Tiger*?"

"Yup. This is you."

Listening and tapping to the beat, Josie said, "You fought for your divorce, and now you're gonna fight for your money. You are the eye of the tiger."

When the song ended, Josie asked, "Are you ready to kick some butt?"

Amy sent her a firm nod and a pretty determined smile. "Ready."

Josie tossed her car keys into her purse and opened the door. Reaching for her briefcase and cane in the back seat, she realized she was ready too.

****

Josie made it a rule never to make her clients wait in the long, dim hallway outside the courtrooms. How demoralizing to be trapped there, sitting on those hard benches, along with a crowd of other miserable souls. Anger, sadness, disgust, along with embarrassment, hovered over them like dark clouds as they waited for their cases to be called and their lives to be determined by strangers, at hundreds of dollars an hour.

As an alternative, Josie advised her clients to bring a book or magazine or download something on their phone to pretend to read, while waiting in the law library or an empty conference room. She promised to text them when they were needed.

And where did she get this nugget of thoughtfulness from? Richard Diamond, all those years ago, during their one case together. A case that altered the course of her legal career. Specifically, it taught her that you can't improve your tennis game by always playing against someone of your same skill level.

Before going up against Diamond, Josie had been practicing family law full-time at a small firm for three years, with an array of middle-class and lower income clients. And she felt like she was on the right track. She was learning a lot, and she earned a decent income.

Talk about a false sense of security.

It was Dan who introduced her to Susan Masterson. She was the daughter of one of his real estate clients. The thirty-six-year-old divorced her husband five years earlier and had primary custody of their two children, with him spending two weekends a month with them, if he wasn't working or otherwise busy.

Susan was recently offered a great job in Seattle, at five times her current salary, and informed her ex-husband that she needed to relocate with the kids. She asked him to meet with her to discuss a workable parenting plan, but he flat out refused. Instead, he accused her of trying to take the kids away from him and of having a boyfriend out there, which she did. Then he hired Richard Diamond to stop her from taking the children out of the state.

Josie met with Susan and decided she had a good faith reason to modify the parenting plan. Knowing full well of Diamond's reputation for chewing up and spitting out his opponents, and the exorbitant rates his affluent clients paid him, Josie worked harder than she'd ever worked on anything to prepare, spending hours rehearsing her legal arguments in front of Daniel who critiqued her without mercy.

Susan had everything going for her. She understood

how important it was for the kids to maintain a good relationship with their dad, even though he showed little interest in them. Instead, they frequently stayed with his parents during his parenting time. Furthermore, expert psychologists and the children's teachers supported the move, and she even had a string of character witnesses praising her parenting abilities and community engagement. They also confirmed that the dad rarely participated in the children's activities. Their testimony couldn't have gone better.

And yet Diamond defeated Josie with so little effort. The judge ruled that the children had a positive relationship with both parents under the current parenting plan, and they were thriving. Changing that plan could result in irreparable harm that he was unwilling to risk.

"Death by a thousand cuts," Dan later described it. After the trial, they'd huddled in a dark booth in the back of a bar where no one knew them, licking their wounds. He hadn't taken another family law case since.

Josie stuck with it, determined not to lose like that again. She analyzed each moment of the trial, over and over again. Since this was pre-pandemic time, courts were open and trials were live, instead of virtual. This provided constant opportunities to observe Diamond and the few others of his caliber in action. In this way, she learned the strategies they employed, along with an assortment of nuanced manipulations that caused the odds to line up in their favor. More than once, she'd marveled, "They can do that? And get away with it?"

Implementing the skills she'd learned, and adding her own twists to fit each situation, Josie's boldness grew, startling opponents who'd underestimated her.

That, along with increased advertising and schmoosing at endless social events, just like Richard and his opponents did, provided new clients with higher socio-economic means and more complicated issues. And higher fees. By the time she took Anne Compton's case nine years later, she had entered the so-called big leagues. Not quite as big as Richard Diamond, but a close enough second. And she'd made sure never to take a case against him.

Josie thought of Amy Castle. With her stashed safely away, she exited the rattling elevator at the fifth floor, fifteen minutes before the hearing was scheduled to begin. As expected, two dozen or so folks spoke in hushed tones to their lawyers. At the same time, they stole glances at their spouses or partners whom they now viewed as enemies.

Josie zeroed in on the court's daily docket, posted halfway down the hallway, outside the scheduling clerk's office. Richard Diamond's laughter boomed from the far end as she spied the Castle case at the top of the second page.

She caught sight of him as she arrived at the assigned courtroom. Per usual, he presented a commanding presence, this time in a dark, pinstriped suit, powder-blue shirt, and a red tie with gold designs on it. His black shoes shined like glass, even from a distance. She knew she looked good too.

Their eyes locked.

Darn it. That wasn't supposed to happen.

"I'll call you back," she heard him say into the phone as he strutted toward her. He raised his arms, palms up. "And here we are again."

Josie couldn't help grinning back. "Good morning."

"You selected a doozy of a case for your comeback."

"I was just thinking the same thing." *Shoot. Why did she let that slip out?*

"You've been involved only a few days. Would you like to discuss the matter before heading straight to the judge? I'd be delighted to give you a crash course about the tumultuous events that transpired over the past four-plus years."

I'm sure you would. "Thanks, but unless you have all the signed documents needed to implement the transfers to my client, I'm all set."

"Are you sure?" he retorted. "Neither my client nor I have any objection to postponing today's hearing. I'm certain the judge would understand."

Josie accepted her opponent's helpful demeanor, identifying it for the garbage it was. In addition, she decided Daniel was right about practicing law. It was just like riding a bike or having sex, because all at once, her prior experience came rushing back. And for the first time in a very long time, she felt like she was standing on solid ground.

"No need." She took a seat on a nearby bench as Richard made a show of glancing at his designer watch.

"All right then, let's get this circus on the road." He rubbed his hands together, all business now. "Where's Mrs. Castle? I don't have much time. I need to be in Bridgeport by noon at the latest."

"She's in the building," Josie answered. "And Mr. Castle?"

Richard's smile faded a degree. He sat next to her, leaning in close enough to peek down her blouse and steal a glimpse of her black lace bra. She even wore her favorite perfume to entice him.

"He's on his way, but it's your client's motion. She needs to be here to testify."

"I think not. He's the one in contempt of court."

A troubled expression crossed his near perfect features. "I'm curious about something."

He paused, waiting for her to prod him on.

"Yes?"

"Why is your client pursuing this? In fact, why are you enabling her? She has already received much more than she deserves. And Mr. Castle decided not to appeal the judge's orders because he felt pity for her. If he did appeal, you and I both know she would have ended up with a heck of a lot less."

Josie arched a questioning brow at him. "Or perhaps not."

Richard tilted his head, as if confused by her response. "Why does she want to spend more money and time continuing this nonsense? She waged a bitter battle against my client, breaking his heart. It lasted for years. Isn't it time to let the wounds start to mend? After everything, they still have two sons together."

Who loathe their father, Josie considered reminding him, but didn't. Nor did she buy the breaking heart claim.

"I could ask you the same thing, Attorney Diamond," Josie answered, keeping her tone light. "You know better than me that court orders are in effect, created out of that bitter battle you mentioned. And your client is violating them. In case you've forgotten, that's why we're here today." As she spoke, she scratched her cheek with her middle finger.

Amusement danced in Richard's dark eyes. "Welcome back, Counselor. We've missed you."

"Oh no. This is a one-time thing."

He cocked his head to one side and winked. "You say that now."

Chapter Twenty-Five

Richard, Thursday Morning

After an hour of waiting, the clerk called the Castle case. Richard purposely sat next to Josie behind the scarred wooden counsel table, as the judge entered the old-style, dark paneled courtroom. Her client, Amy Castle, sat on the other side of her. The woman looked different. Better. Divorce must agree with her.

Josephina leaned toward him, staring straight ahead as she whispered, "Would you please direct your client to follow the court's orders so we can get out of here?"

He moved closer, his lips almost touching her ear. "He's been advised."

"Then convince him to do it."

"You know I can't do that."

"Can't? Or won't?"

"All rise," the court officer commanded, as Judge Myers entered the courtroom. "Hear ye, hear ye, the Family Law Division of the Hartford Judicial Circuit is now open and in session."

Richard continued to stick close to his opponent, to make the judge think they were buddies. Who needs truth when appearances say it all? He was sure the judge knew this was Jensen's first time back in court since the shooting. Above all, he wanted to prevent him from favoring her in any way, even though she sure looked fine. She even smelled good. Nevertheless, the courtroom was not the place for welcome backs and reminiscing, unless of course, it benefited him. And today it would not benefit him. In fact, some might say he was stuck in a rowboat, in the middle of a huge lake, under enormous thunder clouds, without a paddle.

Richard felt the full weight of Judge Myers's icy glare. Then it moved to Jensen, morphing into a welcoming smile.

Richard withheld a snarl.

"Counselors, please identify yourselves for the record," the judge directed.

Before Josie could utter a syllable, Richard blurted out, "Hello, Your Honor. For the record, my name is Richard Diamond, representing Mr. Castle. I presented my motion for a postponement to your clerk. And I am handing a copy to sister counsel now."

He watched Jensen narrow her eyes as he held out the document to her. She declined and pointed to an empty space on the table between them.

Richard addressed the judge. "Your Honor, before we go further, I need to inform you that Judge Calabrese's clerk in Bridgeport called my office a short time ago. I have been ordered to appear there at noon on an urgent child custody situation."

Judge Myers ignored Richard and settled on the woman standing next to him.

"Good morning, Your Honor. Attorney Josephina Jensen, representing Amy Castle who is present here in court."

Still speaking to Josephina, the judge asked, "Is there an agreement regarding the postponement?"

"No," they responded in unison. Richard believed it

was crucial to be seen and heard, especially when the conversation was averse to him. Even when a judge ignored him.

"Attorney Jensen, do you wish to be heard?"

"Thank you, Your Honor. May I inquire of brother counsel whether Mr. Castle is present in the courthouse?"

"Attorney Diamond?"

"Thank you, Judge. Unfortunately, Mr. Castle is stuck at the airport in Miami. He informed me that he was scheduled to fly back to Connecticut last night, but the flight was canceled due to this bad weather the entire eastern seaboard is experiencing." Richard pointed to the windows, showing heavy rain and sleet outside.

Always divert from the issue. Decide what you want the judge to focus on and keep hammering at it. Even if it's garbage.

"Attorney Jensen?"

"May I approach the bench?"

"You may."

"Your Honor, I have here the state marshal's affidavit of service. It proves Mr. Castle was duly served with this subpoena, in-hand, Monday afternoon. The subpoena commanded him to be here this morning. And if you review the court file and my motion for contempt, it's clear that all I am seeking today is his compliance with your financial orders that you issued more than three months ago."

Richard watched her, hiding his amusement and his slight concern. The cane didn't detract at all from her commanding presence, though its origin was unforgiveable. If not for that event, this battle with her could have been very interesting. Fun even.

And to think he was getting paid for putting on this show. Jensen should thank him for his client's pigheadedness. He expected she was making a pretty penny in attorney's fees too.

The judge reviewed the documents, then looked to Richard, who rose. "Attorney Diamond?"

"Yes, Your Honor?"

"Why hasn't your client complied with my orders?"

Richard didn't miss a beat. "Why did the divorce take more than four years, Your Honor?"

The court reporter laughed out loud, and the clerk dropped his pen. It flipped off the table onto the floor.

Score one point for the Diamond charm.

Judge Myers twirled one end of his mustache, just as Richard knew he would. They'd done this dance several times over the past two decades, but even Richard conceded that Mr. Castle was his toughest client to date. Correct that. Second toughest.

"When is he expected back?" the judge asked.

"I believe he is waiting to board, as we speak."

"Is it a direct flight?"

Hmm. Got him there. "I would expect so, Judge."

"Let's hope it is, for his sake." He turned to Jensen. "Your response?"

"Thank you, Your Honor. I have here the transcript of the last contempt hearing three weeks ago. Mr. Castle failed to appear on that date as well. At that time, Attorney Diamond reached him by cell phone and reported to the court that today was his client's next available date. As a result, you accommodated him and ordered that the hearing would not be postponed again." Jensen held up the transcript. "May I approach the bench again?"

"You may."

Richard busied himself by pretending to read something in his file, making sure to keep his expression blank.

Handing the document to the clerk, Jensen added, "I find it suspect why Mr. Castle, knowing he was under subpoena for today, would leave the state." Returning to her place, she added, "I also believe Mr. Castle is out on bail, due to an altercation he had with the police on Monday, while being served the subpoena. Query whether leaving the state is a violation of his bail contract." She paused for the dramatic effect, then continued. "In any event, Mr. Castle knows he is violating the orders you issued when you dissolved the marriage. Hence, I respectfully request you to issue an arrest warrant for him."

Richard scoffed. "Your Honor. I don't think we need to go to such lengths. My client is not responsible for the weather, or for me having an emergency in Bridgeport. Turning next to the subpoena, if you are inclined to issue an arrest warrant, please grant me time to draft a motion to quash it and to present testimony. The state marshal served the subpoena in such an egregious manner, that it must be found void. Moreover, Mr. Castle went to Florida for business purposes and the bail commissioner approved the trip. As you know from the very lengthy trial we had a few months back, he must maintain his very busy schedule if he is to continue to operate his business at its current level and also pay Ms. Castle her twenty-percent share."

"May I respond, Your Honor?" Jensen asked.

"No need, Attorney Jensen. Attorney Diamond?"

"Yes, Your Honor?" Always keep it polite and

contrite, no matter what.

"You and your client are ordered to report here at three o'clock this afternoon. No emergencies or weather issues will prevent us from moving forward. Even if your client doesn't make it."

"Of course, Your Honor. But what if my Bridgeport matter is still proceeding?"

"Then send one of your associates with Mr. Castle."

As the judge spoke, the clerk handed him a folded slip of papers. He read it and said, "And Attorney Diamond?"

"Yes, Your Honor?" Again, polite and contrite. Even when your jaw aches from fake smiling. "The clerk tells me the judgment file is months overdue. Please file it by five o'clock tomorrow." He then switched to Jensen. "Anything else, counsel?"

"Yes, Your Honor. I request an order directing Mr. Castle to pay Ms. Castle's attorney's fees for this morning."

"At what rate?" the judge asked.

A slight pause followed. "At the same rate Attorney Diamond charges his client. The last affidavit of attorney's fees he filed with the court stated seven hundred and fifty dollars per hour." She turned toward the clock over the doorway, then back to the judge. "I would ask for two hours please, with payment being made by bank or trustee account check before five o'clock today."

With no hesitation, the judge said, "So ordered. And Attorney Diamond?"

"Yes, Your Honor?" *This is getting old.*

"Your client might also want to work on settling this matter. Otherwise, I'll settle it for him."

"Message received, Judge."

The judge rose and instructed the court officer, "Please recess court."

"All rise."

Anxious to skedaddle, Richard leaned into Jensen and whispered, "I need to go, but I'll take care of that judgment. It should have been filed right after the divorce."

Always act helpful and cooperative. Or at least make it look that way.

Richard knew it worked when she whispered back, "Safe travels."

He sent her a wave, but once out of her sight, he made a fist pump into the air.

I did it again. I am the master! Then another thought came to mind.

How dare that punk clerk bring the missing judgment to the judge's attention. He just cost Richard a bundle of money. Jensen's going to take the document and run with it. He'd better not plan to work in Hartford after he graduates because Richard will see that it never happens.

Pushing that issue aside, Richard felt pleased overall with the morning's result. It was a close call. He knew his client was skating on paper-thin ice, but as Malcolm said, he had Richard to cover his ass.

He reached the outside door and buttoned his long coat, then opened his umbrella and proceeded to walk to his office. *Who knew what the afternoon would bring? This rainy sleet could change to snow. If it kept up, the courthouse may close early.*

And if not, he would come up with another way to slide through the day. He always did.

Chapter Twenty-Six

Josie

Josie and Amy waited in silence for Richard Diamond to leave the area before venturing from the courtroom. They continued in silence until they reached the conference room on the third floor where Amy waited earlier. She gave Josie a huge hug when they were behind the closed door.

"I can't believe the judge ordered Malcolm to pay my attorney's fees. Do you know how huge that is? And we have court again this afternoon, not a month from now."

They laughed as Josie hugged her back. Then they settled at the table to discuss their next steps. "We still can't be certain what will happen this afternoon," Josie cautioned. "Malcolm isn't going to do anything without a fight."

"Believe me," Amy answered. "After my four-year divorce battle and thirty-five years of marriage, I know we're not even close to being done. But at least the judge knows what Malcolm's been up to. That's a win by itself."

An hour later, Josie left to get lunch from the food truck parked outside.

Alone, she inhaled the rain-soaked air, clearing her thoughts. She liked Amy, but the drama of matching wits and battling with words, while emotions soared, took its toll. Every lawyer was expected to win, while their opponent was expected to do the same. The trouble was, both sides couldn't win at the same time.

Josie's next challenge became figuring out how to juggle food and drinks, along with her cane and an umbrella. Taking advantage of the slowing rain, she stuffed wrapped egg salad sandwiches with bottles of water and chocolate chip cookies inside her large purse and headed back inside.

A text notification sounded from her cell phone as the elevator reached the third floor. "Of course." She blew her bangs out of her eyes and dug through her purse to locate the phone.

—*Please call as soon as you can.*—

Stepping out of the elevator, she punched in the number. "Hi, Rivka, what's up?"

The young woman hesitated. "Um, I don't mean to bother you, but um, you got a delivery."

"What is it?"

"Um."

Josie sat down on a nearby bench and rubbed her forehead. "Should I be worried?"

"Someone sent you a dozen long-stemmed black roses."

"Oh. That's weird. Are you sure they're for me?"

"They were left in front of your office door, with your name typed on notebook paper."

"I'm almost afraid to ask, but do you by any chance know if they could mean something? I mean, is somebody sending me a message?"

"I looked online."

"And?"

133

"Um, one site claimed they symbolized death and mourning. Sometimes people bring them to graveside funerals and place them on the casket. But another site said it could mean a major change or upheaval is coming, though perhaps not bad. They could mean the death of old habits and to inspire confidence and enthusiasm for a new era of hope and joy."

"Talk about a mixed message. Are they kind of pretty? Did they come with baby's breath and ferns?"

Rivka giggled. "They did."

"Great. At least the sender has some class. See if you can find a vase to put them in with some water. I'll deal with them when I come in tonight to teach."

Rivka giggled again. "I'll do that." Then she added, "How are things going in court?"

Josie stood and hoisted her purse strap over her shoulder.

"We're still alive and kicking."

"*Baruch Hashem.*"

"Blessed by God is right. And thank you for calling. I've got to get back now."

The instant Rivka disconnected, a string of swear words escaped Josie's lips. It was surprising how fast old habits reoccur when triggered. She felt like she was right back in her former life, before the shooting, when she jumped from one crisis to another, fighting battle after battle, many times, more than one at the same time. She loved the craziness of it all. She thrived on it. And she was good at it. And then it was all taken away.

Richard's comment repeated in her thoughts. *Welcome back, Counselor.*

It was something to think about. Then she pictured the black roses waiting for her.

No, it's not.

****

Josie returned to the now empty fifth floor hallway with Amy a little after two o'clock. Seated on one of the benches at the other end, Richard Diamond occupied himself with the contents of a manila folder. Josie directed her client to a bench halfway down in the opposite direction, then made her way to him. He offered up an empty acknowledgment and unless Josie was imagining things, she also detected a sneer.

"I'm glad you got here." He held out a document. At the same time, his cell rang. Josie went back to her client as he took the call.

Amy balked at the document. "What's a motion to quash?"

"Diamond wants the judge to invalidate the subpoena."

"But that's just plain wrong. Malcolm was served fair and square."

"You're correct," Josie whispered. "However, he had to retaliate. Malcolm required it."

"Even though he knows his client is drop-dead wrong?" Amy whined.

"Yes. He wins even if he loses because he gets to divert the judge's attention from my motion to hold Malcolm in contempt and run down the clock. Then we won't have time to address the money issues today."

"And the shit starts all over again." Amy sniffled, swallowing back a sob. "That's what he did every time we went to court. I would think we were going to argue about one thing, but we always ended up arguing about something different. That's why the divorce lasted so long and was so expensive."

Josie re-read the motion. "Yup. But don't worry. I anticipated this. Please hand me that list of the accounts and their present-day values." She spoke loud enough for Diamond to overhear her.

Amy held up the paper. "It's right here."

Josie took it and noticed an incoming text on her cell phone.

—*I feel certain our clients are anxious to get us out of here. Join me at the bench around the corner and tell me what you think we can do to make some progress this afternoon—*

She showed it to Amy. "It's from Diamond."

"Go for it."

With a masked effort, Josie made her way back toward her arched rival. As she approached, he scrolled through his phone. She sat down next to him.

"Oh hi."

"Hi, yourself."

Still focused on his phone, he said, "What's it going to take to get us out of here in the next thirty minutes? I need to get back to my Bridgeport case. The police are in the process of issuing an Amber Alert for the grandmother and infant who went missing earlier today."

"And you represent the grandmother?" Josie couldn't contain a bit of snideness. She wasn't even sure she believed him, but it sounded like a case he'd be involved with.

He grunted.

"Your client needs to transfer the accounts, the cottage, the car, and the boat to Amy. I have all the documents necessary."

"I'm sure you do. But it can't happen today. What else?"

"What else? That's why we're here."

Diamond lowered his phone. "Mr. Castle is having a hard time. You and I know he must comply. Just not today. Let me work on him to see if I can get you something."

She met his dark eyes over the rims of her glasses. "He needs to comply with all of the orders and stop wasting everyone's time."

To her surprise, Richard moved very close. A grin overtook his handsome face as he moved his eyebrows up and down. "How about one of them?"

Believe it or not, his theatrics eased the tension. Josie scrunched up her nose to hide a smile. "One? Are you serious?" Then she held up her hand. "Forget I said that. Of course you're serious." She noted the time. Two-nineteen. He was ticking down the clock.

Using the same camaraderie, mixed with a smidge of condescension, he continued. "I'm giving you a choice, Josephina. It's simple. Leave here with nothing and have your client furious with you or leave with a little something so today isn't a total waste. I came across the title to that electric vehicle she wants. I'll work on him to sign it now. Then we can go home."

"What makes you think I'll leave empty-handed? You heard the judge. At minimum, she'll get her fifteen hundred."

Richard stood and stretched his back. "You are forgetting my motion asking the judge to quash your subpoena. My client has no intention of paying your fees. Unless you agree to forget about them, I will insist we address my motion first. And when I prevail, it will no longer be an issue. By that time, it should be close to five o'clock. The judge will adjourn court and your client will leave with nothing. Again."

"Oh, that." She waved it off. "Yeah, you need to withdraw it."

She stood as Richard did a double take, as if unsure he heard her right.

His eyes piercing, he spoke through clenched teeth. "My client claims he was almost killed by your marshal. He has a hospital report to prove his injuries. He has even directed me to file a complaint with the State Marshal's Commission."

Faking a yawn, Josie checked her watch again. Two-forty-two. "You might want to take a peek down the hall, to your left."

****

"Who are they?" Richard asked, surveying the group of men and one woman, huddled together.

"The two marshals involved in serving your client," Josie told him. "And the seven police officers who responded to his theatrical behavior by pulling him over for speeding and reckless driving. They all wore bodycams and they're ready to testify against him. Oh, and about the arrest…"

Josie reached for her cell phone. "Here's the video." She accessed the link from the marshal and held her phone up to him. "Would you like to see it?"

He didn't react.

Josie expected him to play it cool. She surmised he lived by the motto, *Never show surprise unless it works to your advantage.*

Still eying the group, he said, "I will not withdraw it, but if I choose not to pursue it today, will you take the vehicle title and agree to postpone the hearing to next week? Say, Wednesday?"

"No, but it's a start, since your client is in such a generous mood." She pulled a folder from her briefcase. "Here's the deed and the conveyance tax form for him to sign, transferring the beach cottage to Amy. Oh, and have him sign over the boat title as well. I'm sure you have it somewhere in your files. And don't forget about the fifteen hundred in legal fees from this morning's order."

Richard feigned dismay. "Hey, I am good, but my miracle working abilities have their limits."

"Fine. Let's go." Josie motioned to place the folder back into her briefcase.

He cradled his chin between his thumb and forefinger, then released it and held out his hand. "Give it to me. Let me talk to him."

Watching Diamond waltz down the hall, which she decided was odd, she recalled Amy saying she had a buyer for the boat. It would be heading to Turks and Caicos for the winter season if the deal went through by the end of next week.

When Richard re-appeared several minutes later, he skipped down the hall toward Josie. *How odd,* she thought again. *As if he hadn't a care in the world.*

"Here is the vehicle title," he announced, presenting the document as if it was some grand gesture. "He'll sign over the boat, but he says he can't find the title. He thinks your client set fire to it, along with his other valuable papers." He leaned down closer to her. "You know she's off her rocker. You have experience with that kind of client, don't you?"

"As do you," she retorted, hiding the sting and ignoring the bait. She inspected the document, careful to make sure nothing was amiss. Satisfied it was acceptable, she handed him another folder. "You could be right about the boat. Here's an Affidavit of Lost Title. Please have him sign it now, along with the deed for the cottage and the tax form I gave you earlier."

Diamond made of show of checking the time. "It's almost showtime. I don't think I can get him to sign anything else today. The vehicle was difficult enough. And I must get back to the office. Why don't I work on him some more and you and I can touch base on Monday."

"I don't think I heard you right."

Responding with a huff, he said, "Like I said before, at least your client is not leaving empty-handed. She knows how challenging he can be."

"He's challenging and she's off her rocker. Isn't that all the more reason why we should let the judge address this? I'm sure he's expecting us in the courtroom, like now."

Josie made a move, but Richard placed his hand on her shoulder.

Rolling her eyes, she sat down.

"Please understand, Josephina, my client is beyond choked up about this. He loves that cottage. And the boat was like a trophy to him. He just needs a little more time."

Until now, they'd just been trading harmless digs. Now she felt her temper simmer. Careful to silence her renewed potty mouth, she enunciated her words. "Funny. That must be why the poor, choked-up fella just bought a yacht. He keeps it at his new three-million-dollar beach cottage in the Florida Keys. It may be raining here, but it wasn't raining there this morning. I'm told the sunrises are spectacular. No doubt that's why he didn't make it back on time."

Josie stood and lifted her briefcase onto her shoulder. In a lighter tone she added, "Feel free to address your motion to quash first. When it's over, there'll be plenty of time left for my motion for contempt."

Richard rubbed his hands together. "Give me five minutes." With that he skipped back down the hall.

Josie motioned for her witnesses to join her and called Amy on her cell. "Come on down. We're having the hearing."

Inside the courtroom, she requested Thomas Rivers to alert the judge and the court reporter. As she and Amy settled behind the counsel table, her cell phone vibrated.

"Ready?" she asked her client, reaching for it.

Amy gave her a thumbs up in her lap.

While waiting for both Richard and the judge, Josie opened the text from Richard Diamond.

—We've got a problem.—

Then she heard his voice behind her.

"Mister Clerk, can you ask the judge to give us more time? I need to confer with sister counsel. Something has just come up."

Thomas raised a brow at Josie. She turned to find Diamond in the doorway, his expression panic-like. She nodded back to the clerk and said to Amy, "I'll be right back."

Richard ushered her out of the courtroom and down the hall, out of earshot.

"What's happened?" she asked, imagining a slew of ridiculous responses.

"You're going to be mad. Very mad. And you have a right to be."

She stopped. "Why? Because you continue to stall for time?" She tossed him a playful smile. "I expected that."

He raked a hand through his hair. "Excellent. I'm no longer a mystery. But there is something else."

"Don't keep me in suspense."

Darting his gaze everywhere except toward Josie, he said, "Against my advice, my client decided to leave the building and he won't answer his cell. The judge is going to be so pissed."

Josie shrugged. "Funny. I don't see this as a problem at all.

*****

Josie almost enjoyed the next half hour. Listening to Richard Diamond make his excuses reminded her of some of her more difficult clients from the past. Anne Compton included. She knew how it was. She just didn't like that Richard supported their bad behavior, and even made excuses for it. And got paid a ton of money doing so.

Standing before the judge, the very dapper advocate presented a very humbled front. "Your Honor, I am very sorry to report that my client felt he needed to leave the courthouse this afternoon. He continues to feel very distraught over the dissolution of his marriage and the enormous efforts he must now make, alone, to continue his business enterprises. He's exhausted and begs the court's forgiveness."

Josie squeezed Amy's hand, as a warning to remain silent while Richard paused to clear his throat.

Continuing, Richard said, "On the bright side, Your Honor, my client did execute the title to the electric vehicle, the boat, and the deed to the beach cottage.

These documents give Mrs. Castle exclusive ownership of all three assets."

He held them up, as if presenting a straight A report card. Then he handed them to Josie. "I'm sure we can all agree this is major progress. Therefore, I respectfully ask the court to continue this matter to an agreeable date. During that time, I will make my best efforts to ensure that we continue to make good progress."

The judge's face remained expressionless. "Attorney Jensen, what is your client's position on this request?"

Josie stood. "Of course we object, Your Honor. As I've stated earlier, it's been more than three months now since you entered the orders at issue here today. No acceptable excuse has been given for Mr. Castle's refusal to comply with those orders. Meanwhile, the accounts are accruing interest that my client is being denied, and I'm beginning to worry that he may have moved the accounts out of this court's reach."

Richard chuckled. "I can assure, Your Honor, the assets are safe."

The judge cleared his throat. "Attorney Diamond?"

"Yes, Judge?"

"Please inform your client that I am hereby ordering the investment companies to add fifty percent of all interest accrued on the accounts listed in my memorandum of decision, beginning on that date through the date they transfer Ms. Castle's fifty-percent share to her."

Josie stiffened. As did Richard. That could be the order she needed to end this mess, and he knew it. She didn't dare smile. "Thank you, Your Honor."

"And Attorney Jensen? Are you and your client

available next Thursday afternoon for a final hearing date?"

She deferred to Amy, who nodded. "Yes, Your Honor, but if you grant Attorney Diamond's postponement, I respectfully request you to order that an arrest warrant shall issue, in the event Mr. Castle fails to attend the entire proceeding on this next date."

Richard stood. "While I can't agree, I am certain an arrest warrant will not be necessary. I understand where sister counsel is …"

"So ordered," the judge interjected. "Mr. Clerk, please note the file."

"Thank you, Your Honor," Josie said, further cutting Diamond off. "And Your Honor, I request additional attorney's fees to be paid today, for two additional hours, due to Mr. Castle's premature departure, requiring us to waste more time."

"Your Honor," Richard interrupted. "Since my client did substantially follow your orders today involving the cottage, the vehicle, and the boat, I submit that it wasn't a total waste of time at all this afternoon."

The judge settled on Josie.

"None of us should have been here this morning or this afternoon, Your Honor. And six million dollars, plus interest, is still due to my client."

Judge Myers eyed both of them, then at the clock hanging on the wall at the back of the room. "The time is now ten minutes after four. Attorney Diamond, I am ordering your client, through you, to provide Attorney Jensen with certified funds in the amount of three thousand dollars by five o'clock today. I trust you have those funds available?"

"I can do better than that." Richard reached into his

jacket and a produced checkbook. "This is my clients' funds account, and I can represent to the court that Mr. Castle has ample funds in here to cover that amount. I'll write it out now to the order of Ms. Castle, to reimburse her for the fees I suspect she has already paid to Attorney Jensen."

"So ordered," the judge said. "We shall wait as you do so."

Josie heard a low snarl coming from Richard as he signed the check. With a flourish, he presented it to her. "Satisfied?"

She scanned the check and smiled. "Yes. Thank you."

As she handed it to Amy, the judge said, "This hearing is continued to next Thursday at two p.m. Mister Clerk, please block off the entire afternoon."

Josie remained standing, using the table to stay steady as Richard scrolled through his phone calendar and scratched the top of his head. "Ah, Your Honor. Next Thursday is tight for me."

The judge shot him an unsympathetic response. "I'm sure you can rearrange your schedule, and your client's schedule, to accommodate this case one last time, Attorney Diamond. We will start promptly at two o'clock. Oh, and just a reminder…"

"Yes, Your Honor?"

"Please be sure to file that judgment by five o'clock tomorrow."

"Yes, Your Honor."

The judge tilted his head toward the court officer. "That concludes today's business."

The man got to his feet. "All rise."

It was customary to remain standing until the judge

returned to his chambers behind the bench. Waiting, Josie held on to the table. Amy leaned toward her and whispered, "What just happened?"

"Pigs are growing wings," she whispered back, "and Hell is about to experience its first ice storm."

****

Inside the courthouse's rickety elevator, Amy grabbed Josie's arm. "This has been the best day ever. I can't thank you enough. I know we still have a long way to go, but you've accomplished more today than all my other lawyers combined. I got the car, the cottage, and the boat." She pulled out the three-thousand-dollar check from her purse and waved it in the air. "Plus, I got my legal fees! Finally, Malcolm is being held accountable."

Wiggling her brows, Josie smiled. "Remember, the eye of the tiger."

That caused them both to laugh.

Once outside, Josie paused on the landing. Amy joined her.

"Can you play the song again? I want to hear it as we stand at the top of these stairs and absorb today's victory. Every other time I left this building, I ran down those steps, bawling my eyes out."

Josie accessed the play list. "Ready?"

"Ready."

She pushed play and together they moved to the groove, adding a little wiggle and giggle here and there. Heck, it was dark outside, and no one was around. Josie was feeling pretty good too. They sang in unison as they made their way down the ramp and toward the small parking lot. As they rounded the corner, Amy let out a gasp. "What's that on your car?"

Josie stared at the scene, illuminated by the lot's towering lights. "Someone dumped something red all over it."

Chapter Twenty-Seven

Richard, Thursday Afternoon

Richard made a mad dash for the exit as soon as the judge left the bench. The last thing he wanted was to get stuck in that poor excuse for an elevator with Josephina Jensen and her temporarily redeemed client. Four years of Amy Castle and her mood swings were more than enough for anyone.

Back at his office, Richard tossed his briefcase onto the leather couch and dropped into his high-backed desk chair. After loosening his tie, he powered on his laptop and typed notes on the latest installment of the Castle v. Castle fiasco. Grand total for today's theatrics? Four hours, multiplied by one thousand buckaroos per hour. Neither Jensen nor Judge Myers needed to know that he'd increased his hourly rates for this client.

"Not bad at all," Richard said aloud, hitting the print button. He shoved one copy into the Castle file and made another for his bookkeeper. He'd drop it off to the bin on her desk on his way out.

And that was not all that he'd accomplished today. He skimmed the notes from the file involving the missing grandmother and baby grandson. Gotta love her. She and the baby were safe, but she wouldn't give up her location until the parents entered a rehab facility and the court awarded her temporary custody. That had taken up seven hours of his day, thus far, that had started at six a.m.

Then there was an hour spent dealing with two of his other clients who "forgot" to pay their hefty alimony payments last month. And two hours arguing during a virtual mediation, against a father who requested to take the couples' two children to Disney World next month. His parents will be there, visiting from Jerusalem, and wanted to celebrate Chanukah with their grandchildren. Of course, Richard's client, the mother, wouldn't consent to them missing school. And for that, she will pay him at least another ten thousand by the end of the month.

Thank you, Dad, for making such an unreasonable request. Not.

To their credit, Richard and his ex-wife made sure not to argue about stupid stuff like that when their kids were little. Or even now that they were in their mid-twenties.

Richard totaled the hours and his hourly rates and felt the day's stress begin to ooze out through his fingertips. Was it absurd? Without a doubt. Earning several thousand dollars a day because people insisted on being themselves helped him to manage the absurdity of it all.

Still basking, he took a call from Dana. "What's up?"

"Annie Callahan is holding on line three. She said you'd remember her. I checked our client list and found an Anne Compton, maiden name, Callahan, but I couldn't find the file. She says she wants to hire you again."

Dread doused buckets over Richard's good mood.

This can only be bad.

****

Richard eyed his modern version of a grandfather clock that sat regally across the room. He could take the waiting call and still make his dinner date over the border in Springfield, Massachusetts at six. But did he want to?

Anne Compton was using her maiden name now. Callahan. Why was she calling him? They hadn't spoken in over a year. To his knowledge, she was still confined to a locked ward at the state's psychiatric hospital for the criminally insane. She would be there for at least the next ten years.

"Send over the call," he told his assistant.

Half a second later, the transfer button blinked red. He pushed it.

"Good evening, this is Attorney Diamond."

"Richard?"

He winced. "Yes?"

"It's me. Annie."

Hearing the caller's chipper voice, he gripped his pen. "Of course. I hope you have been well."

"Why so formal, my darling? After all, we were once engaged to be married."

"Until you dumped me for a White, Catholic boy, but I digress. How can I help you, Anne?" *Shoot! Why did I say that?*

"Oh Richard, isn't it time to let that go? We were so young. Now we have a chance to make everything right again."

Sitting straighter in his chair, he measured his words. "How do you mean?"

"I'm getting better," she announced in a high-pitched voice. "My doctor said I'm making tremendous progress. I'll be getting day passes soon and I'll be able to leave the grounds. Isn't that wonderful? You can pick me up and we can go out dancing, just like we used to."

"I am glad things are improving," he lied, keeping his voice even.

"My goodness, Richard, how mature and business-like you sound. Not at all like that horny young buck, whispering in my ear, begging to get inside my panties. Oh, how I relive those memories every day. I'm sure you do too."

More like he'd erased them decades ago.

But to this woman, he said, "Thank you for calling, Anne. I need to go now. I have an appointment waiting."

"I'm sure you do. You're a very busy man. Before we hang up, I want to congratulate you on protecting your client today. I know he had to give up something to get that crooked judge off his back, but that horrid wife has no business getting all that money from him. Marriage is until death. If you leave, you leave empty handed. That's what I told that stupid Josephina Jensen, but she didn't listen. It's a sacrilege that she's been allowed back into the courthouse."

Richard's pulse quickened. *What is she talking about?* He debated asking how she knew about this afternoon's court session. And why she cared about it.

Before he could form the words, she added, "I'm beginning to remember things that happened that day. I wanted to thank you for all your help." Then she laughed. "Don't worry, sweetheart. I won't tell. Your secret's safe with me. We need to talk soon about my next hearing. It's scheduled for the end of January. We have a lot to do to prepare. I can't wait to see you again. I'll try to call tomorrow. And soon you'll be able to call me any time.

Just send back the forms saying that you're representing me again. The hospital mailed them to you earlier in the week."

She ended with a shrill laugh. "Goodbye for now, my love."

Richard continued to hold the receiver until the computerized voice came through, directing him to hang up. Then he bolted into action. First, he dialed the hospital's director, leaving a voicemail message asking for a call back as soon as possible. Next, he sent a text, canceling his dinner date, and grabbed his topcoat and car keys. He needed air. Lots of it. And he needed to think.

Chapter Twenty-Eight

Josie, Thursday Afternoon

That morning, Josie had parked facing the shorter side of the courthouse, maybe a foot away from the building. Now, she and Amy stood outside in the parking lot, examining the red stuff, paint she hoped, that covered her car's roof, the hood, and flowed down the sides.

She looked up at the building's seven sets of large windows, one for each story. They were the old-fashioned kind, long and rectangular, encased in black iron. She knew, from several years of working in the building, that they were screenless and opened easily from the inside, especially during the hot, summer months. And they were not alarmed.

She traced a possible route from the top window down to her car. With shaky fingers, she texted Dan, then called the police to report the scene while Amy used her phone to take photos of the car from all angles.

"Malcolm strikes again," Amy declared, her voice filled with authority. "I hope he hasn't trashed my home again." She checked her phone. "So far, I don't have any alerts from my security company."

"Let's go inside to tell the court officers at the door, before the building closes."

Her limp more pronounced from the long day on her feet, Josie reached the top of the ramp and pulled open the heavy brass door. "Can you tell the guard who is stationed at the metal detectors what happened?" she asked Amy. "I'm going to the top floors, to check out the windows that overlook the parking lot. Meet me up there."

Josie's heels and her cane echoed as she traversed the deserted space. She didn't see a soul as she entered another creepy elevator at the opposite end of the hall. On the fifth floor, where they'd spent most of the day, someone tossing something out of a window would be noticed. But if memory served correctly, the higher floors were a different story.

Creaking and hesitating, the shuddering box arrived at the sixth floor. Josie stepped out onto one end of a long, dim hallway. To her knowledge, this part of the building was used for storage and offices for retired · judges. Unless something changed, there wasn't a lot of public activity up here, especially in the afternoons.

She searched around for surveillance cameras. None. That meant someone could have dumped the red stuff out the window, then gone off on their merry way.

At the window now, overlooking the parking lot and her car, Josie was careful not to touch anything, just in case the bad guy left any fingerprints on the crank or the sill. She pressed her cell phone's flashlight app and searched for red residue. Nothing. She then peered down through the window at the lit parking lot below. She didn't see any police vehicles yet, but two security guards were circling her car. One was writing down the license plate.

She dialed Amy. "Where are you?"

"I'm on the first floor, waiting for the elevator."

"Come to the sixth floor. Go to the left when you

leave the elevator."

"Did you find anything?"

"Not yet. We need to check the next floor."

"Yikes," Amy groaned minutes later. "It's so eerie up here."

Agreeing, Josie showed her the window and car below, then they headed up to the top floor. The elevator's strain echoed in the silence before finally coming to a thudding stop.

"It feels like a scary movie," Amy whispered. "When's the creepy music going to start?"

"Never, I hope," Josie shot back.

The doors parted into a dark hallway. A few scattered lamps protruded from the walls, providing little illumination. No sounds came from any of the rooms behind the numerous closed doors.

They aimed their cell phone lights toward the window in question.

"There!" Amy pointed, as they got closer.

They bent down and found small red splatters and larger red smears on the wall under the window and the white parts of the black and white marble floor.

"One of us has to stay here until the police see this," Amy hissed. "It might be an inside job. Malcolm could have hired someone. They could still be here behind one of these doors, watching us now, making sure we see it. Then when we leave to get help, they'll clean it up and we'll be made fools when we show the police."

Josie processed her words.

No longer whispering, Amy added, "I know I sound super paranoid, but that's how Malcolm always got away with everything. He'd trash something at my house or my car, but by the time the police arrived, the evidence was either gone or trampled on. I could never prove anything. Then he and Diamond would call me a vengeful wife. They even accused me of doing the vandalizing myself, then accusing him."

In Josie's active divorce practice, she witnessed firsthand the compounded emotional trauma victims suffered when their perpetrators got away with their vindictive retaliations. She recognized Amy's trauma during their first conversation. She also recalled the Castle's Cakes box being tossed from the truck the other night. Could she prove Malcolm Castle was behind it? No. And if she brought it up to Richard, he'd laugh it off and gaslight her about it. But that didn't mean it didn't happen.

Josie aimed her light for Amy to see her face. "I believe you. You're not being paranoid. Thank you for making the suggestion."

Tears welled in the woman's eyes. She held up her phone. "I'll take photos."

"And I'll go downstairs to get the police." Josie dialed her number. "Stay on the phone with me."

****

When Josie, her bad leg screaming its objections, returned to the seventh floor, two young, male police officers followed her out of the elevator. Amy wasted no time bombarding them with her theory. "Please investigate my ex-husband, Malcolm Castle, because this has his name all over it."

The officers hesitated.

"Ms. Castle could be right," Josie told them, keeping her voice steadier than she felt. "We just finished a few tense hours in the family court downstairs. It didn't go his way and a lot of money was involved."

"Millions," Amy interjected.

The officers inspected the evidence. The taller one taped off the area with yellow crime scene tape while his partner spoke into his shoulder radio, requesting assistance.

Josie and Amy answered their questions, then made their way back downstairs. Outside, as they answered more questions, a black car slowed and pulled to the curb. The passenger window lowered. "Are you all right, ladies?"

Josie turned toward the voice and did a double take.

"It's Richard Diamond," Amy shouted. She ran toward the car, arms flailing, boot heels clattering on the pavement, yelling, "Come see what your f-ing client did!"

****

Intending to shut down her client, Josie reached Amy's side as the sky opened. A drenching monsoon rained down on everything in sight. Together, they watched Richard park his car, then remove two large umbrellas from the trunk and walk toward them.

Josie tugged Amy's jacket sleeve. "I know you're upset. I am too. But let's stay cool." The last thing they needed was Malcolm suing them for defamation. The truth wasn't the point. That kind of fight would allow him to cloud the issues regarding the money he owed Amy, thus creating a perfect excuse to delay things further.

Amy opened her mouth to object, but then backed down.

Richard ducked under one of the umbrellas and held out the other.

"Thank you," Josie mumbled, stepping under it with

Amy as he continued past them, to the officers.

They followed, listening to the exchange.

"Hi, Rich," one of them greeted.

"Hey, fellas. What happened here?"

"Someone dumped this red stuff on Attorney Jensen's car from the seventh-floor window," Amy declared in a tone reeking with accusation.

By this time, variations of pink streaks replaced the red and dripped onto the ground. Richard dipped his forefinger in one of the puddles. "Paint?"

"Not sure," the taller officer replied. "The rain is washing off a lot of it, but we have photographs and samples."

Richard turned to Josie and Amy. "I can understand why you might suspect Mr. Castle had a role in this, but I can assure you that I watched him drive away from here myself."

Amy kept her lips tight together, but her eyes bore into him.

He looked to Josie. "I do not condone anything like this. Please believe me."

She didn't buy it, but nodded anyway, wondering again if he knew anything about her ride home from Amy's the other night.

"I can give you the name of a friend of mine who does auto detailing, if you'd like."

A little surprised, Josie said, "Thanks, but I'm sure my brother knows someone."

As she spoke, a car horn beeped.

"Daniel!" Amy called out and ran toward his car, taking the umbrella with her.

Richard stepped in to cover Josie as Dan emerged. Carrying his own umbrella, he jogged over and held out his hand to Richard. "Dan Jensen."

Richard reciprocated. "Rich Diamond."

"What the hell happened?" Dan asked, examining Josie's car.

"We suspect it's a random act of vandalism," Richard said.

Josie sent Amy a warning and shook her head.

Amy clamped her mouth shut.

Dan faced Richard. "Let's hope." He kept his curious stare glued to the other lawyer a second longer.

"Ms. Jensen, can you come here please?" one of the officers asked. "It's drier in the cruiser. I need a few more questions answered for the report."

To Dan she said, "I don't know how long this is going to take. Can you get Amy home?"

"Sure. Call me if you need a ride."

As they left, Josie realized Richard was following her to the officer's cruiser. When she was fully inside on the passenger seat, he closed the door and slid into the back.

"You don't have to stay," she told him.

"I'll stay."

The officer nodded. "Much of the evidence may be washed away, but we'll have forensics go over the vehicle anyway. Someone will call you tomorrow about the status."

The conversation took several minutes. Afterward, Richard stood with her in the rain, watching her pink-splotched car being raised onto a flatbed truck. "I will bring you home." He looked at his watch. "In fact, how about dinner first? My treat, to take our minds off this unfortunate event."

Before Josie could respond, his dark eyes

glimmered. "While you contemplate the ethical dilemmas raised by my offer, I'll remind you that as a new member of your synagogue, I would appreciate some information regarding that dinner this Friday evening. Since, after all, you are the Shabbat Coordinator."

She laughed. She didn't mean to. It just came out.

Richard Diamond could be so charming. So disarming. And male-model perfect. She envisioned him in a magazine advertisement for expensive watches or suits. Then she thought of those handsome men in those erectile disfunction commercials.

To replace those images, she conjured up a lethal animal who strikes when its prey least expects it. Then it sucks out all the blood, leaving a shriveled-up shell for the vultures to snack on. She didn't want that to be her.

She thanked him for the dinner invitation. "I'm teaching a class at seven-thirty. Could you give me a ride to the law school instead? Perhaps then I could attempt to answer your questions."

He gripped her elbow. "Let's go."

Now on the highway, Richard focused on the traffic. "Mark Jensen, the Rabbi, is your brother."

"Correct."

"And Dan Jensen is?"

"Our older brother."

"You and he handled that custody case we had a long time ago. Masterson. Wasn't it?"

Josie cringed, staring straight ahead. "Also correct."

"The last time I heard, he was representing an oil company who suffered a huge spill into Long Island Sound."

"It sounds familiar."

Richard leaned toward her. "I represented the CEO in his divorce."

She curled her upper lip. "Of course you did."

"And Ms. Castle knows Dan. She called out his name and jumped right into his car. Are they dating? Is that how she found you?"

Josie almost laughed. She decided there was no harm in telling him. "Close. They're cousins through marriage on his mother's side."

Richard crinkled his forehead at her, then re-focused on the road. "You have different mothers?"

"Yes. Our parents divorced other people."

"But you, Dan, and the rabbi have the same father."

She sent him a sideways glance. "Satisfied now?"

"Yes, but…"

"But what?"

Richard took the exit to the law school. "Think about this. If you hadn't stopped practicing, there's a good chance you would have been Amy's lawyer much earlier, instead of those other clowns she hired." His eyes shined with mischief. "What a ride that might have been."

"For both of us," Josie added, considering the situation. Who knows what her life would have been like if she hadn't stepped in front of Anne Compton's bullets.

"Which building?" he asked when they arrived on the campus.

She pointed to the multi-colored stone structure a few hundred yards away. "It's that one to the left."

Josie's cell rang as Richard put the car in park.

"It might be the police," he suggested. "Maybe they have some answers."

She accepted the unfamiliar number. "This is

Josephina Jensen."

"Hello Ms. Jensen. This is Captain Healy from the Hartford Police Department."

"Yes, Captain." She pressed the speaker button to hear better over the rain and windshield wipers.

"We have some more questions for you. Is this a good time?"

She looked to Richard who nodded.

"Sure."

"I don't want to worry you, ma'am, but we did a field test on the red substance from your car. Mind you, the lab will run more tests tomorrow, but I can tell you, it's not paint."

Josie felt the back of her neck burn. "You don't sound happy, Captain. What is it?"

"It's blood, ma'am. From an animal." He paused. "One of my officers found the head of a small pig behind the guardrail near your car. Please try not to worry, but this might be a hate crime. I need to ask you, um, are you by any chance Jewish or Muslim?"

Richard's large hand covered her fist and held tight.

"Yes, Captain. I'm Jewish."

****

Josie said goodnight to the police captain and removed her hand from Richard's. As she opened the passenger door, he reached over her and pulled it shut. "Please wait. Hear me out." Anger filled his words, coordinating with the stone-cold expression on his face.

Josie tried to sort out her emotions and settled on how she felt when Anne Compton pulled out that gun. *Terrified.*

Did Malcolm Castle do this because he had a bad day in court? Did he and Diamond plan it together? If so, how far would they go? And if Diamond wasn't in on it, how far would he let Castle go and still represent him? How unhinged was Castle? Was she facing an Anne Compton repeat? Or was it mere intimidation?

Or, what if it was just a racial thing, from an unknown source? Being the object of unquantifiable hate by strangers who knew nothing about her, reminded her that she had a target on her back. And on her front. Just because of how she chose to honor God.

"If Malcolm Castle did this," Richard said, his words measured. "I will fire him and help you press charges."

Diamond acted so earnest, so distraught. Josie remembered he was Jewish too. And Black. A double whammy. But she didn't buy his words for an instant.

"No, you won't," she countered. "He'd sue you and insist that you reimburse him for all the fees he's paid you."

Richard deflated like a balloon being stabbed by a sharp knife. He rubbed his face with both hands. "What the hell? I just don't want to believe this. Can I tell you something if I make it fast?"

Unaccustomed to the vulnerability in his tone, she nodded. "Sure, if you want to. Just keep in mind that every second we spend together will infuriate both our clients."

They smiled at each other as she added, "I spoke to my assistant at the law school earlier today. She said an anonymous source sent me a bouquet of black roses. They left them at my office door. I almost hope they're from your client, just to end the mystery."

Richard crunched his forehead and threw up his hands. "Black roses?"

"Yup."

"That feels more than a little icky."

"Do you think?"

"I don't know what to think, except that this attack on your car worries me. You are an affluent, educated, white-skinned woman, who also happens to be Jewish. And yet, someone targeted you like this? At a courthouse?"

Richard tapped her hand. "I'm going to tell you something most people don't know. And I'll trust you not to blab, but if you do…" He shrugged his shoulders. "It's fine."

Josie raised her eyebrows, encouraging him to continue. She didn't know what he was going to say, or if he was even being truthful, but curiosity required her attention.

"My family is from Ethiopia. I am a second-generation, black-skinned Jew with some European slave owner blood mixed in. My parents and grandparents have worked beyond hard, scraping and saving to provide me and my sisters with every opportunity this country offered.

"But back in Ethiopia, my relatives face murder and torture and starvation, along with employment and health care discrimination, just because they are Jewish. I started a program several years ago, as my law practice took off, to help them and others who cannot leave due to immigration quotas. And I have a program here in the states, to help those who are lucky enough to make it here, adjust and improve their lives."

"*Tikkun Olam*," Josie said.

"Genesis, chapter 12," he added. "Our obligation to help heal this imperfect world. It started way back when

God and Abraham made their covenant and God commanded that Abraham would be a blessing."

"Yeah. And a thousand years later, when God renewed that covenant with Moses at Mount Sinai, don't you think Moses should have consulted a lawyer first, to discuss the fine print, before signing us all on as the chosen ones?"

A solid laugh erupted from Richard. "Well put, Counselor." He retrieved a bottle of water from the back seat and cracked it open. "Would you like one? I've got another."

"No thanks."

After taking a long swig, he said, "America remains the one beacon of hope left for any person facing peril, just because they were unlucky enough to be born elsewhere. It is the greatest country in the world, and people who come here, legally or not, want to work and make better lives for themselves and their families. And they want to give back to this country, to show their appreciation for that chance. But the increased prejudices make me worry what this country may be turning into. No one is born hateful. It is taught and cultivated."

Knowing she shouldn't, Josie reached out and touched Richard's hand. He covered it with his other one. "When we wrap up the Castle saga, let me know how I can help with your programs."

A slow smile formed on Richard's face. "You already have."

She crinkled her brows.

"Through helping people address medical bills they cannot afford to pay," he told her. "I am aware of a number of families who have benefited from your intervention and generosity."

How could he know that?

He squeezed her hand again, then let go and took another drink. "Do you have a ride home? I can come back around when your class is over."

"I'll be fine. But thank you for offering."

He reached over her again and pushed open the door. "May the force be with you as you teach those lawyer-wannabes some juris prudence." Then he lowered his voice. "And please remind them that they have the power to make positive changes for people whose voices are not being heard."

Josie swallowed hard. Her mother had said the same thing. "I will. Thank you again for the ride."

He lifted his bottle to her as she got out of the car, but he didn't drive away. She hated that he could be watching her limp toward the building. It wasn't an image she was proud of, but what could she do? When she got inside, she waved. He flashed his high beams and sped off.

Chapter Twenty-Nine

Amy Castle, Friday Morning

A woman on a mission, Amy took a right on Main Street in Madison. Her goal was to record the deed to the beach cottage at the town hall. Josie Jensen explained that until then, Malcolm could still transfer the property to someone else or get a mortgage on it and pull out all the equity. She needed to make sure that wouldn't happen. But the clerk's office, where the land records were kept, didn't open until eight-thirty. Her watch read seven-sixteen. She spotted a drive-thru place and ordered a vanilla chai tea latte. Next, she drove to the Castle store in town.

Amy checked her reflection in the car window. The movie stars were right. The short, blonde wig and big sunglasses she wore created a decent disguise. Emotionally crushed when the judge awarded Malcolm the company, she hadn't been able to enter any of the Castle stores. It wasn't that she wanted to run the huge conglomerate herself. No, she fought for it to make him pay attention. The business was the one single thing he cared about, even more than their children. She wanted him to feel the loss, or at least the threat of the loss, to show him how it felt to have his dreams stolen, like he'd stolen hers. And golly gee whiz, she sure did get his attention.

In usual Malcolm-style, times a thousand, he'd refused to consider any compromises regarding ownership or management, or even a financial settlement. Fighting Amy for every dollar, he told the judge he *let her pretend* to work for the company to help fill her days.

That hurt. And it fueled Amy to fight just as hard as he did. She'd insisted on remaining an active part of the business while the divorce was pending, continuing to perform her usual, numerous responsibilities, and the judge agreed.

Maybe that's why it felt like a crash landing with no survivors when Amy read the court's final divorce orders. Even though she retained the rights to the bakeries and catering divisions, and she received a decent percentage of all of the stores' profits for the next several years, the blow still stung. But thanks to Josie Jensen and yesterday's small victories, minus the lawyer's car being vandalized, Amy felt empowered. Today, and from now on, the beach cottage would belong to her. That knowledge gave her the courage to stop at her neighborhood Castle store.

But a scan of the near empty parking lot caused Amy to crinkle her botoxed forehead. Scattered trash blew against the curbs and abandoned shopping carts occupied many of the parking spaces. Others dangled half off the curbs.

Where were the attendants? And the greeters who welcomed customers at the door? This is not the Castle way.

It took her a half hour to push all the stray carts to the front of the store, just like she and Malcolm did eons ago when they didn't have enough money to hire a parking lot attendant. Or a full-time deli person, or a baker. They wore every hat back then, including bagging customers' groceries.

So where is everybody now? I can't believe this. I've only been gone a little over three months!

Entering the store, Amy searched for the sign posted on the wall near the entrance. It listed the manager's names for each department, letting consumers know who to contact for assistance.

The sign was gone.

Where were the holiday decorations? Chanukah started in a few weeks. Christmas came next.

Amy perused the half-empty shelves, aisle after aisle, straightening signs and counting the stock. At the deli counter, six early risers waited in line as one panicked employee rushed to fill the orders.

She moved over to the fish and meat counter. The lobster bay was empty and only one butcher worked behind the glass in the back.

Where were the specialty items? The stuffed shrimp? The steak Florentine? The meatloaf with cheddar and bacon, and the other prepared meals? I know I've filled the orders.

Beyond distraught, Amy rushed to the bakery section and gasped. Each day she sent over fresh breads, cakes, scones, and more. But the shelves were empty. And there were no staff people behind the counter.

I know the business isn't mine anymore, but I poured my heart and soul into it. And I continue to work every day, servicing all the stores. Something just isn't right.

Amy raised her eyes to the office windows that took up the entire upper floor of the building. They surrounded the store, providing a clear view of the happenings below.

They were dark.

What's going on, Malcolm?

****

Amy stormed out of the store and drove to the town hall's brick building in the center of town. She eased into a parking space and turned off the engine. For at least the tenth time, she verified Malcolm's signature on the deed to the beach cottage.

Once in the building, Amy followed the signs to the town clerk's office. The assistant clerk, Marylee Schafer, was a longtime customer at the store. Amy saw her talking on the phone at her desk, behind the service counter.

The woman held up a finger, mouthing, "Just a second."

Amy faked interest in the notices posted to the town's bulletin board. Then her eyes hovered over a familiar address and a popular name. She gasped. *That famous food warehouse company wants to open, right next door to Castle's? The vote is scheduled for next week?*

"Amy, it's so good to see you," Marylee greeted, approaching the counter.

After exchanging pleasantries, Amy asked about the notice.

"Oh yes. It caused quite a flurry at first. Half the town was for it and the other half objected to the commercialism of it, claiming it would hurt local businesses."

The clerk stopped. Her expression softened. "You didn't know about this?"

"No," Amy whispered, humiliated and embarrassed.

The clerk motioned for Amy to come closer.

"Was it in the news?" Amy asked. "I don't know how I could have missed it." But as she spoke, she realized she did know how she missed it. In addition to avoiding the stores, she had stepped back from anything involving the business, other than her role in her own departments.

"What does it mean for Castle's?" she asked. "Didn't Malcolm object?"

She thought of the profit losses the store would suffer in every department with that type of competition so close by. They couldn't begin to match its discount prices and huge inventory.

The clerk lowered her voice. "The company plans to buy your property, too. I heard they've reached an agreement if the zoning board approves the plan."

"I see," Amy replied, not mentioning that she was no longer an owner. *Or am I?*

"I hope I haven't spoken out of turn."

"No, not at all. Um, how long has this been in negotiations?"

The clerk looked over at the multi-year calendar hanging on the wall. "Oh, for almost two years, I'd say. There were a lot of delays."

"Will it pass at this next meeting?"

"It's expected to."

Amy wasn't sure what to say next. A patron came through the door.

"You can take care of them. I'll wait."

Marylee nodded and directed her attention to the newcomers as Amy's thoughts raced with suspicion. She used her phone to take a photo of the zoning board hearing notice. When the other patrons left, she handed the beach cottage deed and the tax form to the clerk, along with the recording fee.

Marylee inspected the documents. She stamped them and typed something into the computer, just as Josie said she would. Then she placed them in a folder with a small pile of other papers and gave Amy a receipt. "I'll mail you back the originals after we copy them and enter them into the current volume." She pointed beyond Amy to an adjoining room filled with shelves holding rows and rows of huge red and white books. "It will take about a week."

"That's fine," Amy said, but she wasn't ready to leave. "Can you help me find the records for the cottage and Castle's store here in town?"

"Sure. Come this way." Marylee walked around the counter and led her to a group of computers against a wall in that adjoining room. "Which address first?"

Amy gave her the home address.

The clerk typed it in. "Here you are. Anything in particular you need?"

Amy hesitated. Madison was a small town. The walls had ears and wagging tongues. But she didn't see any other choice. "I want to make sure there are no liens on the property."

Seconds later, she sighed with relief. *No liens or mortgages. Malcolm had left the property alone. It was hers now, free and clear.*

"Now the store," she said to the clerk. "Can you go back to the time we bought the land?"

"Sure," Marylee replied, her fingernails clicking on the keys.

A phone rang in the office as a new screen of information popped up.

"Here you go. I need to get that but let me know if you have any questions. There

are instructions on the wall near the door to access the physical documents."

At ten o'clock, Amy left the town hall with a pile of revealing documents that served to confirm her suspicions. She texted Josie as soon as she got into her SUV.

—*Call me asap, please. I've got big news. Not sure what to make of it.*—

Then she programed her GPS for the town hall in Mystic.

Chapter Thirty

Josie, Friday

Josie finished teaching her last class of the day and made it back to her office a little before noon. Still reeling from the recent events, she tried to reconcile images of Richard Diamond driving her mad with his client's antics, with the new and improved version he shared with her last night. She almost liked that Richard...Which wasn't good.

Don't get fooled. His bad boy reputation was well earned.

But still...

Stop! Stick to the issues. Did his client arrange to have my car vandalized with pig blood? Or was Luke responsible?

Josie didn't know. She said as much during the meeting with Captain Healy earlier that morning. He released her car, saying it wouldn't be needed. They'd taken plenty of photographs to use as evidence to prosecute any suspects they may apprehend. But he didn't sound hopeful.

Seated at her desk now, Josie mocked the black roses sitting in a white vase on her bookcase. *Sure, the ferns and baby's breath are a nice touch, but who sent them? And why?*

Switching mental challenges, she looked at the time.

Richard Diamond had until five that afternoon to file the Castle judgment. She scrolled down the court docket on the judicial website for the third time. *Nope, not there yet.*

Next, she thought about Debra Tate, Dan's aunt who was ready to start her divorce. Marshal Reed would serve the necessary documents to Debra's husband Sunday night when he arrived home from his fishing trip. So, for now, things were stable there.

Josie then considered her course load. Her classes were moving along toward final exams in a few weeks, and she'd completed the syllabus for each course next term. That left her textbook edits on current family law issues. They were due at the end of December.

Josie tapped her username and password on the desktop's keyboard, then popped open a soda while the machine worked its magic. "Come in," she called out, responding to the knock on her door.

"I can't," a female voice called out. "My hands are full."

Josie opened the door to Rivka, resting her chin on a pile of law books and holding a large, plain box.

"Thanks," she said, out of breath, as Josie grabbed the books before they fell to the ground. "They're from the list you gave the librarian. The most recent tax code for divorcing couples should be here next week."

"At least we'll have a cure for insomnia when that arrives."

Agreeing, the young woman made a space for the box at the corner of the already crowded desk. The office phone rang as Josie located a pair of scissors.

"Do you want me to get that?"

"Please," Josie replied, struggling with the packing

tape. "Unless it's the dean, just take a message."

"Professor Jensen's office. Yes, one moment." Rivka covered the mouthpiece. "It's Attorney Daniel Jensen. He said to tell you to take the call."

"I'm sure he did."

Still fighting with the box, Josie placed the receiver between her ear and shoulder.

"I'll open it," Rivka said, holding her hand out for the scissors.

"Thank you," Josie mouthed. To her brother, she said, "Hi there. What's up?"

"Your cell phone keeps going to voicemail, and that's full," Dan told her. "Is it off? Amy's been trying to reach you. She discovered something about two of the store properties."

"I don't think so. Hold on a sec." Josie pulled her cell from the bottom of her purse and scrolled down the calls and texts. "There's no record of your number or hers."

"Send me a text."

She typed, —*Hello?*— Then pushed the send button. A red X popped up beneath the word.

"Shoot. It says it wasn't delivered.'" She scrolled down. "The last text I received was at eight-eleven last night."

"Call me."

She pushed Dan's speed dial button.

It rang.

Then it connected. But not to him.

****

"My cell phone company answered," Josie told Dan, using her office phone's speaker function. At the same time, she followed the prompts to reach a live human on the cell.

After a few exchanges, she raised her voice. "What do you mean, the account was closed?"

"Hang up the cell and take me off speaker," Dan directed. "We need to talk about Luke."

Josie was just about to challenge the agent, but changed her mind and ended the call. "What about him?"

As she spoke, she wondered if he'd stopped paying the cell phone bill, or if he'd closed the account. She'd forgotten it was in his name because his employer gave him a ten-percent discount.

But Dan's next words pushed that topic from her thoughts.

"Tabor filed a motion to keep your divorce in Harford. He also filed a motion for temporary alimony and attorney's fees. The judge wants to see you in her chambers, with Tabor and Luke, on Monday at ten. I think it's time to call Everett Kramer, or someone."

Josie yanked open the side drawer of her desk and searched for the roll of antacids she kept there for emergencies. "You're saying he wants to humiliate me further by having our dirty laundry aired where I practice?"

"I'm sorry," Dan said. "I know you wanted to avoid this type of scrutiny."

Beyond distraught, Josie noticed Rivka, still preoccupied with opening the box.

"Make the call, Josie," he pushed.

"I will." *Ugh. There goes a pile of money I'll have to pay out in attorney's fees. What a waste.*

"Now."

"Yes, Daniel. I promise." She placed a loose curl behind her ear. "So, what's going on with Amy?"

"Wait till you hear this," Dan challenged, his tone renewed with excitement.

"I'm waiting."

"She's still the record owner of two store properties. The ones in Madison and Mystic. And Malcolm has been in negotiations for the past two years to sell the Madison property to a huge competitor. It wants the land. What do you want to bet the sale price they've been discussing is much higher than the value he reported on his financial affidavit?"

Josie's pulse rate soared. "This means that the numbers the judge used to divide the marital assets were inaccurate."

She pulled out Malcolm's most recent financial affidavit from a box of documents she'd brought to the office that morning. Reviewing it, she said, "He listed the company as the owner of all eleven stores. And Amy didn't question it, or the values he assigned to them."

"I asked her about that," Dan replied. "She said she forgot about it until she was recording the deed to the beach cottage at the town hall this morning. She saw a notice for a zoning board hearing initiated by the competitor and asked the clerk about it."

"But, Dan, why would the buyer negotiate with Malcolm if Amy owned the property? How didn't she know about this?"

"She thinks she might have signed something years ago, giving Malcolm her authority to act on her behalf regarding the business. She's investigating it now."

Josie scratched the scar on her chest. "That would do it. And it means Malcolm intended to go through with the sale, without Amy's knowledge, and keep all the money. Meanwhile, the transaction would reduce the overall profits for Castle's, including Amy's monthly share, along with the money she makes from her two departments. But she wouldn't know anything about it until the orders stopped coming in." She paused. "Do you think Richard Diamond knows about this?"

"I don't doubt it. I've got someone snooping into the details. We should know more soon."

"Thanks." Josie noted the time. "I have to go. But Dan?"

"Yeah?"

"Malcolm's going to flip when I interfere with that sale."

"No worries," he promised. "I'll have a bullet-proof vest and a helmet shipped to you tomorrow."

"That's not funny."

"Yes, it is."

"I hate you," she chided.

"You love me."

She relented. "Always."

"See you tonight?"

"Six-thirty sharp."

Hanging up, Josie heard Rivka gasp. "What is that?"

She dropped the object she was holding onto Josie's desk. The remaining contents in the box fell to the floor.

Josie eyed it from all angles, then used a pencil to flip it over. "Is that a sex toy?" She leaned over the desk to get a better look at the pile on the floor. "Are they all sex toys?"

****

"Really, Luke?" Josie demanded, into the air. "You sent these to my office?" Then she realized Rivka wasn't aware of her marital situation, except what she may have gleaned from the conversation with Dan. And she was still reeling from the contents of the box. Yesterday's flowers didn't help.

But it had to be Luke. Or maybe the bimbo he's boinking?

"I didn't buy these," she told Rivka, using a pen to sort the different colors and sizes and shapes of vibrators and other assorted *toys*.

Rivka examined the items close up. "Oh, I didn't think you did. But whoever sent them sure has an odd sense of humor. Maybe they're from the same person who sent you the flowers. Could it be the ex-husband in that big case you're working on?"

"Could be," Josie answered, returning the items to the box.

When Rivka left, most likely to pray or maybe sneak a peek at the forbidden toys on the Internet, Josie collapsed into the chair. She curled her lip toward her cell phone. Then at the box. And then at the vase of flowers. She thought of her car, doused with animal blood. And being run off the road last Saturday night. And being locked out of her house on Monday, with no electricity, and discovering Luke had looted the place.

What the heck was going on? How did my life get like this?

Fed up, Josie rubbed her tired eyes. With her phone out of commission, she checked her email before calling Amy. And it was a good thing she did. Debra Tate's topped the list of unread mail.

—A State Marshal came to my mother's house today and served me with divorce papers.—

Josie pounded Debra's number into her desk phone. The woman answered on the first ring. "Hello?"

"Hi Debra, it's Josie Jensen."

"Oh Josie, thank you for calling."

To her surprise, Debra's voice sounded animated, almost happy.

"Are you okay?"

"Yes, I'm fine. Really."

"Tell me what happened."

"A man identifying himself as a state marshal came to my mother's door…I mean my door, a little after ten this morning. I was unpacking boxes. I told him I wouldn't open the door, but we agreed he would slip the papers through the kitchen window if I opened it just an inch. Then he thanked me and left."

"Did you have any idea Philip was doing this? Could he have known about your plans?"

"You know, Josie, I've been asking myself the same questions, but I don't have any answers. He spent a lot of time at choir rehearsal this week and I've been asleep when he got home. This morning, he left just after six, to meet his friends for breakfast before taking off on their trip. But that's their usual plan. So, I can't tell you anything."

"Well, on the bright side, he just saved you the thousand dollars it would have cost for you to file."

"That's something," Debra replied, still almost giddy. "Now I can stop feeling so guilty for thinking I would be blindsiding him. Maybe he's been just as unhappy as me."

Ah. "I understand," Josie replied, releasing the stress in her shoulders. It made sense. Guilt was a terrible thing. "Has he called?"

"No. I haven't heard a word from him."

"Okay. I'll file my appearance form with the court to confirm I'm representing you when your divorce shows up on the judicial website. Until then, there's nothing for us to do." Then a thought occurred to her.

"Hey, Debra?"

"Yes?"

"Find the lower third of the first page of the documents the marshal gave you. Did Philip sign the documents himself or is there a lawyer's name typed in and signed?"

"Let me get my glasses. Um, there's a typed name. It says Jonathan Tabor, attorney at law. Is that what you wanted to know?"

Josie tossed her pen into the air and seethed. *Someone's messing with me.*

****

It didn't take long to tackle Josie's cell phone issue. Dan called just as she was hanging up with Debra and walked her through connecting it to his plan over the provider's website.

Josie dialed Amy.

"The details about the two stores are coming back to me now," Amy told her. "I bought the vacant land in my own name, with the funds from a low interest federal loan program for female-owned businesses. The program required me to be the sole owner for a minimum of ten years."

"How long has it been?"

Josie could hear her counting.

"The ten years expired two weeks ago. I just found all the paperwork stuffed in the back of an old filing cabinet in the basement."

"Excellent." Josie located the entries on the land records website. "Tell me how it worked."

"The loan money was used to buy the land and build

the stores in both locations. Then I leased them to the Castle's corporation."

"Dan said you may have given Malcolm authorization to act on your behalf, to make decisions about the properties."

"That's correct," Amy confirmed. "I found the documents in the paperwork. In both cases, I signed them right after I got the land because he was handling the construction and licensing of the stores, and I wasn't always available to sign for things or oversee whatever needed to be done." She paused. Her voice hitched upward when she continued. "But I didn't think he could use it years later to sell a whole store and the land without me knowing about it. I can't believe he fooled me. Once again."

"Don't fret," Josie told her. "I know what we need to do."

At a few minutes after two, she met Amy at the Castle's store in Glastonbury. There, in the parking lot, Amy signed two documents that revoked Malcolm's authority over the buildings and the land located in Madison and Mystic. When they finished, Josie headed home, and Amy left to record them on the land records in both towns. Once accomplished, they would prevent any sale or other action from taking place without her knowledge and consent.

Even better, Josie decided, nearing her exit, since Amy was the sole owner in both situations, there was no requirement to notify Malcolm or Richard Diamond of the recordings. However, she decided she wanted Dan, a guru in commercial real estate, to notify the prospective purchaser of the Madison property. Not that she wanted to blow the deal. Heck no. She felt sure Malcolm negotiated a sweet one, and Dan would make sure of it. She just wanted Amy to have a seat at the table when it was finalized, and her name was on the check when it passed hands.

Josie took the exit toward home and tried to anticipate the fall out when Richard Diamond and his client discovered she knew about their scheme. *Every action creates a reaction...*

An image of Anne Compton, aiming that gun at her husband, came back. Josie pushed it away and decided she had time for a shower, but not a nap before leaving for the evening's service. Except that plan went right out the window when she approached her house.

She grabbed her cell phone and pressed the speed dial button.

"Hey what's up?" Dan answered.

"Why is *our* father's humongous motor home parked in *my* driveway? He told me he was coming tomorrow. And he didn't say anything about bringing that mansion on wheels with him."

****

Dan laughed. "He's such a hot shit."

"Daniel, he's got the entire thing opened up and he's sitting on a lawn chair, next to one of those portable firepit thingies and a small table set up on a fancy rug. And he's drinking a beer with my neighbors. What's going on?"

"How would I know?"

Josie watched her father rise to his full basketball player height. A huge grin took over his already pleasant features as he waved to her. She parked in front of her house and cut the engine. "Your denial tells me you do know. What's he up to? Where's his wife? And their yippy little dog? Did you tell him about my car being red washed?"

"Got to go. See you tonight."

"Don't you dare hang up!"

He hung up.

"Josie!" her dad boomed as he barreled toward her. "You're home!"

Slapping on her most dazzling, braces-enhanced smile, she got out of the car. "It's good to see you, Dad. I thought you were coming tomorrow."

He enveloped her in a huge hug. "So, I'm here now." Acting very pleased with himself, he linked their arms and drew her toward his RV. There, he retrieved a beer from an ice-filled cooler and popped off the cap.

"Hard day?" he asked, his brown eyes filled with mischief. "Here. Have a cold one."

"Thanks." Josie took the bottle and greeted her neighbors.

"I didn't know Pat here just retired," Gabe said. "And he plays golf. We're going out tomorrow to hit some balls."

"That's wonderful."

Pat agreed. As did Rachel, his wife, who was probably glad to get her husband out of her hair for a few hours.

"Thanks for the beer," Pat said, tipping the bottle to her father. "We'll leave you two to your evening."

Gabe tipped his in response. "See you at one tomorrow."

When they were out of earshot, Josie ushered her father inside the house. "Now that you've got your playdate arranged," she paused to point to the RV. "And you're all settled in, how come you didn't tell me you'd be here today? I mean I'm thrilled. I've missed you, but I would have come home earlier."

Josie watched her father's broad smile dim. He placed his jacket on the coat rack, then meandered into her living room and leaned on the fireplace mantel. "Honey, I've been giving things a lot of thought. I think I'm getting ready to start thinking about sort of retiring."

"Oh." She hung her car key on its hook in the kitchen and placed her purse and briefcase in their assigned spots. Then she met him in the living room.

"And I'm worried about you. I'm so sorry Luke is such a putz."

How did he know? Daniel! You are such a dead man.

Deflated, she curled up on the edge of the couch.

Gabe sat across from her on the loveseat. "And your car was vandalized yesterday?" He stretched out his long legs and folded his basketball-sized hands on his substantial stomach. "We'll ignore the fact you didn't tell me."

He stuck his tongue out at her, causing her to laugh back.

"Anyway, with that one tough case you got, and now Daniel's aunt's case too, I'm thinking maybe I could help you out. I could investigate, interview people, protect the witnesses, anything you need. And for Daniel too. I love the whole Perry Mason thing. It'll be fun."

He dropped his eyes to his hands, flexing and unflexing his fists. "You know, I've decided I'm at a point in my life when you, me, Daniel, and Mark can spend some real quality time together. And Mark always needs volunteers at the synagogue. There's a lot I can do up here."

Josie listened to what he said, along with what he didn't say. Something was wrong.

"That would be great, Dad. But how could you do all that from Jersey? You'll need some time to wind down your businesses."

He folded his hands again. "Yeah, but it's not that far of a ride. And ever since Daniel and then you decided to be lawyers, I've been intrigued with the idea myself. So, I contacted the law school here. If I take that test, what do you call it? The ST, or the PAT?"

"The LSAT?" she asked, half in shock, the other half in awe. Her father was always full of surprises. Bossy and nosy, and sometimes a huge pain in her butt, but also kind and generous. And nothing kept him down.

Gabe sat forward. "Yeah, that's it. If I take it by January fifteenth, the results will be back in time for me to get my application in by the deadline. If it goes the way I'm planning, I can start in the fall."

"Here in Hartford?" Jose gulped. "Where I teach?"

"Yup. I can go to school at night and work for you kids during the day. I even signed up for one of those study classes. It starts in a few days." He paused, waiting for Josie's reaction.

"Do you think I'm nuts?"

Josie joined him on the loveseat. "I know you're nuts, but I think it's pretty cool."

"You do?"

"Yeah."

"So, I'm thinking I'll move up here for a while. See how it goes. I could stay in my RV until I figure out something more permanent."

"You could," she agreed. "Or you could stay in the house with me."

Did I just suggest that my father moved in with me?

"Or with Dan," she amended. "He's got plenty of room. And I'm sure Mark will want you to spend time with him too."

"Thanks, babe. We'll see. I don't want to impose on anybody. And I kind of like my privacy."

"Did Roxanne kick you out again?"

Josie watched her father's jowls sag. He sat up and tapped his fingers on his knees. "Sort of."

"Oh Dad." She reached for the hand closest to her. "What did you do this time?"

****

His hooded eyes held a pained look. "Why does everybody always think it's my fault?"

Josie sent him a sympathetic grin. "Because, Dad, it usually is your fault."

He shrugged. "Maybe, but this time, not so much." He adjusted his position to face her, his mouth in a twist.

Josie suspected he was trying to decide how to tell her something but then changed his mind.

"Hey, I'm starved. Unless your cooking skills have improved, let's order a pizza."

She stood to find her cell. "The usual? Sausage, pepperoni, bacon, extra cheese, and mushrooms?"

"Skip the bacon. We're Jewish, you know."

Oh dear. This is bad.

Though Josie's mother grew up in an observant Jewish household, Gabe was raised as a cultural Jew. Meaning, they were not very religious. His father's family survived the Holocaust in Denmark due to the heroic efforts of the gentile countrymen who defied Hitler's henchman. Taking enormous risks, they hid most of the nation's Jews and eventually led them to safety in Sweden. Katrina, his father's girlfriend, was one of those brave people. The couple reunited soon after the war and married. A few years later, they immigrated to the United States and settled in central New Jersey.

Gabe was their oldest child, followed by his two sisters. As a family, they attended the high holy day services and celebrated Chanukah, but they also celebrated Christmas and Easter.

Things changed after Gabe met Josie's mother. As a compromise, by the time Josie was born, they were full members of an active Reform congregation. By then, he'd developed a deep appreciation for his religious heritage, becoming fully engaged in the synagogue's activities. But though they kept kosher at home, an occasional thick, juicy, bacon burger with Swiss cheese or a pizza topped with the works were his favorite, occasional go-tos. He also loved to sing Christmas carols and they always decorated a *Hanamas* tree, as he called it, right after Thanksgiving. It stayed up until New Year's Day.

As Josie waited to place the order, she watched her father scroll through his phone. He reminded her of a big, sad Saint Bernard. That stopped her from reminding him that sausage and pepperoni, with cheese, fell into the same category as bacon. When she finished, she came closer and asked, "How bad is it?"

Gabe leaned his head against the cushion and studied her ceiling. "Roxanne says she's in love with a woman. Oh, and I'm not religious enough for her."

Josie reached for his hand. He squeezed back. "She met this homewrecker at the gym. Shit, the lady's almost my age. And she's Orthodox. They met last year, and now they're in love. They moved in together a month ago."

"And you didn't tell me?" Josie challenged, a hint of humor in her tone.

Gabe rubbed his face with both hands.

They both burst out laughing, then sobered.

"I'm so sorry, Dad."

"I even offered to try a threesome, you know, to see what all the fuss was about, but she said no."

Josie slapped her hands over her ears. "Enough! Yuck!"

He winked. "Just kidding. That's what I told the guys."

"Cute, Daddy-O."

"Of all things. I'm seventy-three. Still active and pretty good looking, I'd say. I got most of my hair and I even had plastic surgery on my eyes. I didn't want Roxanne or other people thinking she was with an old man. And son of a gun, there she goes, falling for an old lady who's got more wrinkles than me."

The images that flooded Josie's imagination...

Gabe returned his attention to the ceiling. "I admit I'm not as religious as I was with your mom, but Roxanne never showed any interest at all. In fact, she told me she was an atheist when we met. She went along with the Jewish stuff for Mark because she could see how it helped get him on the right track."

He stood and paced. "We still belong to the synagogue and the JCC and we go to all the high holy day services. I don't eat wheat products during Passover, and I support Israel. I also sympathize with the Palestinian peoples' plight. At least those who aren't trying to wipe us off the face of the planet. And I'd get more involved if she'd asked me."

Josie gave him a tight hug. "I'm glad you're here."

"I haven't told Daniel," Gabe said, trailing her into the kitchen. He took the white candles she held out and placed them in the silver candlesticks for Shabbat.

"I won't either."

"And on the topic of break-ups, I don't want to interfere, but have you considered going to counseling with Luke? Maybe you could forgive him, and the two of you could work things out."

Josie got out the placemats and the plates. "Even if I did, Dad, I don't think he wants to come back. He's got a girlfriend. From the photos, she's twenty years younger than me."

"Life sure is a trip, ain't it?" He placed silverware and napkins on the table. "You just never know what's next."

Josie filled the glasses with water and ice. "You just never know." After a moment, she added, "You're coming to the service with me, right? Mark is leading and Dan will be there. The synagogue is hosting a small dinner afterward. Consider the pizza a snack."

Gabe's eyes darted about the room as if he were lost.

"Talk to me, Dad."

It took a long moment for his glassy eyes to meet hers. He sniffled. "I doubt God's happy with me, kiddo. I said a bunch of things after Roxanne made her announcement and I haven't been to a service in I don't know how long."

Josie went to him and held his elbows. "You always told me God was strong enough to take all of our pain and anger, and still be there for us, no matter what."

He grunted.

"And besides." She focused on his eyes and smiled.

191

"Your son's a rabbi and your daughter's in charge of the Shabbat services each week. Somewhere along the line, you must have gotten a few things right. I'm sure you get a pass."

Like a little hopeful kid, he raised his bushy eyebrows. "Do you think?"

The doorbell rang. "I do." She smiled. "Food's here."

Chapter Thirty-One

Richard, Friday Evening

Richard stepped out of his car, parked in the same spot across from the synagogue, and stretched his long frame. The service started in thirty minutes. He expected to see Josephina Jensen there tonight. Yesterday's incident with her car still turned his stomach. No doubt it continued to bother her as well.

For years, he'd attended services miles away from where he lived and worked in order to step away from his daily life. And yet now, here he was, in the same city. Maybe he should leave. There were other synagogues in the area.

And yet he kept walking toward the building.

When Richard reached the entrance, he joined the quick-moving crowd toward the sanctuary. Being a new member, he needed to pick up his name badge at the Welcome Table. Moving forward, he heard a now familiar voice giving directions. Josephina's face came into view, along with the rest of her, wearing a flattering blue and white dress with scarlet accents. He wondered if she was wearing the same perfume as yesterday.

As the line moved him closer, Richard's anticipation of her reaction to seeing him increased. Then it was interrupted by another voice behind him.

"*Shabbat Shalom*, Rabbi."

Richard turned and saw Mark Jensen. The young man was responding to an elder man and woman, adding their names to the greeting. His smile widened even more when he recognized Richard, who was now one person away from the Welcome Table.

"*Shabbat Shalom*, Rich," Mark said, "Let me re-introduce you to my sister, Josie."

Richard couldn't stop his double-beamed grin when Jensen saw him standing with her brother. Their paths hadn't crossed in so many years, and now both their personal and professional lives kept running into one another.

"*Shabbat Shalom*," she greeted, rummaging through the box with the name badges.

Richard stopped himself from laughing aloud. "*Shabbat Shalom* to you, Ms. Jensen. We meet again."

Her warning-like smile said, "Yes. I know this is weird, but please behave," as she handed him his badge. "Welcome," she voiced aloud.

Oblivious to their undercurrents, Mark continued with the introductions. "Richard is also an attorney in this area." He paused and nodded to the duffle bag Richard carried. "And he's going to do us the great honor of blowing the shofar this evening."

Josie blinked surprise, but then moved her attention over Richard's shoulder. Her expression melted into genuine affection. Suddenly, he felt displaced.

"Mark, Dad's behind you with Dan."

Greetings were repeated, along with introductions and handshakes.

The Jensens have their own basketball team, Richard realized. Dan wasn't as tall as his towering father, but he had to be at least six foot four. And the rabbi reached at least six feet. As did Josie.

"Richard, please sit with us in the sanctuary," Dan offered. "And join our table for dinner after the service."

"Yeah, that would be great," the older man added. "I don't know anyone here either."

Surprised by the invitation, Richard nodded as Josie looked poised to throttle both family members.

"Thank you. I'd like that." *Even more now, seeing her tripled reaction.*

Dan winked at her.

Richard held back a laugh as he joined his new acquaintances in the sanctuary. He had done some research on Daniel Jensen since meeting him the night before. Like Richard, the guy played in the big leagues. His client list included national companies and a decent number of federal and state politicians and lobbyists. He surmised that many of them flew undetected into the tiny Groton airport, to meet with Dan nearby at his secluded waterfront office.

How intriguing.

Enough, Richard's thoughts scolded. *No more work. Shabbat has arrived.*

But it is so much fun, his mischievous side replied.

Chapter Thirty-Two

Friday Evening

A gruff voice picked up on the first ring. *"Yeah?"*
"Did you do it?"
"Yeah. Just like we said."
"Did you call the cops?"
"I said yeah."
"Good. Let's see how she likes it."

Chapter Thirty-Three

Josie Friday Evening

"Please sit with us," Josie mimicked her brother, slapping the remaining name badges into an envelope. The large reception area was empty now, except for her. She remained at the table, waiting for the last few stragglers.

"Yeah, that would be great. I don't know anyone here either," she added, now mimicking her father.

Ha! The assistant rabbi is also your son, and your other son and daughter were standing right there. Who else do you need to know? And Richard had the audacity to answer, "Thank you, I'd like that."

Josie fumed. She wasn't even sure it was ethical for them to be here together. Last night's bloodied car incident was one thing, but this was over the top. What would their clients think?

In no rush to enter the sanctuary, she crossed the large foyer to the chapel and sat in the last row near the door. The service was live streamed in there for members who preferred a more intimate atmosphere or who needed to stretch or use the restroom during the service. She kept the door open, to permit her to see and hear late arrivals.

Halfway through the service, the heavy outside doors in the foyer squeaked open. Josie hurried out of the chapel, closing the door behind her, and found two police officers. A loud static-filled voice erupted over one of their radios. She thought they were the traffic officers the synagogue hired for the evening. Maybe they wanted to use the restroom or get a bottle of water.

Greeting them, she spoke in a hushed voice. "Thank you for helping out tonight. We should be finished by ten. Do you need anything?"

The shorter officer didn't catch on. His radio went off again and he answered even louder into his shoulder mic.

"Ten four, we arrived at the suspect's address. It's a synagogue."

"Are you requesting back-up?" a voice asked.

Josie made a pleading face, putting her finger to her lips, while attempting to usher them into the larger adjacent room.

They didn't budge.

"We'll let you know," the same one replied into his mic.

The other one looked at the electronic tablet in his hand, then at Josie. "Is Josephina Jensen here?"

She remembered she was on the security call list for emergencies, but where was the security detail?

"Yes," she answered. "I'm Josie. How can I help you?"

"We located the suspect," he said into his shoulder mic.

The shorter officer took a step toward her and removed a set of handcuffs from his belt. "Place both hands on your head, ma'am."

****

"Hey, fellas. What's going on in here?"

Relieved but trembling, Josie heard a familiar male voice behind her as she struggled to keep her hands steady on top of her head and balance without her cane.

It's Jerry Cohen! Our head of security.

"There's a service going on," he continued. "And you're interrupting it. Ms. Jensen, please put your hands down. Let's all go into the next room like civilized folks, out of earshot, and tell me what's going on."

The shorter officer placed his hand close to his holster. "Stand down, sir. We're making an arrest."

The other officer stood within a foot of Josie and reached for her arm.

"You're making no such thing," Jerry declared, now within her sight. "I'm going to reach into my right shirt pocket real slow and pull out my ID. I'm Lieutenant Jerome Cohen, in charge of synagogue security and the Hate Crimes Unit for this county. Mind you, this entire building, including all these rooms, is loaded with surveillance cameras. And I've known this woman for fifteen-plus years. Whatever you think she did, you got the wrong person."

Josie recognized another one of their security officers' voices as it played over Jerry's radio.

"What's going on, Lieutenant? The police scanner says there's an arrest in progress at this address and I'm seeing all of you on screen seven."

"Yeah, Aaron," Jerry answered, keeping his eyes on the officers. "Get Sergeant Flint at the Hartford PD on the line. Pronto. Tell him I've got two officers here whom I just saved from making a serious mistake. I need him to tell them to stand down." He emphasized the *stand down* part. "And keep up the foot patrols and camera surveillance. We don't need anyone getting the idea to bomb the place while I'm cleaning up this little misunderstanding."

Then he spoke to the officers. "Gentlemen, I'm going to ask you one more time. Please come with me. We don't need you making spectacles of yourselves. Or do we?"

The shorter guy started to protest, but before he spoke, his radio went off.

"Officer Reynolds, this is Sergeant Flint. Do as Lieutenant Cohen says. You've got a bunch of bystanders in that building and the situation doesn't warrant causing an unnecessary incident."

****

"What's this all about?" Josie implored from her seat inside the synagogue's security office.

Increased vandalism and terror attacks at houses of worship all over country broke her heart. At the same time, they forced the congregation to dramatically upgrade their security measures. They now employed three full-time officers, including night and weekend shifts, and each staff member was trained to detect threats and handle hostage situations. Many congregants also participated in these trainings.

"You're being charged with reckless driving, risk of injury, evading responsibility with an automobile, and destruction of property," the short officer, now identified as Reynolds, declared.

Josie clenched her fists and shifted her weight off her injured hip in the uncomfortable chair. "How? When? I've been here since six o'clock this evening."

"Here's the video." The less obnoxious officer handed the tablet to Jerry. To her he asked, "What kind of a car do you drive?"

Her mind blanked. *Think, gosh darn it.* "Uh, a white sedan."

"What's the license plate number?"

Josie scratched her forehead. "I'm not sure. AP 3891 or something like that. It's parked midway down on Belvedere Street."

By this time, she wondered if she should have a lawyer with her. In fact, she knew she should. At the same time, she did nothing wrong. And she didn't want to aggravate the situation further.

"What am I seeing here?" Jerry asked, staring at the tablet.

"At six-thirty-four this evening, our surveillance cameras on Lacross Street filmed a white sedan, license plate number AP 3891, jumping the curb in front of a restaurant. It crashed through the metal fence leading to the outdoor patio and came to a stop within a foot of the front window where numerous witnesses watched it coming toward them. The film shows a tall female with dark hair exiting the vehicle and running from the scene."

"I can't run," Josie admonished, holding up her cane to them.

"Where in the building were you at that time?" Jerry asked her.

"At the Welcome Table in the front foyer, handing out name badges. Then I went into the chapel off the main foyer to watch the service live streamed." She looked at the cops. "It's where I came from when you entered the building."

"Did you find it?" Jerry asked Aaron, who sat in front of the wall of surveillance monitors.

The men crowded around the monitors, blocking her

view. She didn't care. She needed to use the restroom, but she didn't dare move. She wanted this mistake cleared up and over.

"Yes sir. There she is," Aaron told them.

Josie shoulders slumped with relief.

"Fast forward one minute at a time," Jerry instructed.

"She's been here the entire time," Aaron reported.

"Yes, that's what I told the officers," Josie reminded them. "But from what you're saying, someone stole my car. Can you find it?"

"Is there surveillance on Belvedere where Ms. Jensen says she parked her car?" Jerry asked.

"Not by us, but we've got a camera at the corner of Belvedere and Lacross. We suspect that's the route they took." Reynolds radioed the precinct and asked for an available patrol to keep an eye out for her car and to pull up the surveillance feed.

"Can I see the video on the tablet?" Josie asked.

Avoiding her eyes, Renyolds held it in front of her and pushed the play button.

Her breath hitched when a vehicle like hers veered around the corner of Belvedere to Lacross Street. "Can you zoom in on the driver?"

The rainstorm that started earlier was at its worst, hammering the windshield. The wipers further blurred the scene. The grainy footage showed a lot of dark colored hair surrounding a blurred face. "That person is wearing a wig. I wore my hair up this evening."

The men took in her upswept curls, then the video, and back to her.

A female voice crackled over Reynold's radio. *"There's no white sedan parked on Belvedere."*

"Thanks," he answered.

Jerry sat back behind his desk. "I think its accurate to say that someone stole Ms. Jensen's car, rammed it into the restaurant, and then took off."

"What's going on?" a male voice interrupted.

Josie's stomach dropped.

Dan, his eyes darting from one face to another, appeared in the doorway. Richard Diamond and her father stood behind him, surveying the scene.

Seeing them, she felt her life swirling downward into an imaginary toilet. "There's an issue with a stolen car," she answered, before the men could respond. To Jerry, she said, "I need to prepare for the Shabbat dinner."

"Sure."

Josie motioned Dan, along with her father and the nosy Richard Diamond into the main lobby. "Before you ask for any details, I need your help. A hundred people expect to be fed when the service ends and a ton of things still need to be done."

Nodding, her father said, "Show us what to do."

Dan's expression showed he was contemplating how to back out without seeming like a jerk. When their father tugged at his elbow, he mumbled, "Oh, yeah. Sure."

"I can help too," Richard offered.

Josie stammered. He was still her mortal enemy, willing to take every opportunity to keep Amy Castle from her money. And yet he'd shown her a decent side of himself last night. And he did have a set of hands.

"Thank you."

Hurrying to the kitchen, she forced herself to push aside the reality that she was almost arrested, but she couldn't stop wondering why this had happened.

How did the police know to find me here at the synagogue?

****

A little after ten, Josie watched the last congregants make their way toward the building's exit while Gabe collapsed into a nearby chair. "Man, oh man! I can't believe we pulled that off."

"Here, here," Richard agreed, pouring four glasses of red wine from a leftover bottle. He held one out to Josie who sat across from him, then to Gabe and Dan. Raising his glass, he said, "*L'chaim!*"

They clinked their glasses together and repeated the blessing. "*L'chaim!*"

To life.

"Is this a private party?"

"Hey, Mark," Josie called out. She pulled over a chair from a nearby table and Richard handed him a filled glass. "The service was magnificent."

Humbled, Mark nodded. "This merger of our congregations is a huge *Mitzvah*. We all benefit."

"And you did a pretty good job of blowing that *shofar*," Gabe told Richard. "It's been at least ten years since I last did it. I'd like to give it another go one of these days."

Josie exchanged tight grins with her brothers.

"Sure, Dad," Mark replied. "Any time."

"You must be a bit rusty," Richard warned, in all seriousness. "Perhaps you should practice, then audition."

Gabe, just as serious, considered this.

Then a smile cracked Richard's serious expression. "I am kidding."

The two men started to laugh, Gabe, a little less certain.

Richard turned serious again. "But not really. I could give you a few refresher pointers if you'd like."

He grinned again and Gabe roared.

Staring at the two clowns having a grand old time, Josie couldn't believe what she was seeing. This wasn't supposed to be happening. Sure, Richard was a huge help tonight, but still…

Dan leaned into Josie and Mark. "Dad's got a new friend."

Josie snapped her mouth tight.

Mark furrowed his eyes as Dan snickered.

"Josie just took on a huge, nasty post-judgment divorce case and Richard is the attorney on the other side."

"Is this true?" Mark asked her.

"Yes. Thanks to Big Brother here."

Catching Josie narrow her eyes at Dan, Mark covered his smile. It reminded her of when he was a kid and wanted to laugh about something but knew he shouldn't.

"Come on," she urged everyone, rising to her feet. "Let's get out of here."

Dan and Mark walked alongside her as the two new best buds followed close behind, continuing their *shofar* discussion.

"How long is he staying?" Josie heard Mark whisper to Dan. "I didn't even know he was coming."

"Not sure," Dan whispered back. "His RV is parked in Josie's driveway."

Mark pushed open the heavy, mahogany door. Though the rain stopped, an icy wind met them, fighting to push the door closed. Outside, they dodged scattered puddles covering the shimmering wet blacktop.

"He and Mom must be arguing again," Mark told them. "I tried to reach her a bunch of times over the past few days, but she hasn't texted or called me back."

There was no way in heck Josie was going to be the one to spill the beans about their parents. "I'm sure she'll contact you soon."

"No doubt." He headed toward his SUV, parked in the *Reserved for Rabbi Jensen* spot, and aimed the remote control to unlock the doors. "Where's everyone's cars?"

"Josie and I are on Belvedere," Dan said. "Richard?"

He pointed in the opposite direction. "On Farmington."

"Hop in," Mark told them. "Our synagogue reminds me of King Harrod's palace at Masada. It's a gorgeous fortress, but outside the walls can be dicey at night."

Josie sat up front, leaving the three big dudes to squish together in the back. Belvedere was right around the corner. It wouldn't kill them to suffer for a bit.

"I'll drop them off first," Mark told Richard, engaging the engine. "Your car is on my way home."

Josie buckled her seatbelt, feeling like she was starring in a horror film. Richard Diamond, with her family, working through a Shabbat dinner, and now sharing a ride? No one watching would suspect they were embroiled in a battle for millions of dollars. She retrieved her keys from her purse as Mark pulled up behind Dan's car.

"Where's your car, Josie?" he asked. "I parked right behind you."

She lowered herself in the seat. She'd forgotten about that. Almost being arrested was one thing. The practicalities of having her car stolen created yet another quagmire. And she didn't want to discuss it with Richard around. "Um, Dan, can you take Dad and me home?"

"Sure, but what about your car?"

Four pairs of eyes waited for her answer. Their owners followed her to Dan's vehicle.

"Josephina?"

That came from her father. It didn't matter how old you were. The roles in the parent-child relationship never wavered.

"Remember when I said our security team and the police were investigating a stolen car?"

"It was your car?" Gabe questioned, looking both ways down the street.

Dan's brows drawn, he moaned, "We just cleaned it up."

"Why didn't you say something sooner?" Mark inquired, frowning in the street's harsh light.

And Richard, the final member of the new quartet chimed in with, "When did this happen?"

I didn't want to, and I don't know, Josie almost shot back.

She knew she was a victim, but she felt so violated. Again. And did Richard honestly give a hoot? Or was he putting on an act to cover for his client?

"I don't have any details yet," she told them. "From what the police said, it happened during the service. I'm sure they'll know more in the morning."

She opened Dan's car door and said, "Night, guys."

Mark went back to his vehicle, but Richard hesitated.

Their eyes met.

Did your client do this? she almost asked.

His expression stoic, he murmured, "Good night," and joined Mark.

Chapter Thirty-Four

Richard, Late Friday Evening

Yanking off his tie, Richard drove into his garage, turned off the engine, and dialed his client. On the speaker phone, he challenged, "What do you know about pig blood being dumped on Attorney Jensen's car yesterday, and that same car being stolen tonight?"

"Hey Dickie, take it easy. Why would you ask me something like that?"

Richard suspected a warning underneath that mock innocence. "You're right, Malcolm, don't answer. I don't want to know. But don't be surprised if the police contact you."

"You're saying somebody's been playing with her car?"

Richard didn't miss the hint of excitement in his client's tone. "It does not serve you to sound so cavalier, since you are the number one suspect."

"Anything else happen?"

"Isn't that enough?"

"Hey, a little blood and a stolen car ain't no big deal. Don't you watch the news? Crime is up everywhere. That's why people got insurance. But let me ask you this. Why are you so hot and bothered? How do you even know about it? Did she call you and accuse me?"

Let him think that, Richard decided. "Let me put it

to you this way, Malcolm. On numerous occasions, Amy has accused you of vandalizing her property. It wouldn't look good for you to have her lawyer making similar claims."

"So what? Those two broads cost me a lot of money yesterday and got me locked up three days before that. They deserve anything they get. It could have been a lot worse."

Richard straightened. "What are you saying?"

"Nothing. Nothing for you to worry about, Dickie," Malcolm answered, more subdued. "I'm just shooting off my mouth. It's late. I gotta go. Call me back when you figure out how to get me out of court on Thursday."

"You're under a subpoena, Malcolm."

"So, fix it," he snapped back. "For the millions I've paid, you can fix anything."

"Not sure I can this time."

"What the frig?" Castle lashed back. "Are you going soft on me? Now? What do you want? You want more money? How much?"

Richard leaned his head against the seat's head rest. "It's about more than the money now. Court orders are in effect. Up until the trial, for the most part, you were able to avoid them. But now that the divorce is over. Things are different. You know this. We've discussed it many times."

"What are you saying, Dickie?"

Richard heaved a deep sigh. "You need to be thinking about wrapping up this situation. You've had a good run and you've done exceedingly well. Now it's time to cut a deal."

A short pause followed. "What if I don't want to cut a deal?"

"Are you hearing yourself, Mal?" When he didn't answer, Richard added, "It's time to move on. No more court and no more legal bills."

"Holy moly. What ever will I do with all my free time and money?"

"Give it some thought and let me know on Monday."

"Don't count on it, Dickie."

The line went dead before Richard could respond.

Weary, he left the car and headed inside his home. In the shower, he stood under the hot water. Malcolm Castle was one of Richard's many clients over the years who'd boxed themselves into a corner. They'd experienced the thrill of dodging and weaving and working the legal system's loopholes, but the system only stretched so far. In time, many of them came to their senses and worked with him to reach an acceptable solution. A few others fired him, or he fired them. And the remainder got themselves into a ton of trouble. Richard wondered which category Castle would choose.

Toweling off, he rewound through the evening's other events. To his surprise, he enjoyed helping out at the dinner with the Jensens. Gabe was a real character. Funny and street smart and proud, but humble during the service. Daniel Jensen, Richard suspected, could be formidable, but good company. And Mark, their rabbi. Well, it has been a privilege to know him. And now to know his family.

A smiling image of Josephina Jensen entered his thoughts.

Yes, her too.

It was a perfect storm.

Yesterday's call from Anne Compton solidified

that.

Richard checked his phone log and uttered an oath. He'd missed the call from the hospital's director. He needed answers, in particular, why did Anne contact him? And how? She'd been almost catatonic for years.

Yes, he knew this because he'd represented her in all of her legal proceedings after the shooting. Her wealthy father, who'd hated his very existence years earlier, begged him to agree, and offered to pay him a million in legal fees. Though Richard loathed Anne and her father, he'd relented. For the money, and the payback, and the guarantee of confidentiality. There was no way he wanted his fellow colleagues, including Josephina Jensen, to know of his involvement.

Richard had handled all the negotiations and leg work to convince the prosecutor Anne was insane. Then he hired a buddy from D.C., who was also licensed to practice law in Connecticut. The guy attended all the court hearings to finalize the psychiatric commitment. He also completed the part of the settlement agreement that involved Anne, who had significant family assets, untouched by the divorce. It included a private trust that would pay all of Jensen's medical bills and expenses for life, even if they weren't related to the shooting. In addition, in conjunction with the lawsuit against the judicial department, Jensen received a large lump sum payment, along with a generous yearly allowance, also for life. It was a sweet deal that could never make up for the horrible situation.

Did Richard regret representing Anne? Until now, no. At the time, it was the smart thing to do. Somebody had to do it. Why not him? It also kept him in the loop. He needed to know what Anne said about him.

No doubt the Jensens would not agree.

During the dark morning hours, Richard fought off horrible scenes from a reoccurring nightmare.

His watch showed it was almost four o'clock. The courthouse was quiet, except for a few hearings scattered throughout the building. He had a trial on the fifth floor, the family law floor. Due to an overly efficient heating system, the door to his courtroom was open. He and the people with him heard the rapid firing. One, two, three, four, five...six.

Richard recognized gun shots from his stint in the military. On his feet, he dialed 911 and darted into the hallway as the court officer assigned to the room shouted into his radio for help. Racing past a fire alarm, Richard doubled back and pulled it. Best to get everyone out of the building.

Alarm sirens echoed through the hall. Richard looked inside each courtroom he passed. Empty. Then he arrived at Courtroom 510. For reasons unknown, it was the only room in the building with double doors made of glass. Anyone passing by could see much of what was taking place inside.

Rescue personnel charged from the opposite end of the corridor as Richard arrived to see the carnage. Josephina Jensen lay on the floor and Anne Compton sat at the counsel table. He was almost certain she sent him a small smile as the first responders rushed past him.

Richard bolted from the bed and walked the room. When his heart rate slowed to normal and the sweat drenching his tee shirt dried cold on his back, he stripped and took another shower.

What, if anything, will Anne do next? And when? And how?

Chapter Thirty-Five

After Midnight, Saturday Morning

"What do you mean, they let Jensen go? Why wasn't she arrested? She needs to know what it feels like. The degradation, the helplessness…"

"The call went out as reckless endangerment and attempted assault with a deadly weapon. Now it's listed as a stolen vehicle. She must have convinced the cops she wasn't driving."

The conversation paused. Then, "It don't matter. I'm sure she's rattled. It's still a win. Follow up with the plans we discussed. But this time, make sure you get the results I'm paying you for."

Chapter Thirty-Six

Josie, Saturday Morning

"Would you consider a four-way conference to try to resolve this?"

Josie pondered Everett Kramer's question as she sat across the desk from him at seven-forty-seven that morning. His New Haven office was located on Templer Street, otherwise known as Lawyers' Row. Bordering the campus of Yale University, it contained one tall, narrow, well-maintained and appointed brownstone after another. Everett, perhaps in his mid-sixties, sported a partial head of salt and peppery hair, cut short. Standing about three inches shorter than her, he'd greeted her at the office door wearing khakis, a white, untucked polo shirt, and two-toned boat shoes. It was Saturday, after all.

"Why don't I just put a gun to my head and blow my brains out?"

Without reacting, Everett watched Josie behind his tortoise-rimmed eyeglasses.

"Let me rethink that." She rose to pace the polished wood floor. "After my past experience with guns, it wouldn't be my first choice." She paused and made a face. "Too messy."

The lawyer stayed quiet, but she noticed his eyes shimmer at her sarcasm.

"You know that's how we met, Luke and me? He

was one of the paramedics at the scene."

Everett granted her a half nod. "I read that somewhere."

She sat back down. "Yup, our romance was all over the grocery store tabloids and social media back then. 'Lawyer shot by crazy client weds medic who saved her life.'"

Josie's voice cracked and her eyes filled. She pulled a tissue from the box at the end of Everett's desk, because that's where all good divorce lawyers placed them, and blew her nose.

Everett jotted a note on a yellow legal pad. "So that would be a no?"

"Correct. I don't want to be anywhere near Luke and his horrendous excuse for a lawyer. Just the suggestion that I sit across the table from someone who betrayed me, and expect me to keep my emotions intact...It's not going to happen." Josie sniffled. "Talk about karma. I feel like I should send an apology to every client I made that suggestion to."

She sniffled again when he said, "You've been married thirty months, give or take a few days, and you have a prenuptial agreement. Are you willing to abide by its terms?"

"Yes, even though I think paying him ten thousand dollars for each year we were married is too generous. But the crook he hired, Jonathan Tabor, wants to break it."

Holding up the documents she'd been served with, Everett nodded. "I saw that."

Josie fiddled with the tissue. "I'm presuming Luke and Tabor are counting on me not wanting a court battle. And this stupid jurisdictional fight tells me Tabor sees my divorce as his cash cow."

"Jonathan Tabor's reputation has reached New Haven and beyond," Everett assured her. "A lot will depend on your husband and how much he's willing to pay him, or reel him in."

Josie crumbled up the used tissue and noticed the pale narrow space her wedding rings used to occupy. "I don't even know who Luke is anymore. I mean, I thought I was a decent judge of character, but I was so wrong about him." She paused to clear her throat. "That fake birthday card, the photos…Even filing the divorce in Hartford and shutting off the utilities…I didn't see this coming."

A heavy silence hung over the room.

She moved her hair behind her ears. "Just like I didn't see Anne Compton shooting off a gun in the courtroom." The images rushed forward as she spoke the words. Just as fast, she shoved them back into their imaginary box in their imaginary closet and double bolted the door shut.

Pen poised, Everett waited for her to continue.

"Anyway, with Luke having a girlfriend, I hoped he'd just want to take his money under the prenup and go away."

Everett made another note. "But then Tabor wouldn't make any money."

"I know."

"All right." He leaned forward and folded his arms on the desk. "You know how this goes. What are your bottom-line thoughts for settlement?"

They spent the next half hour discussing the assets and debts she and Luke owned before the marriage, and what they accumulated since then. When she got to

Luke's toys, Everett brightened. "List them for me."

"There's the sports car, the boat, the motorcycle, two jet skis, the lawn tractor, the record collection, the big screen television, the three keyboards, his guitars and recording equipment.…"

Everett dropped his gaze over his glasses.

"Yeah, he thinks he's a reincarnated rock star."

He suppressed a smile. "In the divorce complaint, Tabor asks for alimony. It's not permitted in the prenup, but you earn close to double what Luke earns. What if he pursues it?"

Heat flash-flooded from her gut and rose to the top of her head. She clenched and unclenched her fists at her sides. "Like you said, it's not even a three-year marriage. And yes, I do make more, but his free ride is over. Let him work overtime if he needs money. He's always saying it's available."

"And if he pushes?"

"Then I'll sell his nudie photos to the tabloids and split the profits with him."

This time, Everett permitted a smile as he wrote. "What about your settlement from the shooting?"

"What about it?" Josie shot back. "The law's clear. He's not entitled to any of it. And where do you think the money for his toys came from? He can keep them all, but nothing else."

Everett kept writing. Josie alternated her attention between watching him and the fancy gold clock on his desk, adding up how much money he was making for each minute that ticked by.

How did her clients stand it?

She thought back over the years of all the sad and angry people who sat across from her, just like this.

Talk about the shoe now being on the other foot.
****

Josie handed Everett the signed retainer agreement, establishing their official attorney-client relationship, along with a credit card for him to charge his fee. Soon after, she was racing up the interstate in Dan's shiny black SUV, hoping to arrive at Torah study on time. The last thing she expected was to see Richard Diamond parking in a spot directly behind her when she arrived.

Stepping out of vehicle, she debated her greeting. Warm and friendly, after last night's mutual efforts? Or professionally distant, due to their opposing clients and her overall distrust of the man? To her surprise, the decision was made for her.

A loud, honking horn made both of them turn to find Josie's father behind the wheel of a huge, bright red pick-up truck. She snapped her jaw closed as he parked alongside Richard in the lot and bounded out of the beast, beaming with pride.

"Hey, guys!"

Richard let out an appreciative whistle and walked toward him. "Well, well, well!"

"Thanks for the tip last night." Gabe gripped the lawyer's outstretched hand. "Your buddy's letting me test drive this for the next few days."

Josie followed as the men pointed out all the truck's cool features and discussed how well it handled on the road.

Oh, brother.

Gabe peeked at her over his shoulder. "Hey, Josie. Dan and Richard know the same car dealer over in Simsbury. I picked this one out on the Internet last night and they dropped it off to me at your place."

Richard sent a boyish grin her way. "We discovered the connection during dinner."

While she was hostessing the meal, unable to sit down for more than a minute at a time. *What else did they talk about?*

Afraid to ask, she led the way to the meeting room, half-listening as they discussed the other vehicles her father planned to test drive. Spotting vacant seats, she made sure to put Gabe in the middle.

"What's this week's lesson about?" he whispered.

Josie started to answer but Richard whispered over her.

"*Jacob's Ladder.*"

"Oh, the one where Jacob runs away from home because his older brother, Esau, is gonna kill him for stealing his birthright?"

"That's the one."

Josie located the passage in her *siddur* as Gabe asked, "Isn't there a girl involved?"

"There's always a girl involved," Richard replied, causing them both to chuckle.

Before the best bros could high five each other, the senior Rabbi, Monica Samson, walked in.

"*Shabbat Shalom,*" she greeted the group. Her youthful appearance made it hard to believe she turned sixty-eight this year. "Today we are in the seventh week of this new year. Our Torah *parsha* is entitled *Vayetze,* from the book of Genesis, chapters 28 through 32."

As she spoke, Josie's phone vibrated. She peeked at it under the table. Amy Castle.

—Please call me as soon as you can. I just discovered something important.—

Josie slouched in her chair. *This is why we aren't*

supposed to answer phones or use electronic devices during Shabbat. The world's distractions are endless.

She excused herself and slipped out to her office. She would watch the remainder of the class live streamed on her phone after speaking with her client.

"You're not going to believe this," Amy declared, answering on the first ring.

Josie closed her door and leaned against the corner of her desk. "Tell me."

"Someone, I have no idea who, sent me an email a few months ago. I just noticed it in my spam folder. They attached account statements in the original name of the company that Malcolm and I formed years ago, with an investment firm I've never heard of. And guess what?"

"I'm ready."

"I was able to access the account online. It's still active and it's worth over a million dollars. Up until last year, he was making monthly deposits, but it's not listed anywhere in the financial information he disclosed to the court."

Josie closed her eyes and rubbed her temples. She'd been worried something like this would pop up. "Do you have a guess as to who sent you the email?"

"No. I'm forwarding it to you now. Maybe we can have it traced."

Dueling emotions hit Josie as she and Amy said goodbye. They started with disappointment at the lies told, after all the years and the money both Castles spent on their divorce. Concern came next.

What other secrets may come to light if Amy probed further? Should we re-evaluate the entire financial picture? Or stick to pursuing the court's orders, plus these new financial findings? Would Amy be willing to leave it alone, so she could move on with her life? Or would she want to keep going?

****

Josie worked non-stop through the rest of the afternoon in her office at the law school until her father called. "Hey, we forgot all about going to Boston today for your birthday. What are your plans tonight?"

She checked the time at the corner of her laptop. "How did it get to be almost six-thirty?"

"Time flies," he joked.

"Yeah, but I'm sure not having any fun."

"Come on home and we'll think of something to do."

"Fine. Be there soon."

A half-hour later, Josie drove up to her house. "Oh, good grief," she muttered. Five cars, along with her father's RV, were parked in the driveway and in front of the house. As she came through the door, she was greeted by Gabe and half a dozen guests, all holding multi-colored helium balloons.

"Happy birthday!"

Josie blushed, accepted their hugs. "So, this is what happens when you give your brothers and your father a key to your home."

As they laughed, she noted that the guest list had Dan written all over it. Amy Castle was there, along with Debra Tate, Linda Reed and her husband, Frank. And he and Mark of course.

Josie appreciated the gesture. These were important people in her life right now. Each for their own reasons. So what if she was now forty-one and almost divorced, and back to doing the one thing she never wanted to do again?

Things have been worse. Right?

Thanks to Amy's talents, the guests helped themselves to seconds and even thirds of her delicious brisket, carrots and mashed potatoes. An unbelievable chocolate fudge cake appeared afterward.

As the evening progressed, Josie spotted her dad spending a lot of time with Debra Tate. And Debra seemed to be enjoying his company.

Isn't that interesting?

During the final round of charades, Josie's cell phone rang. Excusing herself, she decided to answer it, even though she didn't recognize the number on the caller ID. The last time she ignored a call, a state marshal showed up with divorce papers.

"Josie Jensen."

"It's me," a serious male voice replied.

Luke.

Her first instinct was to hang up. But she also didn't want Tabor to run the show. Being a chatty kind of guy, Luke might let their plans slip and then she could somehow short circuit them. Otherwise, this divorce was going to cost them both a fortune, for nothing.

"Thanks for shutting off my cell phone."

"Hey, with all your cash, you could have offered to pay the bill."

Josie clenched and unclenched her free hand. She wanted to lash out at him, but held back. "How about we start over? Hi, Luke. How nice of you to call."

In the background, her guests broke into loud laughter.

"Hello? Josie? What's with the noise? Who's there?"

"Just a sec." She stepped into the garage.

"Josie?" Luke shouted.

"Yes? Calm down. I'm here."

"Who's with you? That's still my house, you know."

Forget starting over. "Why are you calling, Luke?"

"I'm sorry." It came out as a conflicted whisper. "I just wanted to wish you a happy birthday."

A bunch of responses came to mind. Josie settled for the high road. "Thank you."

"I want to see you."

"Why?" The response was automatic. But somehow it felt almost comforting to think that maybe he realized he'd made a mistake. Shit, they had everything. A wonderful life, even with her injuries. And he tossed it all away. For what?

"Just to talk. Let's meet for breakfast tomorrow, before the lawyers turn everything into a circus on Monday."

Ah. Monday. He's worried about court.

"It doesn't have to be a circus, Luke. We have a prenup. I'm willing to keep to the terms, even though you cheated. You can have thirty thousand. That's ten thousand for each year we're married. Plus, your toys and your credit card debt. I'll take care of the joint card account." She didn't want to give him a dime, but she wanted to be rid of him. "It's up to you."

A long pause followed. She exhaled into the phone. "Guess not."

"My lawyer says I can do better."

"You hired the most unrealistic, least respected, and overpriced asshole in all of New England. He pumps his clients up, then tosses them a huge bill when the dust settles, and they end up with nothing close to the results he promised."

"I was worried, Josie. I need to protect myself. I mean, shit. You're a divorce lawyer. A really good one, from what I'm hearing. John was the only one willing to take me. Richard Diamond asked him to do it as a favor."

Josie lost her balance and fell against the door. "What do you mean, he was the only one willing to take you? You spoke with Richard Diamond?"

"Yeah. You always said he was the best. But he said he couldn't do it because you have a big case against each other."

Richard knew of her impending divorce? And he sent Luke to Jonathan Tabor?

She thought about Debra Tate. *Her husband also hired Tabor.*

"Who else did you talk to?"

"Don't worry. They all promised to keep it confidential."

"Yeah, Luke. I'm sure they did. Now everyone in the legal community knows our business. Or at least your side of it. Maybe I should pass around the photos, to show them another perspective. Would you like that? And not for nothing, but if you wanted a divorce, why didn't you just tell me?"

Josie paused, forcing her voice to stay steady. "Never mind, don't answer that."

"Things got messed up." Luke's voice lowered again.

"Gee, do you think?"

"Please, can we meet tomorrow?"

A swirl of emotions churned in her stomach. "Are you willing to go along with the prenup?"

She heard loud breathing through the line.

"I don't know."

That ticked up her temper. "I can't believe that in addition to your infidelity, you came back into the house without telling me, took more things, changed the locks, turned off the electricity and my cell phone, served me at work, and then sent me black roses and sex toys? And now you want to meet? Sorry. I gotta go."

"What?" he squawked. "I didn't send you roses or sex toys."

Josie's eyebrows shot up. "But you admit to the other things? If you didn't send them, why are the charges on your credit card? I checked the account this morning. I've been paying your bills for almost three years now. I'm entitled to review your transactions."

"Since you have access to my account, who's to say you didn't buy them yourself, to frame me?"

She snickered. "Like I have nothing better to do." But his preposterous suggestion worried her. Toxic spouses did frame each other for stupid things, and it made for wild courtroom drama. Is that what she needed to plan for? But why? Luke wasn't like that. Then she recalled receiving the photos. *Maybe he was like that. Maybe I never knew him at all.*

"I guess we'll leave it to the lawyers," he said. "Shit, Joe, this is gonna cost me a hell of a lot of money and I bet that asshole you hired in New Haven won't charge you at all."

She swallowed back the brisket and cake hovering in her throat. *How did he know who I hired?*

"Greed is expensive, Luke. Your legal bill is on you. I'm hanging up now. See you Monday."

Josie composed herself before rejoining the party. Her phone dinged. A text from Luke lit up.

—*Fine, have it your way. You better bring your*

checkbook on Monday 'cuz my lawyer's asking the judge to make you pay my legal fees. And I want to move back into the house.—

****

Josie's guests left after an hour, but each minute ticked by as if in slow motion. When she closed the front door behind the last one, she braced herself and returned to her family in the living room.

"Can I see the video surveillance from your SUV?" she asked Dan. "Luke called me a little while ago. He let it slip that he knew I hired a New Haven lawyer to represent me in our divorce. Was I right? Am I being tracked?"

He stood, meeting her eyes. "Yes. Let me get my tablet. It's in the kitchen."

Gabe leaned forward on the couch, a fistful of peanuts in his hand. "Who's tracking Josie?"

"Who's Everett Kramer?" Mark asked, sitting next to him.

"My divorce lawyer."

"Wait." Mark settled on his sister. "You're getting a divorce? What happened?"

Josie refilled their wine glasses. "It's the typical long story that ended with photos of Luke being naked with some girl who wasn't me. I'll tell you later."

"Why didn't I know Josie was being tracked?" Gabe challenged.

Dan returned and placed the tablet on the coffee table. "Because we didn't have any evidence." He tapped a few keys to access a program. "Until now. My SUV that she's driving is loaded with surveillance cameras. I dropped it off to her this morning and she drove me home on her way to the lawyer's office. I watched the feed before the party. Everybody get close and check this out."

"So that's why you were gone when I woke up," Gabe said. "I was gonna offer you a ride, but you'd already left."

Dan did a few maneuvers to zoom in on a gray, midsized hatchback with tinted windows. "This guy showed up all around you today. He picked you up this morning from here and followed you to my house, then to Everett's office. He waited there, then followed you to the law school. I can't tell how long he stayed there, but he tailed you back here."

Silence quaked the room.

Gabe opened the front door. After a moment, he closed it and rejoined them. "I don't see anyone now. He must have called it a night."

"I sent the license plate number to a buddy of mine," Dan told them. "He'll let me know when they ID the car's owner. You should also ask the police to search for a GPS device when they locate your car."

"I repeat, why wasn't I told about this earlier?" Gabe leaned against the fireplace, tapping his foot, all parent-like.

Josie gave him a sideways hug. "I asked Dan to wait. I didn't want to worry you. And I wasn't sure if I was just being paranoid."

"About getting pig blood thrown all over your car?" he implored. "Wasn't that enough of a hint? Why do you think I raced up here yesterday?"

She cocked an eyebrow toward Dan. "How does Dad know about that?"

He sent her a lopsided smile. "Shoot me."

She threw a pillow at him instead.

"But the kicker was Josie's car being stolen last night," Dan added, catching it.

"That's not all that happened last night," Mark chimed in, reaching for one of Amy Castle's mini cherry cheesecakes. "And by the way, what about me? I know I'm the youngest, but pig blood sounds like something I should know about."

"I promise to add those details to my divorce saga," Josie assured him. "I already told Dan about last night."

Huffing, Gabe returned to the couch and snagged another handful of peanuts. Fixing his eyes on his youngest son, he asked, "And what do you and Josie and Dan know that I don't?"

Mark swallowed. "Uh, I got a call from Jerry Cohen this morning. He's our chief of security at the synagogue."

"And?"

His eyes darted to Josie, who glared at him, then back to their father. "Last night, when Josie told us her car was stolen, she forgot to mention that the cops we met were there to arrest her. They suspected she used her car to crash into a restaurant, then drive away. By the time Jerry showed up, they had the cuffs out, ready to roll."

"Thank you, brother dear, for that very unsanitized version of events." She carried dirty plates and glasses into the kitchen, avoiding her father's stare. And the sound of his fist slamming into the palm of his other hand. Over and over again.

Returning, she leaned against the loveseat. "The police said they would contact me if they found my car. Other than that, the matter is closed. On a less dramatic note, during the call with my soon-to-be ex-husband, he told me he met with Richard Diamond about representing him in our divorce."

Mark frowned. "Ouch."

"Yeah. Here I am, in the middle of a huge case, and my arch nemesis knows my personal business. And while it was very gracious of him to decline, he's the one who referred Luke to Jonathan Tabor."

Frowning, Dan shook his head. "Given Tabor's reputation, Richard wasn't doing either of you a favor." To Gabe and Mark, he said, "The guy's a real worm."

"Oh, but it gets better." She twirled the stem of her wine glass. "Tabor is also representing Debra Tate's husband. She's my other client."

Mark reached for another cheesecake. "That doesn't sound like a coincidence."

Josie pushed her hair away from her face. "No kidding. I think it has something to do with the guy tailing me."

"Do you have any idea who that might be?" Gabe asked.

She shrugged. "Amy Castle's claimed more than once that Malcolm has her followed. Why not me? It's either him or his lawyer, Richard Diamond, or both of them."

Chapter Thirty-Seven

Josie

"I hate to think Richard's involved," Mark told them. "I've known him for more than six years now. He's been nothing but great to me and everyone in the congregation. I think we have a good rapport. Do you want me to talk to him?"

"No!" Josie and Dan shouted.

He shot his hands up in surrender mode. "All right already."

"I hate to think so too," Gabe added, his arms stretched over the top cushion. "I kinda like the guy."

Mark stood. "It's getting late. I need to head out. Ice hockey practice with the synagogue's teens at seven a.m. sharp tomorrow."

Gabe and Dan snickered.

"Good luck with that," their older brother added.

Hugging Josie goodbye at the door, Mark said, "Let me know when you're ready to fill me in on your divorce and that other thing. Oh, and when you have some time, a woman I know would like to talk to you about getting a divorce." He half-frowned. "She's Orthodox and embarrassed."

Josie was well aware of the snags in that particular scenario. The last thing she wanted was another high stress case, but if Mark was asking, she'd at least try to help. "Give her my number. She can call any time."

As he drove off, she re-checked her street. Nothing questionable stood out. Back in the living room, her frustration continued to simmer.

"Do you think its Luke who's been following you?" Gabe asked. "How else would he know about your lawyer this fast? You just met with him today."

Finishing her wine, Josie weighed the possibilities. "He has a tight schedule at work and wouldn't have the extra money to pay someone." Then she added, "But he used his credit card to send me black roses and sex toys."

Dan almost choked on the cupcake he'd stuffed in his mouth, and their father perked up, ready to add something he thought was clever.

She held up the palm of her hand to him. "Don't. Keep it to yourself."

His jowls flushed as he bit back a chuckle. "I was just going to ask where you put the sex toys."

She sent him a warning over her glasses. "At my office." Then she positioned herself on the loveseat to see them both. "I want to run an idea by both of you and get your opinion."

Gabe perked up again while Dan opened a bottle of water.

"I'd like to hire Dad as my assistant for Amy Castle's case. He will keep everything he hears and learns confidential. I've got a similar arrangement with the girl who works with me at the law school, but she can't handle what I need done. Are you up for it?"

Gabe's eyes twinkled as he rubbed his hands together. "Cool. I'm getting a jump start on my legal career already. What's my first assignment?"

Josie paused, hoping she was making the right

decision. *But what were the alternatives?*

"The assignment involves picking up a dozen certified copies of Amy's divorce judgment from the court clerk's office and delivering them to the state marshal."

Gabe nodded. "That sounds easy enough."

"I'd do it myself, but I'm being followed, and I don't want anyone to figure out what I'm doing."

Dan inspected the remainder of the cupcake and cheesecake selection. "What are you hoping to accomplish?"

"The marshal's going to serve the copies on the banks and brokerage houses where Malcolm Castle has accounts here in Connecticut."

"How will that help?" Gabe asked.

Dan smiled wide. "I bet I know."

Amused with his enthusiasm, Josie gave him the floor.

Looking positively gleeful, he stood and placed his hands on his hips, like he did when he was addressing a jury on a very important point. "I suspect you are interpreting the judge's orders in the judgment to direct the banks and brokerage houses to transfer to Amy her half share in the accounts, without needing her ex-husband's consent. Am I right?"

Josie sucked in air through her teeth. "That's how I read it."

"And if it works, Amy will get her money and her battle with Malcolm will be over."

Gabe whistled. "Will they do that?"

"They can if they want to," she replied. "Yesterday, the judge issued another order directing them to include in the transfer fifty percent of any interest that's accrued in those accounts. I think that helps our cause."

"Yes!" Dan shouted, giving her a high five.

"I got the certified copies of that order and gave them to Linda before she left tonight. So, we're all set there."

Pensive, Josie folded her arms to her chest. "But the whole scenario terrifies me, because if they make the transfers…"

"The crap is going to fly," Dan finished, devouring another cupcake.

Gabe grunted. "Better crap than bullets."

"And if they don't, the crap will still fly because I'm sure they'll tell Malcolm Castle what I'm asking them to do, and he'll have a cow." Josie tried not to imagine what that might involve.

"But it will also put him in the hot seat," Gabe reasoned. "Right? Because he was supposed to make the transfers months ago."

"It sure will," Dan answered, impressed with the plan. "It's a win win scenario."

This time, father and son high fived each other. "She's got your brains, Dad."

"Yeah, but you convinced her to go to law school."

As they sat back, glowing in their contributions to her brilliance, Josie interrupted. "Can we please move on?"

To Gabe, she asked, "Would you like to help?"

He sat up like a Saint Bernard puppy, begging for a cookie. "I sure would."

"Good. How about this? On Monday morning, while I'm at the hearing with Luke, can you wait for the certified copies at the clerk's office? I already ordered and paid for them online, but that was late last night, after we got home. The staff will need some time to prepare them."

"Yeah. Just tell me where to go."

"I will. Next, you need to get them to the marshal."

Gabe scratched the top of his head. "Hey, do you think me and Dan are being followed, too?"

"The entire world's watching you, Dad," Dan replied. "In your very inconspicuous, deluxe motor home that blocks everyone's view of the road. And now in that fire engine red monster truck you're driving."

"Then probably not?" Gabe sounded almost disappointed.

"Probably not," Josie repeated, but then she reconsidered. "You know, Dad, from the very beginning, this whole case has been way over the top. I think we need to presume that perhaps you are being followed. That means we need to come up with a good cover for you to get the copies to Linda."

"Linda?" Gabe asked.

"She's the marshal," Dan told him. "The blonde woman who was here tonight. With her husband."

Gabe mulled this over. "Man, millions of dollars up for grabs, pretty women marshals, people following my daughter and almost getting her arrested, and sex toys too? I got here just in time."

Josie smiled, thinking maybe he was right.

"What about my Aunt Debra?" Dan suggested. "She's more than trustworthy and I'm sure she'd be willing to meet up with Linda somewhere."

"Maybe," Josie answered, thinking it through. "But how do we get the docs from Dad to her?"

"Who's Debra?" Gabe asked.

"She's my aunt on my stepfather's side. You spent

most of the night talking with her in the kitchen." Dan chided.

"Oh, Debbie." He blushed. "The cute girl in jeans and the red and white sweater."

"I saw you, too," Josie added, in a warning tone. "Please, Dad. Do not make a move on my client."

Gabe laughed, all innocent-like. "Who's making a move? We were just making conversation. I know we're both still married. But not for long. And we're not dead, you know."

Josie's jaw dropped, then opened with, "'We?' You're already talking 'we'?"

Dan snickered as their father blushed again.

Josie slapped her hands over her ears. "I don't want to hear any more."

Ignoring her, Gabe asked, "How about this? What if Debbie and I meet at a restaurant? We could pretend to be on one of those Internet first date kind of things. We'll get a table and order something and Debbie can meet the marshal in the ladies' room. They can both be carrying one of those big purses. No one will be the wiser."

Josie imagined the scene, step by step, acknowledging that this was one of those times it was better to be safe than sorry. And maybe it would help her father and Debra feel like a part of something. To help counteract the upheaval taking place in their personal lives.

"Josie?"

She faced her brother. "Ask her."

"No." Gabe held up his phone, grinning like a kid. "She gave me her number. I'll text her." He started typing.

Josie rolled her eyes toward Dan who returned the

gesture.

Her cell rang. "It's Amy." She hit the green button. "Hi, what's up?"

"Oh, Josie," she gasped. "Thank you for answering. I know it's late, and it's your birthday, but my neighbor, Laura, needs you. She just found out her husband has a second family in Miami. There's a thirty-year-old wife and two kids. One's older than hers, and the other is younger."

****

On Monday morning, Josie waited outside the courthouse with a mid-sized group, some hovering under windblown umbrellas, others without. At three minutes after nine, a court officer opened the brass doors. Six minutes later, she made it through the metal detector and to the elevator.

*So, this is what it feels like to be a party in a case, instead of the lawye*r.

She didn't like it. Not one bit.

Sticking to her own rule, she intended to hide out until she was needed. Then she heard someone call her name. Josie turned to find a harried clerk she recognized from years earlier.

"Attorney Jensen, I'm so glad I found you. Judge Steward wants all of you in her chambers as soon as you're all here. She's in 502."

"Thank you," Josie replied, reaching a new height of humiliation.

She drafted a text to Everett. As she hit the send button, her inane distrust of the legal system clouded her thoughts. She, like other experienced litigators, accepted that so many things could go wrong, especially in a case that seems open and shut. People lie. Innocent people go to prison and corporate America triumphs over the little guys they step on every day. And yet good things happened too, wrapped up in a set of bad circumstances.

These thoughts swirled as Josie sat in the judge's chambers with Everett and Luke, listening to Jonathan Tabor stretch the dictionary definition of a lie. She clamped her mouth shut and gripped the side arms of the chair to prevent herself from lunging at him.

When Tabor concluded his monologue of verbal diarrhea, Judge Steward, who was scary even on a good day, drum rolled her fuchsia painted nails on top of her desk's shiny surface. Finally, she asked, "Attorney Tabor, why are we here this morning?"

Tabor narrowed his beady eyes and pouted. "What do you mean? I thought my position was clear. The couple lives in the Hartford circuit. The divorce should take place there."

"The facts you provided do not agree with that statement, Attorney Tabor." The judge held up a document from the file in front of her. "The couple's marital home may be in Hartford, but this divorce summons you filed with this court lists an address for your client in Colchester. As you should be aware, Colchester is in the New London circuit. Therefore, you and Ms. Jensen had a choice. Either of you could have filed the divorce in Hartford or in New London. She chose New London and filed there before you filed here. So, what's the problem?"

"But my marshal served her first."

"And she filed first."

When Tabor fumbled for a response, she leaned forward. "And even if you did beat her to it, we have a court rule to address divorcing attorneys and it is very clear. Are you familiar with it?"

She handed him the rule book that was lying open on her desk. "I'm paraphrasing: 'The jurisdiction to address a divorce, or any other civil action where an attorney is a party, shall not be in the same jurisdiction where they practice.' So, answer me this, Attorney Tabor. Were you aware that Ms. Jensen was practicing as an attorney in an active case in Hartford before you filed the divorce action here?"

His eyes darted around the room. "I don't recall."

Josie scribbled a message to Everett while fumbling for her phone.

"One moment, Your Honor," he requested.

"Sure."

Josie handed it to Everett and pointed to Luke's text.

Everette cleared his throat. "Your Honor?"

"Yes, Attorney Kramer?"

He held up the phone. "Ms. Jensen has texts here from her husband dated last Tuesday, two days before Attorney Tabor filed the divorce in Hartford. It shows that both of them knew she had an active case here."

Tabor opened his mouth, but Judge Steward silenced him with a steely glare. "Here's what we're going to do. We're going to go into the courtroom. Then, Attorney Tabor, you are going to put your argument to keep the case in Hartford on the record. I am going to deny it and grant Attorney Kramer's motion to dismiss this action. I am also going to order your client to pay Ms. Jensen attorney's fees for today's complete waste of time in my court."

Tabor shot up. "But Your Honor. I also filed a motion for attorney's fees for Mr. Penway. I need to be heard."

She looked down her nose at him. "No, you don't. Denied."

His eyes narrowed. "I object."

"What a surprise. Save it for the record and feel free to appeal."

Josie watched Luke whisper something to Tabor.

"Uh, excuse me, Judge. One more thing."

"Yes, Mr. Tabor?"

"My client wishes to move back into the marital home. I filed a motion for that as well."

"I have a response to that." Everett held out the birthday card and photos of Luke and his girlfriend to the judge and handed Tabor a copy.

"Not only does Mr. Penway reside in Colchester, according to his message inside this card which he sent to his wife, he couldn't wait to leave the marital residence to be with his paramour there. Accordingly, we ask you to deny his motion and instead grant Ms. Jensen exclusive use and possession of the marital residence."

Tabor started to object again.

The judge held up her hand. "Noted."

She read the card and flipped through the photos. After a long expressionless moment, she said to Tabor, "I have a gut feeling someone wants to instigate a domestic violence situation and incur thousands of dollars in unnecessary legal fees and proceedings. And that someone is not Ms. Jensen or her attorney."

She returned the card and photos to Everett and closed the file folder in front of her. "Therefore, to prevent that situation, the couple shall not reside together. I will grant Ms. Jensen exclusive use and possession of the marital residence and I will make sure my orders today are made part of the New London file, along with a transcript of the proceedings."

The judge stood and reached for her black robe hanging on the brass rack behind her. "I will meet you all in the courtroom."

Josie felt too relieved to move. Catching up to Everett, she stopped him and whispered her thoughts.

"Are you sure?" he asked.

"Yes." She pointed her chin toward the empty bench. "The judge is giving us time to work this out. Let's try. If Tabor goes for it and we reach an agreement, he'll have waived his right to appeal or to raise the issues again in the New London case."

Everett went to speak with the opposing attorney.

"May I suggest," he said, as Josie eavesdropped. "That you withdraw this Hartford action now, and we agree to proceed with this divorce in New London? In addition, we will agree that Ms. Jensen has exclusive use and possession of the marital home. Furthermore, neither party will seek alimony from the other, and each party is responsible for their own attorney's fees. All these orders will be transferred to the New London court's file and will remain in effect for the duration of the case."

Tabor puffed out his chest. "Why would I agree to that?"

"Excuse us, please." Everett ushered the reluctant lawyer to the other end of the room. Luke stood where he was, lost and confused. Josie moved close enough to hear Everett's harsh, yet patient whisper, as if reprimanding a child.

"Because, Mr. Tabor, as the judge just told you, she will not award you any of the bullshit you asked for. It's not even a three-year marriage and your guy walked out. Therefore, agreeing to the terms I just outlined will save face for you and your client."

Everett paused, then raised his voice. "And it saves your client from paying my five-thousand-dollar legal bill for today's debacle."

"We agree!" Luke interjected. He approached the lawyers and repeated his decision to Tabor who waved him off, feigning dismay.

Josie noticed that the tips of Luke's ears and his nose burned red against his pale complexion as Tabor tried to talk with him, but he held firm.

To Everett, he said, "Draft up what you just offered, and I'll sign it. Quick. I want to get out of here."

****

Everett walked alongside Josie as they exited the courthouse and used the ramp to reach Lincoln Street. "Your thoughts?" he asked.

Welcoming the faint December sun, Josie took in the cool air. "We don't get many home runs like that very often."

"No, we don't. But it was the right call. For both your sakes, I hope Luke recognizes this as a preview of what to expect if he continues to go along with Tabor's plan to challenge the prenup."

"Time will tell."

They said their goodbyes and headed in opposite directions. Josie reached Dan's SUV, but then remembered her father was in the courthouse, waiting for the certified copies of Amy Castle's divorce judgment.

Back in the building, she rounded the corner leading to the clerk's office and heard her father's unmistakable bellow. "Did you see that pass he made in last night's game?"

"It was the best play all season," Richard Diamond

replied, equally enthusiastic.

Jonathan Tabor joined in. "Super Bowl here we come."

Scratching her chest scar, Josie observing the scene, trying to decide if she was seeing Huey, Dewy, and Louie in action, or the Three Stooges, or a combination of both.

They must have felt the force of her presence because they stopped and spotted her.

Gabe's face broke into a supersized grin. "Oh hi, Josie."

Tabor slinked away in the opposite direction as Richard said, "I must run. Good seeing you again, Gabe." He sent Josie a half wave and took off.

At that moment, one of the younger staff members stepped into the hall from the clerk's office. She held out an oversized, spicy mustard-colored envelope to her father.

"I've got the copies of the judgment you requested, Mr. Jensen."

Josie tensed. She looked through the panel of windows to her left as he accepted the package. It showed a small courtyard, then another panel of windows across the way. Richard Diamond was walking down that hall. He stopped and half turned, listening for more. Then he caught her watching him.

Neither smiled.

He resumed walking.

****

Josie hurried her father out of the courthouse as fast as his bad knees and her bad hip could go. "We need to move up the timetable. I thought the clerk would take longer with the copies and I'm sure Diamond heard her announcement. He knows something's up."

Gabe dismissed her concern. "I told him I was picking up some records for one of your old cases. The client wants to bring her ex-husband back to court to help pay for the kid's college tuition."

Once inside Dan's vehicle, Josie said, "That was smart thinking."

"I thought so too. See, all those times you'd tell me about your cases, thinking I wasn't listening? Well, I was."

"Still, I wonder if Debra and the marshal could meet you sooner."

Gabe engaged the engine, then reached for his cell. "They're just waiting for my text. We're on one of those group chats."

Josie stared at him. "You're loving this."

Gabe broadened his usual good-natured grin. "What? We might be old, but we keep up with the times. Debbie got the marshal's number off that website for the judicial departments."

Josie squeezed his hand. "Anything else I need to know?"

He did a U-turn in the middle of Lincoln Street and headed for the highway. "I think we've got the situation covered. I'm taking you to school now and I'll let you know as soon as Linda gets the documents. She said she'll get in touch with you too. And you can call me to pick you up when you're ready to go home."

"Thank you."

He tapped a popular tune on the steering wheel, moving to the groove. "So, this is what it will be like when I pass the bar exam." He slowed for traffic. "I was thinking we should call our firm, Jensen, Jensen, and

Jensen, Attorneys at Law. It's got a nice ring to it, doesn't it?"

Chapter Thirty-Eight

Richard, Before Dawn, Thursday Morning

Richard's ringing cell phone pierced the dark silence, startling him awake. Blurry-eyed, he realized he'd fallen asleep in the recliner in his home office. The digital clock he'd affixed over the door for evenings like this glowed three-ten. The phone erupted again from the corner of his desk. He stood and stretched his tense muscles. A call at this hour usually meant one of two things. Either someone got in trouble for doing something they should not have done, or a tragedy occurred.

His children's faces came to mind.

Richard hoped for the first.

The number on the phone told him it could be either. Perhaps both.

"Good morning, Malcolm."

"The witch you told me not to worry about stole more than four million from my accounts. How did you let this happen?" He enunciated each syllable in an ominous tone.

Oh yeah. It could be both.

Richard made his way to his state-of-the-art kitchen and settled on a shocked-like response. "How do you know this, Malcolm? What happened? Can the funds be traced? Are they sure it wasn't some kind of hack?"

To himself, he gave credit where credit was due. Josephina Jensen took the same action he would have taken. Except, he wished she hadn't acted so fast. He would have waited a few more months and a few more court hearings, to be sure he'd made at least another fifty thousand before pulling the cord. She would have benefited too. That's why he had held back filing the judgment Amy's former attorney had sent to him a week after the divorce was finalized.

Anticipating this scenario, Richard had wondered if perhaps Jensen's experience with Anne Compton would have caused her to hold off for a while.

I guess not.

"It's no hack," Malcolm barked back. "I just got a call from one of my brokers. Those vampires never sleep. He was checking my accounts and discovered money was missing. It happened right after midnight. He said the money went into Amy's accounts that she'd created for this purpose. The notes say it was authorized by a court order."

With hardly a pause he continued. "You gotta stop this, Dickie. You got to get my money back and stop Jensen from touching the other accounts. I want her law license. And go after those brokerage houses too. All of them. I want it all over social media what they did without my authority. I'm gonna ruin those assholes. No one will ever put their money with them after I get through with them. They didn't even give me the courtesy of some notice. They just took my money!"

Loading the cappuccino maker, Richard decided now was not the time to tell his client he was shit out of luck. Remaining calm, but with a sufficient amount of feigned concern and exaggerated authority, he said,

"This is appalling. Let me see what we can do. It is a good thing we are in court today. Two o'clock. Meet me there at one-thirty."

"Who the hell does Jensen think she is? And Amy too. After all I did for that woman. She'd be nothing without me. And she's too much of a ninny to come up with this all by herself. Tell that Tabor jackass to turn up the heat on Jensen's divorce. Keep her humiliated about her own life so she'll leave me alone. Why did he think we gave him her husband and that other sloth, Tate, or whoever, as clients?"

"I will call you back when I find out what happened," Richard told him. "And Malcolm?"

"Yeah?"

"I suggest you keep all of this to yourself for now. You can deal with the brokerage houses at another time."

"Fine, but keep this in mind, Dickie." A pause followed.

"Yes, Malcolm?"

"You'd better come up with something good. Are you hearing me? 'Cuz if you don't, nobody's gonna like the end result."

"I hear you, Malcolm. Loud and clear."

Were Castle's threats serious? Richard wasn't sure. He knew this new development hit him big. His ego included. But how big? Big enough for him to act out more than usual?

Richard switched on the cappuccino maker, wondering where Jensen was this fine morning.

Chapter Thirty-Nine

Josie, Thursday Morning

"Thanks for coming in before your class to help with this," Josie told Rivka. They sat opposite each other on the floor in her office at the law school, working through the first two of five file boxes Laura Schofield left with her the day before.

Josie's cell buzzed. She read the text from her dad and sent back a response.

"What do you want to happen at this Schofield hearing tomorrow?" Rivka asked as she organized the files.

"We need to extend the emergency custody and financial orders the judge awarded when I was in court with her on Tuesday. The husband's been missing ever since his wife confronted him, but he might show up for the hearing and contest them."

The young woman looked at her through thick lenses. "Thank you for asking me to help. This is such great experience."

Josie smiled, then noticed something on a bank statement.

"What do you see?" Rivka asked.

She pointed to a transaction. "I don't recognize that account number." As she spoke, she reached for a yellow sticky note pad. Three loud knocks drew her attention to the door. A tall dark figure showed through the frosted glass.

Rivka stood. "Who can that be? It's not even seven-thirty."

Josie's pulse raced as her assistant opened the door to Richard Diamond. He ducked under the door frame and entered, causing Rivka to step back. He glared at her, then at Josie on the floor.

"Good morning," she greeted, mustering up a calm exterior.

"A word, please." It came out as a menacing whisper. And it wasn't a request.

No doubt he was here because Malcolm learned about the account transfers. Amy had called her a few minutes past midnight with the good news.

"Rivka Abrams, this is Attorney Richard Diamond. He and I have a case together." As she spoke, she hoped Richard's sense of propriety would hold, at least in Rivka's presence.

"Good to meet you," he said, but his gaze remained fixed on Josie.

Rivka cleared her throat and reached for her purse. "Why don't I go down to my office." Then she added to Josie, "Unless you want me to stay."

"Do I need her to stay, Attorney Diamond?"

With both women now staring at him, Richard frowned, indignant-like. "What?"

Unhurried, Josie placed the documents she and her assistant were reviewing in a box. "You look like a thug, Richard. A well-dressed thug, but still a thug."

Rivka gasped. Her hand flew to her mouth.

Richard blinked, as if not comprehending. Then the lightbulb switched on. Recovering, the corners of his mouth hitched up just enough to knock the tension down a notch.

"Excuse me, ladies." He used both hands to smooth his hair in place. "I do apologize. It has been a long morning, and it is about to get even longer." To Rivka he said, "You can go, Ms. Abrams. I promise to behave."

Josie nodded to her. "We'll be fine."

Richard closed the door after her and faced Josie. Extending her a hand, he said, "Please stand up. I don't want anyone who may come in here to think I am overpowering you."

"You mean when you scold me? Because you're acting like that's what you're gonna do." She scrunched up her nose. "But I'm not sure why. If this was any case, except yours, you'd be congratulating me. And you would have done the same thing months ago."

Richard didn't comment. Instead, he tried to pace around the box-covered floor. Exasperated, he held out his arms, motioning, "What is with all of this mess? Don't you have a table somewhere?"

Josie patted an empty spot on the floor. "Join me."

His appalled expression made her laugh.

"Fine."

She pretended not to watch him manage to sit crisscross applesauce a few feet across from her, biting her lip to keep it from curving.

"This reminds me of yoga class."

"Good for you."

He scoffed. "I hate yoga. And what's with the *Frummer*?"

"Very observant and also very smart. She plans to be a lawyer."

"They are letting girls do that? Since when?"

Acting like an authority on the subject, Josie replied, "A good number of Orthodox women have careers now. Rivka's mother is a pharmacist. And another woman she knows is a judge in Boston."

Richard raised a skeptical eyebrow. "Are you recruiting?"

Josie grinned. "Maybe."

"*Oy vey*. Another one of you?"

"Let's hope so."

His eyes bugged out. Then he straightened, perfecting a *Sukhasana* pose, minus the arms. "My client is furious, Josephina. Did you have to subpoena his private banker? And you may have blown a multi-million-dollar real estate deal on the Madison property when you recorded that revocation notice, divesting him of his authority, at the town hall."

"You mean that deal your client kept secret, with no intention of sharing the profits?" she shot back. Without missing a beat, she added, "What was the alternative, Richard? What would you have done under the circumstances?"

Richard's slight change of expression told Josie she wasn't wrong. Then he huffed. "He also wants to know how you located that old investment account."

Josie's temper soared to its boiling point. "And Amy and I want to know why your client lied on his financial affidavit multiple times and thought he could get away with it." She held up both hands in frustration. "It is beyond fascinating how you and your client behave as if you're in charge of this…"

He tilted his head to one side and formed an almost smile. "Shit show?"

Josie raised an eyebrow and sort of smiled back.

And just like that, the tension in the air defused.

"Please turn around. I'm all cramped up and need to stand. I don't want you watching the process."

Richard got on his knees and held out both hands to her. "Grab hold. We will pull each other up."

"I won't be steady when I stand."

"I can handle you."

Fire flashed in Josie's eyes.

Quickly, he corrected himself. "I mean I can get you to your feet."

"Your client will be mad if he finds out you helped me."

"He's just plain mad."

To that they agreed and without warning, Richard lifted her to an upright position. As their eyes met, she felt the protective strength of his arms around her. More than protective perhaps. They stood there, neither moving. Then a cell phone dinged, sending an echo into the silence.

In unison, they touched their foreheads together and sighed, then disentangled. Josie used the edge of her desk to reach her chair and Richard collapsed into the chair across from her and pulled out his phone. He sighed again and held it up to her. "Guess who?"

Josie watched him silence the phone and return it to his jacket pocket before she said, "Let's start again." She folded her hands on her desk. "How about, 'Mr. Castle is very distressed to learn that certain real estate he undervalued and hoped to sell has been encumbered, and that half the values, plus interest, in a number of financial accounts, though not all of them, have been rightly transferred to his ex-wife.' "

A burst of laughter erupted from Richard. "Well

said, Counselor." Then his good humor faded. "I cannot convince him to give up another dime, Josie."

She swatted the air. "Relax. The judge will do it for you. And please inform your client that the number has gone up. The judgment calls for a fifty/fifty split of everything, disclosed or not. That includes whatever the Madison property deal goes for and the recently located account."

"What about the Mystic store and property?"

"You mean the one Amy also just found out she owns? Does he want to continue leasing it from her? Or does he want to buy it?"

"You expect all of this to be determined today? The calculations alone require professionals and will cost money."

Josie looked at him over the rims of her glasses. "I doubt the calculations will ever be perfect. Amy's reaching for the close enough range. Too much has happened for her or me to back down now."

Richard furrowed his brows. "You mean the car incidents?"

"And a heck of a lot more."

"Explain."

"What do you mean, 'explain'?"

"Humor me."

"I'm not sure I want to."

He raised one perfect brow. "Because you believe I may have been implicit with my client in these acts of vandalism?"

Josie fiddled with a paperclip. That was one reason, which was bad enough. The other was that Richard Diamond was not her friend. Sure, he'd been very kind, and he'd shared some of his personal story with her. But was that the real him? Or does he use his engaging appearance and personality to lure people, like her, into a false sense of security so she'll blurt out information he may later use against her?

What did it matter?

"Jonathan Tabor, the clown you and my father were talking to the other day, is representing my husband in our divorce." She tossed the paperclip in the trash can. "Luke let it slip that he'd been to see you. After he told you his tale of woe, you declined to represent him but referred him to Tabor." As she spoke, she noticed the black roses were starting to wilt.

Richard crossed one leg over the other and nodded, as if to say, "Please continue."

"That's not humiliating at all, knowing that my rival is privy to my marital disaster." She waited for his reaction. There was none. "Then I learned the husband of my other client told her Tabor contacted him, warning him that his wife met with a divorce lawyer. Tabor, of course, being the good guy he is, offered to help out the fella. That means I get to deal with the buffoon on two cases." She shook her head at him. "I don't believe in coincidences, Richard."

He shrugged at her concerns. "You'll slice and dice Tabor so fast, he won't even know what's happening."

Josie leaned forward. "That's your response? I should thank you for sending that nitwit in my direction?"

Richard tilted his head. "Only if you want to assume it's true."

"To assume… To make an ass out of you and me. Cute."

Now it was her turn to smooth her hair in place. "As

a courtesy, I'll tell you that a security camera across the street from the courthouse filmed the person tossing the pig blood out the seventh-floor window onto my car. They wore a face mask, but a delivery van from Castle's was parked down the street during the estimated time of the incident. Of course it could be just another coincidence." She shrugged. "The police are investigating."

Richard didn't react.

Josie decided not to bring up Richard's promise to fire his client if it was determined the jerk had anything to do with the event. She never expected him to keep his word. Instead, she said, "I'm driving my brother's SUV. It's got all sorts of cameras. They picked up that I'm being followed, which now makes total sense. The police intend to make an arrest for stalking." She stopped and asked, "Shall I continue?"

Richard's mouth twisted. "Can I stop you?"

Josie had fibbed about the arrest. The police told her the offending car was leased to a corporation, which made their investigation more cumbersome. But unless he was involved, he wouldn't know that.

"Let's just end with I've been run off the road, my electricity and cell phone were turned off, and the locks on my doors at home were changed. I think I already told you about the black roses, but did I mention the sex toys that were delivered here last week? They were a nice touch."

Richard sprang to his feet. "Hold it. Sex toys?"

"Good to know you're paying attention." Josie removed a vibrator, wrapped in plastic, from her desk drawer and held it up.

Richard snapped his open mouth shut, failing to hide

256

his amusement. "I had nothing to do with that, but I will keep it in mind for future situations."

Josie's desk phone rang. He used it as the perfect excuse to make his exit.

"Wave to my father in the parking lot."

He turned back to her as he opened the door.

She grinned and waved her fingers.

"You knew I was coming up here."

She added a wink to her grin.

Relief replaced the grin the instant the door clicked shut behind him. *Time to get ready for the next round at court today.*

****

Josie settled Amy into the same conference room on the courthouse's third floor, then rode the elevator to the fifth floor. As the doors parted, she stepped forward, right into a squat, balding man with small, steel-rimmed glasses and black hooded eyes.

He didn't budge.

"So, you're the thief who stole my money."

Startled, Josie realized this was her first live introduction to Malcolm Castle. Most short, chubby, bald men emitted a certain unique charm and humor. This clown chose to rely on intimidation. Josie wasn't impressed.

Castle came closer, pointing his stubby finger at her chest. She towered above him, refusing to retreat into the elevator as he yelled, "You think you're so smart, I bet you don't know your hubby's been dipping his wick into high priced hookers for years. Becky's one of them, but they fell for each other. She's been financing his lawyer to wipe the floor with you."

Before she could react, Richard appeared out of

nowhere. Dark eyes blazing, he grabbed his client's fat forearm. "Let's go, Malcolm."

Castle shook him off. "What? I'm just giving her some advice. Public service, don't you know? The lady should get herself checked out. Who knows what diseases Luke's been spreading to her."

"Enough!" Richard commanded, this time yanking Castle out of Josie's way. She maneuvered around them as Castle continued to struggle, but the lawyer held tight and directed him down the hall.

"What's wrong, Dickie?" His shout echoed. "Don't you think she's entitled to know? And that reminds me. How did it feel to get shot? After seeing her in action, it's a wonder her client didn't aim for her first."

"Shut up!" Josie heard Richard warn, shoving his client into a conference room and slamming the door behind them.

Josie ignored the handful of gawkers who witnessed the scene and headed to the lawyer's lounge at the far end of the floor. Thankful it was empty, she reached the large window and stared out, not seeing the city skyline. If Castle was right, which she suspected he was, she should thank him for filling in some of the blanks about her so-called happy marriage.

****

Josie wasn't sure how long she'd been in the lawyer's lounge when she heard a loud knock. The door opened. Richard Diamond closed it behind him and leaned against it to prevent anyone from entering.

"My client's behavior is deplorable. I can't apologize enough for him. But for me, please accept my personal apology. For everything."

For everything? What was that supposed to mean?

258

And should I believe him or was this just a good guy, bad guy routine?

Projecting a conciliatory tone and straight face, she said, "Perhaps we should consider it foreplay, leading up to the climax where my client gets all her money, and we close this file for good."

Diamond's brows rose.

She pursed her lips into a smile.

He matched it.

She arched a questioning brow.

"Uh…I think not."

Josie retrieved her phone and checked the time. "It's one-forty-six. We've got to get into court. I'll alert the witnesses."

Following her to the door, he said, "You might want to hold off on that."

She stepped into the hall, then paused and raised her eyebrows. "What aren't you telling me?"

He sucked in a deep breath, avoiding her stare.

"Rich?"

He scratched the space between his eyebrows. "Mr. Castle just fired me."

"And you wasted these past few minutes making sure he had just enough time to get out of the building before I ran after him?"

"I knew you were going to say that."

"Of course you did."

Walking next to her now toward the courtroom, he explained. "The way I see it, there were two choices. I could permit my very angry client to shoot off his mouth to the judge. But then he would be held in contempt, and he would surely fire me…"

"Or, you could have him fire you now to avoid such

a scene," Josie finished.

"He chose that one."

"Of course he did."

"He even filed a self-represented appearance form to replace me and a motion to postpone today's hearing, to give him time to obtain new counsel."

They reached the courtroom. Richard held the door open for her.

"How thorough of him. And of you."

He tilted his head and joined her inside. "I thought so."

At the counsel table now with Amy, Josie bit back a smile as Richard resumed his same chair, dragging it even closer to her so that their legs touched under the table.

It took several minutes for Judge Myers to come to the bench. He admonished Diamond for his client's failure to attend the hearing, yet again. Then, before accepting Castle's self-represented appearance form, he ruled that all the transfers made by the financial institutions to Amy were valid and were not to be reversed.

Before adjourning, the judge added, "There will be a five thousand dollar per day fine for each day, beginning at five o'clock p.m. tomorrow, that Mr. Castle refuses to permit or otherwise interferes with the transfer of the remaining funds due to Ms. Castle."

All contrite, Richard answered, "Understood, Your Honor."

"And Attorney Diamond, you are hereby ordered to convey these orders to Mr. Castle by five o'clock today. Email, telephone, voice mail, or abode service by a marshal will suffice."

"I will take care of it."

"And I'm directing my clerk, Mr. Rivers, to schedule the next hearing for this case with me in New Haven, three Fridays from today. Attorney Diamond?"

"Yes, Judge?"

"When you communicate the financial orders to Mr. Castle, please add that he is to show up at that hearing, with or without counsel, on time. If he is not there, the arrest warrant referenced in last week's order will be issued."

Without waiting for a reply, Judge Myers motioned to the court officer. "We are adjourned for the day."

"All rise."

When the judge disappeared into his chambers, Josie sent a text. Then she told Amy, "My father is parked in front of the courthouse, waiting for us. I'll meet you there in a few minutes. I want to order today's transcript from the court reporter. Linda can serve it on the other financial institutions who questioned the judgment."

Unexpected melancholy drifted over her a minute later, as she finished with the court reporter and entered the scary elevator. The Castle case, without Richard Diamond, felt boring somehow.

Exiting on the main floor, her thoughts countered, *But that's how you want things. Boring and predictable.*

Josie considered this as she approached the building's exit. Then she heard Amy's voice. She looked to her left and found the woman racing toward her, her eyes wide and her arms waving in the air.

"Josie!"

"Please don't tell me someone vandalized Dan's SUV."

"No." The woman stopped and gasped for air. "The Madison store is on fire. The security company just called me. There was an explosion."

Chapter Forty

Richard, Friday Morning

For the second night in a row, Richard's cell phone rang before dawn. At least this time it was closer to five o'clock, his usual wake up time. And he was in bed, not snoozing on the recliner in his office.

He reached for the phone, thinking it was a good thing he did not require a lot of sleep. His business would not permit it. Thus far that day, he needed to be in court by ten for three cases. That would occupy him until at least one o'clock. Afterward, he had appointments with two new clients, followed by his accountant in the next town over. From there, he planned to attend the sixty-thirty Shabbat service.

The cell rang again as Richard read the screen.

Blocked number. He cocked an eyebrow as he hit the green button. Police Department holding areas and hospitals tended to come up as blocked numbers. "Richard Diamond here."

"Happy anniversary, darling."

Richard's internal alarm raged red. He sat up, chastising himself for not returning the hospital director's voicemail message yesterday. Feigning ignorance, he asked, "Excuse me? Who is this, please?"

"It's me, silly. Who'd you think it is? Wake up. Rise and shine. It's a great day!"

"Anne? What…"

She interrupted before he could get any further. "Don't you remember? In a few hours, it will be our anniversary."

Richard racked his memory for clues of any event involving this woman that warranted a celebration. "I am not sure what you are saying, Anne."

"Oh, darling," she chided. "You can be so dense sometimes. Four years ago today, you helped me smuggle my gun into the courthouse. That was a huge accomplishment, with all the security in that place. I was just about to lose my nerve and leave when I spotted you. My Richard. No one would think to question you, or anyone with you."

He swallowed the sudden flow of bile burning his esophagus and wiped the beads of perspiration forming at his hairline. This was the first time Anne, or anyone else, linked him to her hideous act. He suspected she'd duped him the instant he spotted the gun near her at the counsel table. That tiny smile she sent him before the first responders pushed past him cinched it.

He'd always expected this day to come. Now he wondered how far she would go with it. Exposure? Blackmail to prevent the exposure?

"And I put that homewrecker out of business," she screeched.

Richard hit the speaker button and yanked on a pair of jeans and a sweatshirt, presuming she was referring to Josephina Jensen as the homewrecker.

"She was supposed to stop the divorce, Richard. Like you do with all your cases. Drag it out as long as possible. Years, not just a few months. I needed the time to find a way to end my adulterous husband's life. Then

I'd be a widow. Even if I was caught and convicted here on earth, God would forgive me because adultery and divorce are cardinal sins, and I would be righting Peter's wrongs."

She paused in between wretched sobs. "I wanted to hire you, Richard. I knew you'd understand. But my father wouldn't let me. He controlled my money and stuck me with her. That stupid woman stopped the bullets meant for Peter, letting him and everyone else get away. If I'd known she'd do that, I would have aimed for her first, then knocked off him and the judge."

Rage mixed with Anne's sobs. "And now she's back, taking up handicapped parking spaces that are reserved for the innocent. And she's giving you a hard time too. I can't believe that judge allowed all those account transfers. They belong to the poor husband. He said over and over during the divorce that he'd forgive his wife and take her back, but she refused to reconcile. In God's eyes, that means she walks away with nothing."

Richard paced, listening to Anne's rant, seeking clues into her current thought process. The off hour of the call demonstrated she'd managed to circumvent the hospital's protocols and the staff. He had no doubt she'd either stolen the phone she was using, or someone gave it to her. But where was she, to be able to make this call? That worried him more.

He sat on the edge of the bed and held his head in his hands. *How could she know where Josephina Jensen parked her car? Was she, and not Malcolm Castle, somehow responsible for the pig blood vandalism at the courthouse and Jensen's car being stolen? And how could she know the outcome of the Castle hearing yesterday? None of this made any sense.*

The woman quieted, sniffled, then cleared her throat. "Don't you worry, Richard. Everything is in place. In just a few more hours, all will be as it should be."

What does that mean?

He had to keep her talking. Using his most sympathetic tone, he asked, "Why are you sad, Annie? What is in place? What is upsetting you?"

Adding to his further confusion, she laughed. Hard and loud. "I'm not sad or upset, darling. Can't you tell? I'm elated. You'll see very soon. And this time, you won't need to do a thing."

He tried again. "Annie…"

"Got to go now, my love," she whispered, in a sudden rush. "We'll be together soon. Don't worry. I've taken care of everything."

"Anne! Wait! Where are you?" Then he realized she'd hung up.

Throughout the criminal proceedings and the psychiatric commitment process, Anne repeatedly insisted that she had no recollection of planning to shoot anybody. Nor did she recall getting the gun into the courthouse or using it. Three psychiatrists agreed on a traumatic amnesia diagnosis, but Richard always had his doubts. And now, Anne just proved him right. She knew what she had done in that courtroom, both at the time, and every minute since. And she was not remorseful. As for her continuing the fantasy that they were a couple, that was just nuts.

But Anne was right about one thing. The shooting took place four years ago today. Before Josephina Jensen joined the Castle case, he'd kept the memory buried deep. But seeing her with that cane yanked at his conscience. And it infuriated him that he liked her. He liked her family too. And he didn't like too many people. If Anne persisted, Richard knew those relationships would evaporate. They would never forgive him for his role in what happened that day.

The images resurfaced.

He stood waiting in the long line to enter the courthouse. It was close to nine-twenty. He needed to file a motion in the clerk's office before his hearing started at nine-thirty.

Rushed, he hadn't paid attention to the petite woman with short dark hair, standing a handful of people in front of him, except to groan when the metal detector beeped as she walked through. He then noticed she'd worn a heavy winter coat, a huge metal buckle on her belt, and numerous silver bracelets and necklaces.

Her eyes downcast, and her cheeks red with embarrassment, she removed each item, fumbling with clasps and repeating apologies.

"I'm so sorry. I forgot about the security. I'm so nervous. I'm getting divorced today."

People in line grew agitated, along with the lone court security officer assigned for that day. He directed the woman to stand aside, beyond the metal detector, and allowed the rest of the line to proceed while she continued to remove the metal items.

As Richard cleared the detector, a familiar female voice called out to him, each syllable dripping with desperation.

"Richard? Richard Diamond?"

He turned to the source, finding the same annoying woman waving at him.

"It's me, Annie. I'm getting divorced this morning

and I can't be late. Will you vouch for me?"

Before he could respond, the phone on the court officer's desk rang. Impatient now, the officer glared at both of them.

"Go ahead," he barked, picking up the phone's receiver.

Anne shoved her belongings into her coat pockets and caught up with Richard. When they entered the main lobby, she stopped him and stood on her tippy toes to give him a peck on his cheek.

"Thank you, love." Then she took off.

Richard dismissed the event and went to work. All hell broke loose later that afternoon.

Soon after the fact, he concluded that Anne's choice of accessories was intentional. She knew she needed to cause a scene that would get her inside the building at its busiest time, without a thorough search. And it worked. But to this day, he hadn't figured out where she'd hidden the gun.

Richard paced back and forth the length of his living room.

What did Anne mean when she said, 'all will be as it should be?' What will happen in a few hours? Where? And how?

****

The rain outside pounded on the roof of Richard's house. He wondered who, if anyone, he could contact at this hour to address what Anne just told him. Should he call the police? Or was he overreacting? Perhaps Anne was just delusional. After all, she was not out walking the streets. Or was she? How did she get away with making that call?

He started with the hospital.

A tired sounding male voice answered on the third ring. "Nurses station, fourth floor west."

Richard introduced himself, then said, "I apologize for the hour, but I am calling about Anne Compton. Her maiden name is Callahan."

"Hey, Attorney Diamond. This is Robert Townsend. We met a few years ago when Annie was first admitted. She talks about you all the time."

Richard stifled a groan at the thought of what she might be saying. "Thank you for taking this call," he said. "I hope you have been well."

"Can't complain. The wife and I have a two-year-old now, and another one on the way. It makes life busy."

"How wonderful. I recall those days well. Best wishes." He paused, hoping he'd sounded sincere. "As I mentioned, I'm calling about Anne."

"Yeah, she said you'd be calling. She gave us permission to speak with you. She had a gallbladder attack after dinner last night. She spent the night at the hospital and last I heard, she's on her way back here. We'll settle her in on our medical wing."

That explains her phone access.

"Oh dear. Can you transfer me to the medical wing? I have a busy day coming up, but I want her to know I am checking on her."

"Let me make a call. Hold on."

The line went dead. Richard fumed and dialed again.

Townsend picked up on the first ring. "Sorry about that, Attorney Diamond. Hang on."

His patience waning, Richard counted the rings as he squeezed his chin between his thumb and forefinger.

"Eight, nine…"

"N wing, medical."

"Good morning, this is Attorney Richard Diamond. I believe Anne Callahan will be heading your way soon?"

"Yes, Attorney Diamond. I'm hearing that, too. I just got off the phone with Robert. How can I help you?"

"I'd like to visit her, but I need to be in court at ten today. Would it be possible for me to see her before then? Perhaps at seven-thirty, or thereabouts?"

A pause followed.

"She's been asking me to visit," Richard added, to support his request. "As I told Robert, I don't want her to feel that I have forgotten about her."

"I suspect she'll be sedated."

"That's fine. I'll keep it brief."

"Fine," the nurse answered, after a moment. "We're in the N wing, third floor."

"Thank you. I'm on my way."

Through the kitchen window, Richard viewed a flash of lightning illuminating his backyard. A loud rumble came next.

Weird weather for December.

He pondered Anne's words again. Perhaps he dreamt the whole thing. No, he wasn't that daft yet. That meant she believed she was going to somehow harm Josephina Jensen today.

Thunder rattled his windows.

A horrible thought occurred to him. He dashed into his home office and accessed the judicial website. As he pounded the last letter of Josephina's name on the keyboard, a violent crash made the house feel as if it had been knocked off its foundation.

Richard swore, dreading what he suspected.

One, two, three… The computer screen, along with the lights in the office and in the hallway, faded to black. *Lightning must have struck a nearby transformer.*

Chapter Forty-One

Josie, Friday Morning

Gabe Jensen, acting as chauffeur and security guard, delivered a freshly showered and fully caffeinated Josie to the law school just before seven that morning. She needed to finish preparing for Laura Schofield's hearing, scheduled for eleven o'clock. In between, she had a class to teach.

Laura had called her last night to say that Trent showed up at their home, raging like a lunatic. He didn't calm down until she threatened to call the police. He revved up again and stormed out of the house when she handed him the emergency custody and financial orders, with the notice of today's court proceeding.

Printing off two copies of the motions she'd be presenting to the judge that morning, Josie paused in thought. *Do I really want to be doing this again?*

As Dan had pointed out, Amy Castle's case was easy. If you put aside the explosion at the Madison store, and the vandalism, and being stalked, the divorce itself was over and no kids were involved. But the Schofield situation was just the opposite. It could get really nasty.

Josie stood before the mirror behind her office door and studied her reflection. For now, she was committed to help. And she was as ready as she could be. She grabbed what she needed for class and joined a student in the elevator. Her phone vibrated in her purse but before she could reach for it, the new corporate law professor, Shane Wilburn, a fresh-faced, ginger-headed fella, sought her out at the door to her lecture hall.

"Hi, Josie, did you get a chance to read my email?"

She grimaced. "So sorry for not getting back to you, Shane. Of course I'll speak with your class about the impact of divorce on businesses. It's an important topic."

"Great. Does Wednesday at three o'clock work?"

"I'll be there." Watching him rush down the hall, she realized he was cute. She wondered if he was married.

Stop that!

Chapter Forty-Two

Richard

Richard walked behind a female nurse wearing pink scrubs down a mint green coordinator, his tasseled loafers echoing on the speckled tile floor. A slight antiseptic smell lingered in the air. He heard a whimper as the nurse slowed and entered a room on the right. Richard remained at the door.

A petite young woman with long straight blonde hair hovered over the thrashing patient in the hospital bed. "Just rest, Mommy. Everything is fine."

Richard didn't recognize the woman in the bed, whom he'd loved years ago. Aside from one stick-thin arm and her head, a pile of blankets hid her tiny form. Short, gray and white spiky hair framed her pale, heavily lined face. Her vacant eyes rimmed red and purple.

She's aged so much.

The blonde woman returned to the chair next to the bed, holding Anne's hand.

"That's Rebecca, Anne's daughter," the nurse whispered.

Her daughter? Richard forgot Anne left two children when she pulled that stunt. A girl and a boy, somewhere in their late teens. To Richard's knowledge, they'd stayed with her parents, at least during the time he spent cleaning up her mess. Seeing Rebecca here, he realized they were now adults.

"Why is Anne upset?" Richard asked the nurse.

"We're not sure. The ambulance crew who brought her back here from the hospital said it started during the ride. She began screaming and carrying on, saying she had to repent, and she was sorry for what she had done. She called for her children over and over again, begging their forgiveness. She cried out for you too, asking you to forgive her for what she'd done to you. She got so worked up, they had to sedate her. It took quite a while and a lot of medication to get her down to this level."

"Richard?" Anne cried out, seeing him in the doorway. "Thank you for coming." She shook off her daughter and held out two toneless arms to him from the bed. "I'm so sorry I broke our engagement. I know I hurt you so much. I was so wrong. We were meant to be together, but I rejected you. And then I did that other horrible thing. Today it will be four years, won't it? Do you remember? I'm so sorry I involved you, my love. But don't worry. I'll keep our secret. Even if I'm stuck here for the rest of my days on earth with no one to love me."

Richard entered the room and stood near the bed, but out of reach. Anne's bloodshot gaze locked on him. She dropped her arms. Her chest rose and fell under the hospital gown.

"I love you, Mommy," the girl said, her voice cracking as she took the woman's hands. "I will always love you. You'll be better real soon. I'll help you."

Anne studied the girl as if trying to recall who she was.

Observing the interchange, Richard's emotions raced back and forth between utter loathing and pity. He carried a plastic chair from the far corner of the room to the bed, opposite Anne's daughter. Sitting down, he didn't want to touch her, but relented when she pushed away her daughter's hand and grabbed his. Her grip was tight, much stronger than he expected since she was supposed to be heavily sedated.

"Everything all good here?" The nurse asked from the doorway. "I've got to do rounds. Just hit the red call button on the bed's remote control if you need anything."

"Thank you," Anne replied in a babyish voice.

When she was gone, Anne assessed him up and down, still holding onto his hand.

"Thank you for coming, Richard." She spoke in a clear, almost formal tone. No more sobs and no more tears. The corners of her pale chapped lips twitched. "I knew you would."

Richard's gut clenched.

This is so weird.

He watched Rebecca from the corner of his eye. Busy on her phone, she seemed not to notice the change in her mother's demeanor. Before he could say anything, Anne sat up in the bed, wild eyed, her jaw clenched. She increased her grip, pushing her nails into his skin.

"When the bitch gets hers, think of me." Then she laid back and closed her eyes. Her hand slipped from his and she either fainted or fell asleep. He wasn't sure which.

****

While Richard recoiled from Anne, confused by what he'd witnessed, Rebecca maintained her focus on her phone.

"Did you hear what your mother just said?"

No response.

"Rebecca?"

The young woman didn't look up. "You mean when she thanked you?"

"No, after that."

She shrugged. "I didn't hear anything else."

Unsure what to do, Richard stood. The girl wasn't interested in talking and the urgency occupying his thoughts had reached a tipping point.

Was Anne lucid when she last spoke? Is she fake sleeping now? Or did the drugs kick in? "I am going to leave now."

She shrugged again, still occupied.

Richard looked at Anne one last time, then walked out of the room, still unsure what just took place. He decided to speak with Anne's caseworker.

"Ms. Lembo is in a meeting," the receptionist on the second floor, outside her office, told him. "Would you like me to have her call you?"

"Yes. Thank you." He retrieved his business card and jotted down his cell number.

In the parking lot now, Richard recognized Anne's daughter swiftly walking several rows of cars ahead. Her blonde hair swung side to side. She wore a long, black coat and her boots smacked the asphalt. He considered calling out to her as she stopped at a gold compact. Then he decided against it.

What was the point?

He thought about Josephina Jensen. Should he warn her to be extra careful today? If so, careful of what? Anne was in no position to cause her harm. And earlier, when his electricity returned, he accessed Josie's court schedule. She did not have any hearings today. That meant that whatever Anne had planned, it would not be like last time, at the courthouse.

So, what was Anne talking about? And what caused her personality to change? What am I missing?

Richard walked to his car. He would make it to court on time, which was good, but the haunting feeling he'd been plagued with since getting Anne's call that morning hiked up to a new level. He reached for his phone and dialed Josie.

Counting the rings, impatience soared. When her voicemail kicked on, he said, "This is Richard Diamond. Please call me at your earliest convenience. It's urgent."

He disconnected and texted her the same message, then drove out of the parking lot. Less than a minute later, his cell vibrated on the seat next to him.

"Thank goodness," he whispered, engaging the hands-free option.

Instead of Josie, his assistant said, "I'm glad you picked up. It's been crazy here. You've got two new potentials and they both require your immediate attention. One involves court today."

"Start with that one. What is it about?" Veering into the left lane, he accelerated beyond the sixty-five-mile speed limit.

"His name is Trent Schofield. He's left three voicemails in the past hour. He claims his wife has a very nasty female lawyer." She paused to add, "I left out the swear words he used."

"I'm sure."

"She obtained emergency custody and financial orders against him this past Tuesday and the hearing is at eleven today in Hartford."

Richard pressed his foot harder to the accelerator. "Every hour is booked today."

Dana laughed. "No kidding."

"Can I presume you identified the very nasty female lawyer?"

"I did."

"Please tell me she is not Josephina Jensen."

"I can't do that."

"What? No way." Richard took a sharp curve and whizzed past an unmarked state trooper hiding behind a bush. "I already checked the court docket. She doesn't have anything scheduled for today."

He alternated his attention front and back to make sure the unmarked was not behind him. When it pulled out onto the road, he released a litany of expletives in his native language. Then chuckled when the cop flashed its lights at the tractor trailer Richard had passed.

"I checked too and told Mr. Schofield the same thing. He said it's a write-in."

Going into another curve, Richard repeated Josie's favorite catch phrase. "Of course it is."

"What should I do?" Dana asked.

"Call him back. Tell him my rate is seven-fifty an hour. He needs to pay for one hour now, over the phone. If he pays, file my appearance form with the court for the sole limited purpose of postponing today's proceedings. And then file the motion to postpone the hearing to sometime next week. Be sure to include that we agree all current orders will remain in effect until the next hearing. Then call Valerie Gordon at the clerk's office to let her know. And email Jensen a copy of the limited appearance form and the motion. If Schofield wants to meet with me, set up a half-hour appointment sometime on Monday. It can be by phone or video chat. Tell him if he wants to hire me, and I agree to represent him, he'll need to pay a fifteen-thousand-dollar retainer, before I do anything else."

"Got it."

"Just make sure you clarify to him that for now, I am only available to help him get out of today's hearing. And no, the seven-fifty he pays now will not count later toward his bill if he decides to hire me."

"Understood."

Richard glanced at his speed and the gas gauge. "What is the other call about?"

"It's from Luke Penway. He said it's an emergency. Didn't you speak with him last week?"

Richard recognized the name right away. "Yes. Why is he calling again? He already has a lawyer."

"He said it's about his wife, Josie Penway, who is also Josie Jen…"

"Jensen. Yes, thankfully for all of us, there is only one of her."

Dana sent what sounded like a snort through the line. "Anyway, he said it's not about the divorce. He needs to warn her about something bad, but she won't take his calls or respond to his texts. He left a number. Do you want it?"

Recalling Anne's last words to him, he said, "Please text it to my cell. Is there anything else?

"Yes. Malcolm Castle called."

"I'm sure he did. Please let him know I am in court and ask him for a good call back time for late this afternoon."

Richard ended with Dana and dialed Jensen again. "Pick up the phone!" he commanded into the air, when the call went to voicemail again. At the prompt, he left more of a terse message this time. "This is Richard

Diamond for the second time, calling for a different reason, although the other situation remains urgent. I expect to be filing a limited appearance for Trent Schofield, along with a motion to postpone today's hearing. Please do not object and call me at your earliest convenience."

As he ended the call, a text came in from Dana, containing Luke Penway's number. He pushed the number to dial, wondering what the man wanted to warn his soon-to-be ex-wife about.

****

Crossing into Farmington, Richard swore after the third ring.

"Come on, Penway. Answer!" He moved to hang up after two more rings, when a hurried, male voice came on the line. "This is Luke."

"Attorney Diamond here. I am returning your call."

"Thank you, sir. Listen, I think Josie might be in trouble, but she won't take my calls. I get it. I messed up. But I've got to reach her."

"And you think I can do something?"

"Can't you? You know each other. You've got that big case you're both working on. You gotta…"

"Fine. How is she in trouble?" Richard interrupted. "I cannot give her a message like that without an explanation."

"Uh, my girlfriend, or the woman who I thought was my girlfriend, hates Josie. I mean, over-the-top hate."

"You mean the woman you left your wife for?'

There was a pause. "Yeah. That one."

"Under the circumstances, no one would expect them to be best friends."

"I know, but it's weird, man. This is gonna sound

281

crazy, but I think she's two people."

Richard straightened in his seat. "Elaborate please." Up ahead, he saw the highway sign for the law school. He decided to take the exit.

"I, um, found a wig. It's got dark, curly hair. And different kinds of clothes. Stuff my girl would never even buy."

He tightened his grip on the steering wheel. "When and how did you find them?"

"Last night. I got home after my midnight shift and noticed her car had a flat tire. I went inside to tell her, but she was asleep. I went back out and changed it so she could get to work on time in the morning. The clothes and wig were stashed in the back of her trunk, under the spare tire."

"And?"

"You're gonna think this is nuts."

Richard leaned his elbow on the window and rested his head against his hand. "Try me."

"They're the kind of clothes Josie's assistant wears. And the wig looks like her same kind of hair."

Richard thought back to the morning before in Josie's office. "You mean the Orthodox girl?"

"Yeah. Like Rivka."

"How would you know her?"

Richard heard him sigh. "Because before our, um, break up...I guess you could call it that...I hung out at the law school a lot. I helped out with events, and I took some undergrad courses, so I'd use the law library to study. And I'd take Josie to lunch or dinner at least twice a week, picking her up there."

The bile from earlier that morning returned with a vengeance. He forced it down. "What is your girlfriend's name?"

"Becky."

Richard fought to keep control of the steering wheel as every nerve in his being fired off rockets. He thought back to the young woman at the hospital with Anne.

Becky is short for Rebecca and Rebecca is the English equivalent of the Hebrew, Rivka.

"Describe your girlfriend," he commanded, though he suspected he already knew.

"She's got long blonde hair. Thin and maybe five feet, one. She's hot. And she doesn't wear clothes like Rivka's."

Richard pressed the accelerator harder. "Does she know about your discovery?"

"No. I put them back. We didn't get to talk this morning. She left before I woke up. Her note said her mother was sick and she was going to visit her."

How considerate. That fits too.

"What kind of car does your girlfriend drive?"

"A small, goldish, beige one."

"Son of a…" Richard swerved onto the road leading to the law school. Without realizing it, he mumbled, "Anne might be locked up, but her daughter is not."

"What did you say?" Luke demanded.

The campus came into view at the same time Richard recognized the gold car turning into the school's entrance. It entered a parking lot to the left of the main building. Richard turned right, into the large front lot, scouting out a space where he could keep Rebecca in sight.

Through clenched teeth, he said, "I believe I met your girlfriend this morning at the hospital while she was visiting her sick mother, Anne Compton. Remember

Anne, Luke? The woman who shot your wife? Today is the four-year anniversary of that fiasco. I believe your girlfriend is Anne's daughter. And I believe she intends to recreate the carnage today, on behalf of her mother."

"No," he insisted, his voice cracking with fear. "That's impossible."

"Afraid not. She just arrived at the law school. I am watching her now."

"What? You gotta stop her. What should I do?"

"Believe me. You've done enough on all accounts. Don't contact her or let her know we figured it out. Someone will be in touch."

"But what…?"

"But what, indeed," Richard repeated, hanging up. *Schmuck*! He dialed his office.

"This is Attorney Richard Diamond's office. How can I help you?"

"Dana, it's me. Please call the Hartford court now and tell the clerk an emergency has come up. I need all my hearings canceled for today, not just Schofield. Then call our clients and the lawyers on the other side to let them know."

"All right. Anything else?"

Richard hung up without answering, fixating his attention on the gold car. Its tinted windows prevented him from seeing inside but his patience was rewarded when a petite girl with dark curly hair and glasses, wearing a long black coat and boots, stepped out and walked to the building.

Planning his next moves, memories from the past came rushing to the forefront. Richard pounded another number on his phone. He didn't know Anne's plan, or Rebecca's role, but under no circumstances would he permit history to repeat itself.

Chapter Forty-Three

Josie, Friday

Keeping her promise, Josie spent the last hour of class devoted to her students' questions about being a family law lawyer. She picked out another folded piece of paper from several in the basket she'd passed around at the beginning of the lecture and read aloud, "What do you do when a client doesn't pay your bill?"

Josie heard a few snickers as she hobbled around the room. "The answer is, not much. If you sue your client to collect your fees, many of them flip the table and sue you for legal malpractice."

"How is that permitted?" a woman in the front questioned.

"What if you did nothing wrong?" a male from the back of the room challenged.

Josie acknowledged both of them. "It's obnoxious, but believe me, it's true. Keep in mind, the bigger your fee, the bigger the fight that took place. People are mad. And very few are happy when the dust settles. Even if they got what they wanted, they're still stuck with a huge legal bill, and that pisses them off all over again."

Making her way to the front of the room, she added, "A common complaint goes something like, 'But it wasn't my fault. I didn't want a divorce. I didn't cheat. Why should I have to pay for a lawyer?' Or, 'My spouse was a lazy bum. I had to pay for everything when we were together, and now I have to pay more, just to get rid of him or her?' " She held out her arms and flicked her wrists. "So of course they'll sue their own lawyers. They have nothing to lose."

Indignation written all over his face, a male student in the front of the class shot up his hand.

"Nathan?"

"What about the time the divorce lawyer has to spend defending themselves against the malpractice claim? Sure, their malpractice insurance carrier will give them a lawyer, but every minute spent to get that lawyer up to speed and then the litigation process itself is wasted because they lose out on making money on their other cases."

"And they have to worry about the result," the woman next to him added.

Understanding, Josie nodded. "You're right. It can be quite annoying. That's why we strive to get a lot of money up front, before we start work."

"That's the retainer fee, right?"

"Yes. And when the retainer amount is close to being spent, if the case is still ongoing, it's a good idea to require your client to 'refresh it,' " she said, using finger quotes. "Granted, many clients don't like it, but keep this in mind. We didn't cause our clients' problems. They came to us for help, and no one wants to work for free."

She pulled out another question. "How much does the average divorce cost?"

Again, grins and snickers.

"A lot," she answered. "But do you know why?"

They looked at her, eyes wide with anticipation.

"I'll tell you what a brilliant, self-made, wealthy, well-respected pain in the butt, and sometimes ethically challenged divorce lawyer once told me."

"What?" multiple voices shouted out.

"He said…"

Before Josie could finish, a deep male voice interjected, "Divorce is expensive because it is worth it."

She spun toward the voice. Her face ignited as her former opponent waved from the doorway.

"Richard?"

****

Replacing shock with enthusiasm, Josie walked toward the unexpected visitor and announced with a flourishing arm gesture, "Here he is, class. Mr. Divorce Lawyer himself, Richard Diamond."

They clapped, then many shot their hands up in the air for questions. Gracious, Richard called on the bald man to his left.

"Is it easier to represent men or women?"

Josie recognized his most charming grin as he replied, "Neither. Nastiness does not discriminate."

That made them laugh.

Another student shouted, "What one trait makes a lawyer successful?"

"Ingenuity," Richard answered, without hesitation, moving closer to Josie. "Which is what your professor and I need right now because our clients are misbehaving and require our immediate attention."

That caused another round of laughter. Richard sent them a big wave and ushered Josie to the exit, grabbing her cane and purse on the way. "Sorry for cutting your class short," he told them, over his shoulder. "Good luck on your final exams and enjoy your holiday break."

"What's going on?" Josie questioned, once they were through the door. Classes were still in session, leaving the halls clear.

Without responding, Richard propelled her forward toward the stairwell. Gripping her around her waist, he lifted her off the ground and raced down the steps. "Please listen to me and don't argue." His warm breath touched her ear as they neared the second-floor landing. She opened her mouth protest, then closed it.

"Your assistant, Rivka, is Anne Compton's daughter. They are scheming to hurt you today."

Josie's legs nearly gave out, but Richard held tight. She searched her memory for details of Anne's actual divorce. Vaguely, she recalled the woman had children, but custody and children support were not issues. She hadn't needed to consider them. From the beginning, Anne's husband had conceded full custody to her and requested a minimum visitation schedule, at Anne's discretion. He hadn't even balked at paying child support above the court's recommended guidelines. In fact, he hadn't balked at anything. Anne was the problem.

Josie recalled the husband's lawyer telling her the husband would agree to almost anything Anne wanted. "He just wants this over."

Josie conveyed this to Anne, who dictated an over-the-top list of demands. To call her greedy would be a compliment, and yet her husband went along with all of them. Then Anne changed her mind, insisting on more. The same situation repeated itself three more times. Just when they'd finalize an agreement to bring to the judge to make it official, Anne would renege. At the last hearing, prior to the shooting, the judge scheduled a final date. He told the parties they could either get divorced by nine-forty-five on that date or be prepared to start the trial.

To everyone's dismay, at nine-thirty-nine, after both sides had spent untold hours hammering out yet another final agreement, Anne decided to go to trial.

"Divorce is a sin," she told Josie, once they were alone in a conference room. Wearing a black tweed suit, with black tights, a black blouse, and black pumps, she sat primly across the table, her back ruler straight. She grasped a gold crucifix in her lap, speaking to Josie as if she was a troublesome child.

"If I agree to this divorce, it makes me even a worse sinner. Let the judge decide. Let him have my soul on his conscience."

Anne didn't understand the implications of her decision until her husband took the witness stand and began describing their bizarre relationship. Almost immediately, she started sobbing and shouting at him from the counsel table, calling him names and refuting his version of their life together. At first, the judge, experienced with divorce cases, showed patience. He offered breaks to let her to compose herself and he asked the clerk to fetch her a box of tissues. But when Anne renewed her rant, he threatened, more than once, to have her removed from the courtroom.

The lunch recess couldn't come soon enough. Anne jotted a note to Josie as the others left the courtroom.

—I want to settle. Take the last agreement we reached.—

Josie nodded and left to find the opposing counsel. She wasn't surprised when he reported that all deals were off. Anne's husband had decided to let the judge deal with their sordid mess.

Anne took the news with little comment. In fact, she maintained her silence throughout the remainder of her husband's testimony, including Josie's cross examination. When he finished and his lawyer called Anne to the witness stand, she pulled out the gun.

Josie locked up the remaining memories of that day as Richard told her, "Hang on," in between heavy breaths, getting them down the next flight.

"I've already alerted the police and courthouse security, but it turns out Rivka is here."

"She told me she had a history quiz this morning." Josie countered, her feet still off the ground. "The class is across campus in one of the undergrad buildings."

"Maybe."

They reached the first-floor landing that led outside to a parking lot. Richard lowered her to a standing position, then released his grip.

"Minutes ago, I watched her enter this building. You need to get away from here."

"How do you know all this?" Josie demanded, fumbling to place the long strap of her purse across her chest.

Without answering, Richard pushed open the double glass doors and grabbed her free hand. "Come on. My car is the black one, around the corner on the right."

They raced, as fast as she could hobble, across the lot's freshly paved asphalt. Almost to the vehicle, he held up its remote to unlock the doors. They reached the passenger side, then stopped as a black pickup truck came from the opposite end of the lot, its tires screeching to a halt several hundred yards ahead. A young woman, wearing a long black coat, barged out the building's side door.

****

Richard tugged Josie's arm. "Duck."

"Rivka?" Josie sunk to his level to peer through his tinted windows. "And that looks like Luke's truck. What the—?"

The young woman marched up to the truck and shouted at the driver through the window. "What the hell are you doing here?"

When the driver emerged, Josie gasped. "It is Luke. Why is he here? Why is she yelling at him?"

Richard put a tight hold around her waist and yanked her down. "It's not good," he whispered. "I'll explain, but not now. Please stay down and quiet."

His urgent tone convinced her to listen. He loosened his grip and used his other hand to find his phone. She heard him speak to someone in a hushed tone as she fixated on the couple, curious yet bracing herself for their next words.

They stood about a foot apart. Rivka continued to shout, pointing her index finger up at Luke's face. Pale, his lips pursed, he balanced his weight from one foot to the other and back again, like a prize fighter in the ring, calculating his next move. When she stepped closer, he grabbed her finger and pulled her to him.

Rivka struggled to shake free. "Let go! You're hurting me!"

"Then stop!"

And she did.

Both breathing hard, they took a step back from each other.

Then Rivka placed her hands at her hips and again berated him.

Luke interlocked the fingers of both hands at the

back of his head. He circled around a few times, then dropped his arms to his sides.

"Why, Becky?" he cried, his face distorted with anguish. "We love each other. I gave up everything for you."

As Josie repeated Luke's words to herself, each syllable replaced confusion with comprehension. Becky, the woman Luke left her for, was Rivka. And Richard claimed that Rivka was Anne's daughter.

She swayed to one side. Her thighs and back burned from remaining bent over.

Richard steadied her, placing his mouth to her ear. "It's almost over. Help is coming."

Rivka laughed, hard and nasty.

Luke's eyes narrowed. "You won't get away with it. Diamond knows you're Anne Compton's daughter. He also knows that you tricked me into leaving Josie and what you're planning to do today."

Rivka spat back a response, too low for Josie to hear.

Luke laughed this time, saying something equally low.

Rivka lunged at him. He tried to push her away, but she kept coming at him. He grabbed hold of her hair, his hand clenching her brunette curls as she stumbled, crying out, falling to the ground. And yet, he still held onto her hair.

Josie looked back at the young woman, not sure what she was seeing. *Was Rivka bald?* Then she understood. She wasn't bald. She was wearing a flesh-toned skull cap. Luke was holding a wig.

Discarding it, he ran to her. "Becky! Are you hurt?"

She swatted him away, warning, "Don't you dare come near me."

A horn beeped from an older model hatchback entering the parking lot from a side road. It stopped a few feet away and a young man climbed out without cutting the engine. He ran to Rivka.

Josie recognized him before the woman shouted his name.

"Tommy! This moron hurt me. And he told Richard Diamond about me."

"What's he doing here?" Richard whispered.

Josie dared not blink. It made sense that Thomas Rivers, her student and the court clerk, might know Rivka. Though not a law student, she was an undergrad and worked in the law school's registrar's office. And she was cute, even with her conservative clothing. But why would he care what Luke told Richard about her?

Josie watched Thomas lift Rivka to her feet. "Let's go. It's over."

Protesting, Rivka struggled against him. "No. It can't be over. Mommy needs this to happen today."

"Mommy?" Josie whispered to Richard.

"Anne had a son, too," he replied. "This might be him."

Thomas urged her toward his vehicle. Staying calm, he said, "She's crazy, Becky. This ends, now."

Josie flashed back to meeting Thomas in class the year before, and then last week at the courthouse. *He'd always been pleasant toward me. Even helpful. How could he be Rivka's brother, and Anne's son?*

As Rivka continued to resist, police sirens filled the air, coming from all directions. Like a caged animal, she broke through Thomas's hold and drew something out of her pocket. Three rolls of angry thunder followed.

Luke fell to the pavement, clutching his stomach.

On impulse, Josie ran toward him. "Luke!"

But she tripped, landing hard on her bad hip. She tried to get up, but the pain was paralyzing. Then she realized she was out in the open. Rivka stepped toward her, closer and closer, both hands gripping the gun.

Josie no longer recognized this person. Minus the dark hair and thick eyeglasses, her eyes narrowed to slits and the remainder of her face seethed with rage. Crazy rage.

"You were supposed to stop the divorce. You were supposed to make sure it never happened. Even if it meant Daddy had to die."

Unable to move, Josie braced herself for the inevitable.

Shots rang out just as a force lifted Josie off the ground and knocked her several feet away. "You're safe," Richard whispered into her ear. "We're behind a car."

He started to climb off of her, but another round of shots caused him to flatten them onto the ground. From under the car, they watched Rivka's body crumble downward. She fought it, convulsing and flailing, struggling to reach the gun she'd dropped.

Richard reached her, kicking the gun away. Josie's leg refused to cooperate, but she crawled her way to them. She took off her suit jacket and used it to cover Rivka's trembling body.

The girl spewed hatred at her. Then she switched to Richard, mocking him. Through chattering teeth and a gargled laugh, she said something to him, but Josie couldn't decipher the words. Rivka's body convulsed again, then stilled.

From the corner of her eye, Josie spotted Thomas.

He'd moved away from them. The gun he'd fired at Rivka was now aimed at his own throat.

"Thomas!" she shouted, struggling to reach him.

As Richard ran toward him, the young man, his eyes rimmed red, said to Josie, "I'm sorry."

She shook her head. "No! Please!"

Two officers tackled him from behind. But it was too late. He'd already pulled the trigger.

Lightheaded and nauseous, Josie coiled into a ball. Then she remembered Luke.

Richard helped her get to him. Blood flowed from both corners of his mouth. He opened his eyes. Recognizing her, he tried to lift his head, but it fell back. Gurgling sounds came from his throat. "Come...closer."

Wiping her dripping nose and eyes, Josie leaned in.

"This is like déjà vu. Except we traded places." A coughing spasm seized him.

Josie used one hand to squeeze his and the other to brush his hair away from his face. "Hold on, Luke. Stay awake."

His eyes flickered open. He tried to laugh but ended up wincing and coughing up blood. He moved his gaze to Richard. "Take care of her." Then he lost consciousness.

Blinded by tears, Josie hovered—until the first responders pronounced her husband dead.

Chapter Forty-Four

Josie, Twelve Days Later, The First Night of Chanukah

Josie stared at her reflection in the large mirror above the sink in the ladies' room at the synagogue. Hindsight provided some explanations regarding the events of the past weeks, but the deaths of Anne Compton's children all but guaranteed she would never know the full story. Since learning her plan had failed, and her children's fates, Anne had returned to her near-catatonic state, uttering at most, semi-silent sobs.

After endless discussions with the police, Richard, and her family, Josie surmised that Anne had passed down her mental health challenges, as well as her grudge against Josie, to her children. Becky was seventeen and Thomas had just turned twenty when Anne was committed to the psych hospital. The visitors' logs showed they were regular visitors. Their loyalty to her must have been so fierce that it motivated them to legally change their last names and basically stalk Josie, beginning perhaps when she started teaching at the law school.

Thinking back, Thomas projected the image of the perfect student in both classes he took with her. The fact that he was also the courtroom clerk for the Castle case was just plain weird. And yet Josie decided that perhaps it saved her life. Thomas got to know her at school, and then in action. Maybe he realized she wasn't as awful as his mother described.

Then there was Becky, aka Rivka. Josie had no words for her emotions. She'd grown fond of the young woman. To think that this person finagled her way into a job at the school where she'd be working with Josie was beyond imaginable. Seducing her foolish husband and scheming to embarrass her through the divorce proceedings was no less than diabolical.

Josie must have surprised the trio by agreeing to represent Amy Castle and that may have exacerbated Anne's need for revenge. And their plan, scheduled to take place on the anniversary of the first shooting, almost succeeded. Both Rivka and Thomas were armed. They didn't need to risk going through courthouse security. A shot taken on the street or at the school would have done the job.

Thanks to Luke's inadvertent assistance, Richard spoiled their grand finale.

Josie blinked back a few tears. *Funny how things work out.*

She was a widow now. She'd decided to forget the past month and remember Luke as the happy-go-lucky, smiling, and caring man she'd fallen in love with. And much to Jonathan Tabor's chagrin, Luke's death ended their divorce action, meaning he lost a ton of unnecessary legal fees.

Having re-injured her bad hip in the fall, Josie ended up back in the hospital for additional surgery and therapy. Richard didn't visit, but he sent her a dozen different colored roses, except not black. A card containing a humorous lawyer joke accompanied the delivery.

Josie wasn't up to carrying on witty, verbal conversations. Instead, she sent a text, thanking him for saving her life and for the flowers. Richard responded and they went back and forth for a bit. Nothing serious or meaningful.

Wiping the smudged mascara from under her eyes, Josie considered what was left of her so-called law practice.

Amy Castle's post judgment proceedings were still ongoing but moving forward. Amy learned that the business's original accountant had sent her the email about the old account. They planned to meet for coffee next week. As for the Madison store explosion, the fire marshal continued to suspect foul play. Amy told them to focus their investigation on Malcolm.

Speaking of Malcolm, no one had heard a peep from him or a lawyer claiming to represent him. The next court date was coming up. Josie and Amy were prepared to go forward, with or without him.

On a happier note, Amy had a grandchild on the way. That kept her smiling.

Next, Josie considered Debra Tate. Her divorce would be finalized in two weeks. To everyone's surprise, her husband fired Tabor and agreed to a fair settlement, without all the drama Debra feared earlier. And she and Josie's father, Gabe, had become quite chummy. His divorce with Roxanne was moving forward and he brought Debra here with him tonight, to enjoy the festivities.

Josie's thoughts turned to Laura Schofield. Nothing was expected to happen there soon, if ever. Her husband entered rehab for alcohol and gambling and swore he didn't have a second family. Instead, he claimed he was being extorted by the thugs he owed money to for gambling debts.

Laura didn't know what to think. She decided not to push anything until Trent was discharged. Financially, she was stable, and she and her kids had Amy Castle as a wonderful support system.

Josie did speak with the woman Mark had mentioned the night of her birthday party. She wanted a divorce, but her husband disagreed and refused to provide a *Get,* which is required to dissolve an Orthodox marriage. Josie answered her questions and gave her some solid advice. The woman would think about things and call when she was ready.

Josie nodded into the mirror. *And that, as they say, is that.* Her life had returned to its usual routine of continued medical exams and physical therapy, final exams and grading, preparing for next term, finishing her textbook, and addressing her role at the synagogue.

It was a good life.

A knock on the door interrupted her thoughts.

"Josie?" Dan called out. "It's time to light the menorahs."

"Coming."

Using a walker, she joined her father and brothers, admiring the holiday-decorated auditorium. They stood, along with the roomful of congregants, including tons of very excited children, at blue and white covered tables in front of their varied menorahs. Priming their lighters, the room erupted with the countdown. "One, two, three!"

Josie's cell phone vibrated on the table as she lit her candle. Amy Castle's name glowed, along with a three-word message.

—Urgent! Please Call!—

"Oh goodness," she whispered. "What happened now?"

She excused herself to another room and dialed her client.

"Josie!" Amy exclaimed. "A friend of a friend of mine just got a call from the Madison police department. There's a warrant out for her arrest. They want her to turn herself in."

"Okay. Slow down. Where is she now?"

Amy hesitated. "She's out. Not home."

"Understood. She's afraid they'll come to the house. Okay, what are the charges?"

"We don't know. But a state marshal served her divorce papers earlier today. Her husband is in the hospital and even though she's his wife, none of the medical staff or his adult children from his first marriage will speak with her or let her see him. And they won't tell her why."

"That's because there is a criminal restraining order against her," a familiar voice interjected behind Josie.

She whirled around to find Richard Diamond.

Her defenses up, she made a face. "Of course there is."

As usual, he presented a commanding, elegant presence in a navy suit with a matching tie and blizzard white shirt. She knew he was at the event tonight. He'd been talking with Gabe and Dan earlier, while she assisted with the final preparations.

To Amy she said, "I'm at a synagogue function right now. Have the woman call me in an hour if she wants my help. And don't let her turn herself in."

"Okay. Thanks."

"The lady is accused of elder abuse and fraud," Richard continued. "There's a twenty-six-year age difference between the couple. The gentlemen's children hired me to protect him from her and regain the assets she stole from him."

Josie looked over the tops of her gold rims at him. "Of course they did." She started to suggest that they return to the celebration. After all, she hadn't been hired yet. But to her surprise, he placed his hands in his pockets and whistled a tune, as if all was well with the world.

"And there's something about a tortoise."

Josie gawked. "A what?"

"According to your new client, he's twelve years old and has lived with the couple since their marriage. Maybe he can shed some light on their situation."

Richard's piercing eyes twinkled their mischief as he flashed her a double-watted grin. Heading back to the celebration, he called out over his shoulder, "Welcome back, Counselor. See you soon."

Thank you for purchasing
this publication of The Wild Rose Press, Inc.

For questions or more information
contact us at
info@thewildrosepress.com.

The Wild Rose Press, Inc.
www.thewildrosepress.com

9 781509 259250